"Chai Spice Murder"

Le Doux Mysteries #6

By Abigail Lynn Thornton

CHAI SPICE AND MURDER

First edition. May 23, 2022.

Written by Abigail Lynn Thornton.

DEDICATION

To Mr. Brown, my English Teacher.
Not only are you a wonderful teacher,
but your lessons have lasted a lifetime.
Thank you.

ACKNOWLEDGEMENTS

No author works alone. Thank you, Cathy.
Your cover work is beautiful!
And to Laura, for your timely and thorough editing!

CHAPTER 1

"Thank you so much for coming," Wynona said with a tight smile. She ignored Violet's snickering as she and Sajia, a mountain troll, stood from their seats. Wynona reached across her desk, doing her best not to wince at the troll's too-firm grip.

"I good help!" Sajia shouted, rattling the books on the shelves.

Wynona put her hands on her desk to stop it from shaking. "I'll let you know by the end of the week," she said in a calm but firm tone.

The troll nodded and stomped her way out of the room, bumping the walls as she went.

Trolls weren't bad creatures, most of the time, but Wynona's shop definitely hadn't been built to have one inside. She had an outside patio to accommodate her bigger guests, though it wasn't nearly as busy as the inside. Most extra-large paranormals weren't as interested in a quiet, peaceful tea party.

We wouldn't have any china left if you hired her, Violet said as she scrambled out from under the bookcase.

Wynona sighed and slumped into her seat. "Don't I know it." She rubbed her forehead.

Heal it.

Wynona perked up. "Why can't I ever remember that I can do those things?"

Violet chittered and went straight to her plate of cookie crumbles in the corner of Wynona's desk.

Concentrating, Wynona sent the slightest bit of magic down her arm, through her fingers and into her forehead. When the pain dissipated, she sighed in relief and laid her head back against the chair.

A knock on her door was followed by it cracking open.

3

Wynona felt him right before she saw him. "Hello, handsome," she said with a tired smile.

Rascal winked and walked across the room before leaving a kiss on her forehead. "I don't think I even have to ask how it's going."

Wynona laughed softly. "I've had three interviews today. The latest was a mountain troll who shouted when she spoke and nearly brought down my bookcases. Not to mention she couldn't walk through the shop without bumping into every piece of furniture."

His low chuckle sent pixies darting around her stomach. Even after nearly a year of dating and realizing a couple months back that they were true soulmates, Wynona still reacted like this every time they were together.

"I'm sure she was a wonderful creature," Wynona continued, "but her ability to work a tea room probably wasn't very realistic."

Rascal grabbed a chair and brought it around the desk so he could sit next to Wynona. "Were any of them worthwhile?"

Wynona shook her head. "Not yet. Interview number two was a unicorn shifter who grew a horn every time she sneezed."

Rascal pinched his lips as if to keep from laughing. "I'm guessing she sneezed a lot?"

Wynona nodded. "She's allergic to dust..." Her eyes darted to the corner of her desk. "And mice."

Who cared about the horn, Violet said snippily. *That allergy made her totally unacceptable.*

Rascal's laughter grew.

"It's not funny!" Wynona scolded, though she was smiling. "If I'm going to keep helping the police with any of your cases, then I have to have help. Truth is, I need help in general."

Rascal nodded, slowly bringing his laughter under control. "I know, I'm not really trying to make light of it, but it *is* kind of funny."

Wynna gave him a look.

Rascal took her hand and kissed the back of it. "You'll find someone," he assured her. "Give it a little more time."

Wynona sighed. "I've been interviewing for a week. I'm starting to get worried."

Rascal shook his head. "The weirdos always show up first," he said. "Plus, you're the president's daughter, so it makes sense that some people would come simply to meet you, rather than actually be looking for a job."

Wynona had closed her eyes, head leaning back. "I'm guessing that was interview number one this morning." She cracked open an eye. "After asking for my autograph, she admitted she didn't know matcha from lavender and promptly walked out."

Rascal shrugged. "You'll run out of those eventually. Then the serious ones will make it in."

Wynona glanced at the clock. "I do have one more today. I suppose there's always hope."

Violet began grooming herself. *It's a fairy.*

Rascal raised his eyebrows. "Is that a problem?"

Violet gave him a look. *They flutter.*

Rascal shared an amused look with Wynona. "Come on, Vi. What's wrong with fluttering?"

Violet sniffed. *Messes up the fur.*

Rascal nodded sagely. "Got it. No fluttering near a groomed mouse."

Or a napping one. Without saying goodbye, Violet scampered down the desk and disappeared under the bookcase again.

Wynona shook her head. "Traitor."

I heard that.

Rascal smiled. "You'll probably have an easier time without her."

Heard that too.

Wynona laughed under her breath. "Are you on lunch break?" she asked Rascal. "Are you hungry?"

Rascal gave her a look. "Do you really have to ask?"

Wynona rose to her feet. "Then come on, Wolf. We'll get you taken care of." She held his hand, guiding him down the hall and into the kitchen. There wasn't a lot of food in the shop, since she only served finger foods, but there were enough leftover pieces to at least take off the edge of his hunger.

Standing at the refrigerator, Wynona began handing Rascal storage containers filled with food.

Lusgu, her brownie janitor, stood at the sink, supervising as his magic washed the dishes from the morning.

"Thank you, Lusgu," Wynona called out as they headed back out. "We'll eat in the dining room."

"Thanks, Lu!" Rascal shouted.

Lusgu glared over his shoulder, then huffed and went back to his work.

"Rascal," she scolded. "You need to stop calling him that."

Rascal shrugged. "If he wanted me to stop, he'd do more than just glare."

Wynona shook her head, but let it go. It was apparently too much to ask that the men in her life get along.

"So...when's Celia moving in?" Rascal grumbled around a mouthful of chicken salad.

Wynona pinched her lips. "I'm not sure. As far as I know, she doesn't have the grimoires yet." Wynona leaned forward on the table. "Do you think I should let her move in first? I thought the grimoires would be useful since Granny isn't around to teach me anymore, but maybe it was too much to ask."

Rascal growled and shook his head. "No. She needs to prove that she's serious about this. I know your grandmother trusted her, but I don't. But if you at least get something good out of it, maybe it won't be a complete loss."

Wynona gave him a sad smile and leaned back. She knew they disagreed on Celia moving in, but Wynona couldn't help but think it's what her grandmother would have wanted.

When Granny had ended up being pushed beyond the veil and into the afterlife, Wynona had gotten the distinct impression that Wynona saving Celia had all been part of the plan.

Or maybe that's just my guilty conscience, Wynona thought to herself after double checking that her mind barrier was up. Rascal didn't like her blaming herself for the way the last case ended, where Wynona had created a portal to the afterlife that had saved them from dozens of possessed ghost cats, but had also taken away her grandmother forever.

They had gotten the murderers, or at least Rascal and Daemon had run them down, but Wynona had been left to deal with her interfering family. And the results had been a mix of devastating and helpful. She'd lost her grandmother's ghost, but gained a little distance from her parents.

When she'd finally wrangled her magic enough to close the portal, Wynona had also sent her three family members away. She'd later learned that they had been ported back to the castle and hadn't been able to leave the castle for a full twenty four hours.

Rascal, at the time, had commented that she needed to figure out how to do that trick again, but Wynona was a little fearful of pulling on that much magic again if she didn't have to, though porting around the city didn't sound too bad.

The wall clock struck the hour and Wynona jerked to attention. "Oh man, my next interview should be here any second."

Rascal wiped his mouth and stood up. "According to my mom, she would already be late." He leaned forward and kissed Wynona's cheek. "I'll let you get to it." He grinned. "As always, thanks for feeding me."

"Anytime," she said softly.

Rascal pumped his eyebrows. "I'll treat you to dinner on Friday. Seven?"

She nodded enthusiastically. It had been a long time since they'd had a date. A little time alone sounded like just the break she needed.

With one last wink, Rascal hurried toward the door, disappearing around a corner. "Hello," he said, his tone congenial from the entrance to the shop.

Wynona stood and walked to the front entry.

Rascal pulled the door open farther. "Wy, I'm guessing this is your one o'clock."

A young woman, her wings fluttering ever so slightly, looked nervously at Wynona. Her teal hair was pulled into a tight bun, complementing her light pink outfit.

"Thallia?" Wynona asked.

Thallia nodded. "Yes!" She walked in, her hand outstretched.

Wynona met the greeting. "Why don't we go to my office, and we can talk in there."

Thallia nodded, her eyes moving all over the entryway. The smile on her face said she enjoyed what she saw. Wynona led the way through the dining room and turned to the hall, but the girl stopped and gasped.

"Oh my word...it's so beautiful," Thallia gushed, her wings lifting her off the floor ever so slightly. She was in her human form, making her nearly the same size as Wynona. "Look at all the teacups!" She turned her bright eyes to Wynona. "Where did you collect them all?"

Wynona found herself smiling. All the worries she'd been harboring from the disasters this morning began to fade. "Most of them are from antique or thrift shops."

"Perfect," Thallia whispered in awe. Her eyes widened. "Would you be willing to make me a tea? So I can see how it's all done?"

"If you were working here, you wouldn't actually be making teas," Wynona clarified. "You'd simply be serving or building pre-mixed tinctures."

"Oh, I know," Thallia said easily. "I just thought it might help me know what experience your patrons go through. That way I can be sure to give them the best help possible."

Wynona relaxed even further. She tilted her head and let her tea senses come to the forefront. "Valerian and lion's mane." Wynona blinked. A tea for happiness and clarity was a unique one for someone as young and perky as Thallia, but...

"Sounds delicious." Thallia flounced to a table and sat down, folding her hands on top of the table.

Sitting across from her, Wynona spun her finger in the air, using her growing magic to prepare the tray and tea. Both of those herbs were ones she kept on hand. "So, Thallia," Wynona said as the tray came out the door and settled on the table.

Thallia put her hands over her mouth to cover another excited squeal.

"Tell me about yourself." As the young woman began to eagerly talk, Wynona's worries became fleeting and the tension in her shoulders a distant memory. Violet was right, the fairy did *flutter*, but she was bright, energetic, excited for the job and best of all...wasn't allergic to anything.

CHAPTER 2

*Y*ou're really sure about this? Rascal asked through their soulmate connection. He huffed as he lifted a box full of jars and began walking out of the room.

Wynona gave him a wry smile. "Nope. But I'm doing it anyway."

A low grumble came out as he moved down the hallway. "If she so much as leaves a scratch on you, I'm letting my wolf eat her."

Wynon laughed softly, though the sound did little to cover her erratic heartbeat. She knew Rascal could hear it, but there was nothing for it. Wynona was far from ready for her sister to move in, but there was little to do at this point.

If she turns me pink, I'm moving in with Wolfy, Violet added.

Wynona paused and rolled her eyes. "No one is using magic on anyone." She pointed to Violet. "Including you, or me or anything else. There will be rules for her living here and I definitely don't plan on this becoming a permanent situation." Wynona threw her hands to the side. "But she's my *sister.*"

Rascal opened his mouth and Wynona held up her hand.

"I know she's been horrible. I get it. I do. But I don't think who she's been is who she wants to be." Wynona sighed and her shoulders drooped. "I believe my parents are the root of the problem and if I can help Celia escape the same way Granny did for me...then I'm going to do it."

Rascal pinched his lips but nodded. "You're right. Without help, you wouldn't have made it out and I'd have never met you." He walked back her way and wrapped his arms around her, pulling Wynona's head tightly against his sternum.

She let her arms wind around his torso and snuggled in. Rascals hugs were the best. He was so strong and warm, and she felt as if nothing bad could ever touch her when he held her just like this.

He kissed the top of her head. "You're amazing. You know that?"

Wynona tilted her head back. "You're the only one who thinks so, but I'll take it."

He chuckled and kissed the tip of her nose. "We're still on for our date though, right?"

Wynona nodded. "We haven't had a date in forever, no way am I letting this get in the way."

"Perfect." Rascal stepped back. "What else do you need me to carry?"

"I think we about got it," Wynona said, studying the room. It was completely bare at this point. Wynona came with nothing, so she hadn't had much stored in the space except extra jars and doo-dads for her teas. She'd have to reorganize the greenhouse in order to find a place for everything, but it wouldn't be that big of a deal. There was probably some room at the shop as well, if she got desperate.

"Do you even know when she's coming?" Rascal asked, heading to the kitchen.

Wynona smiled as she walked behind him. He was always led by his stomach. "No. But I suppose it'll be whenever she manages to snag those grimoires." Wynona scrunched her nose. "It could take Celia months to figure out how to do that."

No sooner had they entered the kitchen than a knock came on the front door.

Wynona paused and looked toward Rascal, who was scowling.

"Speak of the devil," he muttered.

Wynona gave him a look. "Be nice." She turned to the mouse racing across the floor. "You too, Violet."

Neither answered her as Wynona walked to the front door. The fact that Celia had knocked instead of bursting in actually was a good omen. Before, her sister would never have cared about Wynona's privacy or respected her boundaries. This could only be a good sign.

"Hello, Celia," Wynona said with a small smile. She hoped her sister couldn't tell how nervous she was. Though Wynona spoke as if all would be well, there were bound to be some unpleasant circumstances ahead.

Celia raised an eyebrow. "I don't have them."

"Okay..."

"But I need to move in anyway."

Wynona folded her arms over her chest. "I thought we had a deal." Wynona's eyes wandered over her sister. Celia looked...worn. Her hair was pulled into a tight ponytail, her eyes slightly red-rimmed and her pale skin paler. Sympathy immediately began to build in her core, but Wynona forced it down. She wasn't naive enough to think this would be easy. She needed to lay down some ground rules and it would be better to have everything done from the start. The deal had been that Celia would have the grimoires. Wynona couldn't break it so quickly.

"I know," Celia snapped. Her eyes flashed silver. "But it's not going to be as easy as I had hoped."

"I didn't expect it to be easy," Wynona said calmly. "But you're asking me to turn my life upside down and welcome someone into my home who would have gladly killed me only a couple months ago. If you want me to believe you're serious in changing, then I need you to bring me something that's a sacrifice."

"You want those books because you want to build your powers," Celia accused.

Wynona shook her head. "No. I want those books because I want to understand my powers...and control them." She worked very hard to stay low in her tone, though she was tempted to fight back. Anger, however, wouldn't help the situation. Celia was upset enough for the both of them.

Celia huffed and wiped at her eyes. "I said I would get them."

"And I said you could move in when you did." Wynona could feel Rascal getting restless behind her. He wanted to come tell Celia to go away until she had finished her side of the bargain. Wynona sent soothing vibes back to him through their mental link. She understood the sentiment, but she was doing alright.

"If I wait," Celia choked out, "I might not be alive in order to retrieve them."

The words hung in the air between the sisters like sharp lightning waiting for a place to strike.

Wynona was tense, but unsure. Celia was often a drama queen, but Wynona was also very aware of who their parents were. "Are you saying Dad is trying to kill you?" she asked slowly and warily.

Rascal was done waiting, and he stepped up behind her back. "Are you claiming a threat on your life?"

Celia huffed and rolled her eyes, then sniffed. Slowly, the sneer she'd been wearing trembled off her face and her eyes filled with tears. "He didn't flat out say he would kill me," she murmured. "But he's made it clear I'm of no more use to him."

"And the grimoires?"

Celia shook her head. "They're somewhere in Mom's personal library. I haven't figured out how to get inside the vault yet."

Wynona frowned. "Mom has a secret library?"

Celia laughed a little through her tears. "Be grateful you weren't exposed to it. There's some scary stuff in there." She pushed out a breath. "It's where she practices her magic."

Wynona nodded. Lots of witches had a room where they did their work. Hers was the greenhouse, though Wynona didn't practice anything big in there. All that glass made things a little too...fragile.

"She has a bunch of wards on it that keep me from getting inside without her."

Wynona considered her sister. Celia was asking for refuge, and hadn't come with any luggage. Wynona knew her sister had enough clothes to cover a small country three times over. Either she was a wonderful actress and they had planned for her to come empty hand-ed, or she really was desperate. "Do they know you're here?"

Celia shook her head. "Not yet. But I only had a small window while they were at a press conference." She smirked. "Airian helped keep an eye out so I made it out of the castle without being detected." Her triumphant grin fell. "I've been on watch ever since Mom and Dad failed to bring you back."

What do you think? Wynona sent to Rascal.

Rascal growled softly, answering her without words.

Celia pinched her lips together. "So that's it, then? Without the books, I'm expected to just go back and let them suck the life out of me?"

Wynona closed her eyes. "No," she said softly. She looked at her sister. "I need those books. But I don't expect you to risk your life get-ting them." Wynona stepped back. "Come on in." She ignored Vio-let's snarky comments in her mind as Celia cautiously stepped inside. "There are no booby traps waiting for you," Wynona said wryly.

"Maybe not, but Wolf–" Celia caught herself and swallowed hard. "It doesn't take a genius to figure out your boyfriend doesn't want me here."

Rather than try to smooth things over, Wynona decided to go with the truth. "He doesn't. He thinks you're going to betray me and that this is just another ploy from the family to bring me back against my will."

Celia was quiet and her eyes were on the ground. Finally, she looked up from under her lashes. "Why did you let me in?"

Wynona didn't miss the fact that Celia hadn't denied the allega-tions. She put her hands on her hips. "Because Granny wanted me to take care of you. And this is the best way I know how." She hesitated for just a moment. "Would you like some tea?"

Celia's brows pulled together and she tilted her head. It took several seconds before she responded. "Okay."

Wynona spun on her heel, took Rascal's hand and led the way farther in the house. "It's not very large," she said. "But I like it." She waved toward the kitchen table. "Have a seat."

Rascal stayed near Wynona, just shy of hovering as she got the water ready. She looked back at her sister and studied her. "Lemon balm and thyme," she murmured before turning back to the cupboard.

"Grandma used to do that," Celia said softly.

Wynona walked back to the table and sat down, the tea fixing itself behind her. "She taught me."

Celia nodded, watching her tapping fingers. "I know."

Wynona continued to watch her sister. She was a shell of her former self. Wynona would have almost preferred her snarky, egotistical sibling to the quiet broken one in front of her. She wiggled her fingers and the tea settled itself in front of Celia. "Give it a couple minutes to steep and it'll be ready."

Celia nodded.

Rascal joined Wynona at the table and Violet ran across the floor, scrambling up the table leg and up Wynona's arm.

Celia watched the creature with a curious eye. She fiddled with her teacup. "Is it true that's your familiar?"

Wynona reached up to pet Violet, slightly hesitant to answer, but knowing there was little way to hide it.

She more than likely heard it from your mother.

Wynona nodded subtly. "Yes," she said out loud.

Celia winced, her eyes going between the mouse and her sister. "I'm sorry," she said softly, more than likely referring to the fact that she had tried to kill Violet during their first meeting.

Wynona's hesitancy melted away and she found herself reaching out. "You didn't know." She patted her sister's hand, then pulled back, not wanting to overstep any boundaries. "Tell me what's going on with our parents."

Celia snorted. "What's not going on with them?" She brought the cup to her nose and took a deep sniff. A small smile played on her lips. "You know...this smells a lot like what Grandma used to make."

"Like I said, she's the one who taught me how to make teas, I'm sure most of what I do will remind you of her."

Celia nodded. After a tentative sip, she drank a little deeper. Sitting straighter, Celia set her shoulders back, looking more confident and a little closer to herself. "So...I know this isn't going to be easy on either of us, but I wanted to say thank you for taking me in."

Wynona leaned back, thankful that Rascal's arm was across the back of her chair. "You're right. This isn't going to be easy. But you didn't seem happy and I wanted to give you a chance to..." She shrugged. "Find yourself? Make your own decisions? Be your own person?"

"All of the above?" Celia finished. She shrugged and pursed her lips. "Truth is, I don't really know what I want." Her eyes were on the teacup. "But the crazier Dad got, the more I knew I needed to get out." She shivered. "He was starting to send me on really weird errands."

Rascal jerked to attention. "What do you mean?"

Celia leaned back. "I don't have any hard evidence that he's up to anything," she said quickly, her color disappearing again. "I just thought it was weird."

Rascal narrowed his eyes and Wynona could practically hear him thinking.

"What kind of errands did you do?" she asked. Granny had been so insistent that Wynona take over Hex Haven in order to get their crooked father out of office. If they found a way to have him arrested instead...it would save her from even thinking about staging a coup.

Celia ticked her head back and forth. "Did you know that I visited both the Roseburg mansion and Silvaria's apartment before the whole murder thing?"

Wynona's eyebrows went up. "Dad told you to go there?"

Celia nodded, drinking more of her tea.

"Well? What did you do?"

Celia shook her head. "I was delivering messages."

"What were the messages?" Rascal pressed, his tone becoming a little dark.

She scowled at him. "They were sealed envelopes, *Officer*. How was I supposed to know?"

Violet chittered. *Any witch worth her salt would have read them.*

Then isn't it a good thing Celia has more integrity than that? Wynona shot back.

"They were sealed with a ward. I couldn't do a thing about it." Celia sneered. The tea was obviously working a little too well.

Ha! Forget integrity. She just wasn't strong enough. Violet seemed a little too pleased with that observation.

"Do you think Dad had something to do with the murder?" Wynona asked, a fleeting fear that she'd been wrong crossing her mind.

Celia shook her head. "No. At least...I don't think so. But it does seem odd." She leaned forward. "Plus...why didn't he just mail them? He's been having me take letters all over to creatures for the last couple of years and I'm not sure why."

"Are any others tied to people who have been killed?" Rascal asked. His hold on the back of Wynona's chair was so tight she could hear the squeak of the wood.

Reaching over her shoulder, she pried his hand off and rubbed his fingers soothingly. His growl changed to a more pleasant rumble and Wynona smiled.

Celia, however, wasn't nearly as thrilled. "Is this what I'm going to have to watch? You two playing lovers all day?"

Wynona tried to keep the heat creeping up her neck at bay, but she knew her face was flushed when she responded. "I suppose it is," she said tightly. "If you're going to move into my home, then you're going to have to deal with my lifestyle." Pushing away from the table, Wynona said, "I'll show you to your room and find you something to wear. Tomorrow we can figure out what you're going to do about clothes and such."

Celia sighed, but followed.

"I don't have a bed yet," Wynona announced, flipping on the light in the room. "I wasn't sure when you would be here or what you would bring along."

"Nothing," Celia said, crossing her hands over her chest.

"I'm sure we can fix that, but not tonight." Wynona continued to ignore her sister's rudeness. She was growing tired. They would have to talk about rules tomorrow. But they *would* talk about them.

Darn right, Violet agreed.

"You're welcome to the couch," Wynona said. "Or a pile of blankets, if you prefer. But until tomorrow, that's all I've got."

Celia opened her mouth, then seemed to think better of it and closed it. "I'll take the couch, thanks."

"Sounds good," Wynona said primly. She stuck her chin in the air. "I'm going to go say goodnight to Rascal. If you don't want to see us being...lovers...then I'd recommend you wait a few minutes before coming out." With that parting shot, Wynona came back down the hall and walked right into her soulmate's waiting arms.

This is a disaster, he sent to her.

I know, Wynona admitted. *But what else can I do? And now she thinks Dad is up to something?* Wynona leaned back enough to see his face. *I have to try and figure this out.*

You have to stay safe. He bent down for a sweet kiss. "Please put wards on your room as well as on the house."

Wynona nodded and gave him an encouraging smile. "I will."

"Okay, lover," he teased with a wink. After one more lingering kiss, he slipped out into the dark.

Wynona sighed. Their date couldn't come fast enough. She needed that time with him and *only* him.

Clingy, Violet muttered.

Wynona picked the mouse off her shoulder and scratched behind her ears. "Come on, Violet. Let's go to bed."

Still clingy, the mouse said, though she leaned into the scratching.

Wynona let out a long breath. Just once, she wished her life would get easier instead of harder. But it seemed that tonight was definitely not the start of a smooth patch. And if Celia was right about their father...there might not be a smooth patch for a very long time.

CHAPTER 3

"When the dishes are dirty, just bring them back to the sink," Wynona explained, walking through the kitchen door. She paused to let Thallia follow, then waved an arm. "Washing dishes is mostly taken care of by Lusgu, but if we have a busy day, you might be helping out in there as well."

Lusgu grunted, never turning to face the newcomers.

Wynona knew he wasn't happy having a new face in the shop, but she simply couldn't keep doing it all. Not only did the shop suffer when she helped the police, but she also needed time to learn her magic. Maybe once she felt like she had a handle on everything, she could go back to working alone, but until then...

Thallia nodded. "Yeah...okay. I'm sure I can handle that."

Wynona frowned. "Have you ever washed dishes before?"

The young woman shrugged. "No. But it can't be that hard, right?"

Wynona blinked several times. "Uh, no...it's not that hard. You clean the dishes with soap and water, then rinse them with non-soapy water, dry them and put them away."

Thallia's eyes widened. "Huh. I guess my parents should pay our servants more. That sounds like a lot of work."

Wynona nodded. She hadn't realized the young woman still lived at home, nor did she realize Thallia had come from a wealthy family. Not a lot of wealthy paranormals were out getting part time jobs at tea shops. *Good for her, I suppose,* Wynona thought. *Maybe this will give her real world experience?*

Are you sure you want her getting that experience in YOUR shop? Violet shot back.

"Your mouse is so cute," Thallia gushed, clasping her hands together and her wings fluttering. She leaned in to where Violet was resting on Wynona's shoulder. "Can I hold it?"

It!

"She's not exactly stranger friendly," Wynona said with a tight smile. She was already regretting, ever so slightly, hiring the young woman. She had been so personable and sounded very capable in their interview, but ever since then, Thallia had been interested in everything *except* how the tea shop ran.

"Awww..." Thallia pouted, then winked at the purple mouse. "Someday I won't be a stranger, though, right?"

Not if I can help it.

Wynona coughed, grateful no one but herself and Rascal could hear Violet's snarkiness. The back door to the kitchen opened and Wynona sighed. "Oh. Kyoz and Gnuq are here." She smiled at Thallia. "They're my bakers. They bring in fresh pastries every morning."

The two imps sauntered in, looking like they owned the world, though they were only six inches tall. Trays of baked goods floated through the air behind them and Wynona immediately put up her guard. Those two might be wonderful bakers, but they were also top notch troublemakers.

They're imps, Violet said. *What did you expect when you hired them?*

Wynona ignored her familiar and welcomed her guests. "Good morning, Kyoz, Gnuq. You can leave the trays in the normal spot, please." She waved to a countertop they kept free of other debris just for this delivery.

With a swirl of their fingers, the trays all settled into position. Kyoz and Gnuq stood, smirking at Wynona as if waiting for something.

"Thank you," she said sincerely, then motioned to Thallia. "This is Thallia. She'll be helping me out in the dining room." Wynona's voice grew firm. "And she's under the same protection we discussed before." She left no room for arguing in her tone. When the imps had first begun to work for Wynona, they had wreaked havoc on everyone and everything. She often lost food or had her dishes thrown to the floor by their magic when they scurried out the back door in a hurry of giggles and laughter. But when they'd taken to pinching anyone who was in the building, Wynona had taken a stand.

Prim had threatened more than once to filet the two imps, but Wynona kept her best friend at bay and did her best to simply keep them apart altogether. If Prim came over in the mornings, Wynona made sure they waited in the office, especially since Kyoz seemed to have developed a crush on Prim after her latest threats.

He's obviously attracted to danger, Violet said with a yawn. *It makes no sense otherwise.*

Gnuq and Kyoz made faces and chattered quietly with each other, more than likely discussing Wynona's statement. When Kyoz finally glared at WYnona and nodded, she let the breath she'd been holding slowly leak out of her lungs.

"Thank you," Wynona said regally. "I appreciate you honoring our agreement." Then she clasped her hands in front of her and waited for the imps to leave.

The brother and sister were still arguing as they headed out the door, which was more than likely why Wynona thought they would get away without seeing a showing of the imp magic, but the twins weren't quite so accommodating.

Just before the door closed, a whirl of wind slid into the room and made a pointed journey around the space, sending every pot to banging, every hair into disarray and every napkin sailing everywhere but where it belonged.

Wynona sighed and pinched the bridge of her nose. "Those two can never seem to leave without doing something they find funny."

Thallia huffed and brushed at her hair. "My father would have fired the lot of them." She sniffed, then her eyes widened as if she realized how that sounded to her new boss. "Not that you're doing it wrong," Thallia said quickly, her smile wide and accommodating. "He just has a short fuse." Her wings twitched. "He doesn't work with anyone very long!"

That definitely didn't make Wynona feel any better, but she brushed it aside. Thallia was young. She'd learn. And honestly, Wynona knew she could probably find creatures who were easier to work with but still made good food, but she hated the idea of firing them. Everyone deserved a chance to shine and ones that were more difficult to get along with, like Kyoz and Gnuq, didn't always get the opportunities to do that.

Wynona knew what it was like to be on the outside looking in and she worked hard to give others in that position the same chance she got. A chance to survive and thrive.

Wynona glanced at her watch. "The first patrons will be here in just a few minutes. Why don't you start filling up some trays the way I showed you earlier so they're ready as soon as we have visitors?"

Thallia nodded. "Sure." She walked to the other side of the kitchen and Wynona headed back out to the dining room.

She waved her fingers and began to pull certain teacups from her antique display that sat in the far back of the dining area. Just like she had a knack for knowing what tea a creature needed, she also often felt drawn to certain cups.

Her friend, Officer Daemon Skymaw, who was able to see magic, told her that the antique cups she had collected all held residual magic and that it was speaking to her the same way the teas did.

Wynona couldn't see the magic, but she felt the pull and now that she knew what it was, she allowed it to guide her even more as she prepared herself for the ladies who always showed up on her doorstep immediately after opening.

When the clock rang eleven, Wynona walked to the front door. "Hello, Jubilee. It's so good to see you this morning."

The tiny pixie floated inside with a laugh. "I think at this point you see me more than my family does," the older creature teased.

Wynona laughed with her. "Well, a woman has to eat, right? And a few minutes of quiet with a good cup of tea can go a long way in helping prepare a body for the day ahead."

"Well said," Mrs. Maganti, an older witch and another regular patron, said as she followed the pixie inside.

It seemed that the elderly creatures were always the first ones to arrive in the mornings, though Wynona catered to a wide variety of ages. The late afternoons and evenings were more likely to find the younger tea drinkers, while lunchtime often found family groupings.

None of it truly mattered, but the pattern had surprised Wynona at first. Now, however, she had become accustomed to the schedule and often prepared her food and teas with the ages in mind.

For the next several hours, everything went well and Wynona was beginning to relax about Thallia. The young woman might be slightly spoiled, but she was putting in a good effort and Wynona couldn't fault her rapport with the customers. The fairy truly had a knack for striking up a conversation about anything and everything. In fact, the only problem thus far had been Wynona having to remind Thallia there was still work to do, after she became too caught up in a certain topic and spent too much time at one table.

A gentle nudge, however, had been enough to have the fairy pulling back with a smile and going about helping the others.

The front door opened and Wynona began to make her way to the front entry. "Hello," she said as she crossed the threshold, then came to a stop. "Oh." Her smile was slightly confused, but she tried to stay professional.

A young man with dark gray skin and shoulder length hair, even blacker than Wynona's, stood in the doorway. His muscles were clearly defined and he stood a full head and shoulders above Wynona as he stared her down. "Where's Thallia?"

Wynona frowned. "I'm sorry. Who are you?"

"Dralo. Her boyfriend."

Something about the young man rubbed Wynona the wrong way. He wasn't threatening her, but every word held a hint of...something. Like there was a second meaning, but she couldn't quite grasp what it was. "I'm sorry. Thallia is working right now. Perhaps you could visit her when her shift is done?"

Shaking his head, the young man walked farther in, ignoring Wynona's demands to stop.

"Thallia!" he shouted, marching into the dining room.

Thallia was just coming out of the kitchen and her whole face lit up when she spotted who had arrived. "Dralo!" she squealed. Her wings began to flutter and she hovered off the ground, floating straight to her boyfriend.

When Dralo's arms opened and Wynona realized she was about to have a teenage make-out session on her hands. She didn't like it, but Wynona knew she had to intervene. Holding up her hand, she stopped Thallia mid-flight.

Thallia squeaked in shock, nearly dropping the tray she was holding.

With her other hand, Wynona took the tray and sent it to the table it belonged to. The shifter waiting for the tray didn't even pay attention. She, like everyone else in the room, was caught up in the impending love scene.

"Hey!" Dralo shouted, turning to Wynona, his hands clenched into large fists.

Wynona had never seen a dark elf before, but from the sharply pointed ears poking through his hair, she was positive that that was exactly what she was dealing with at the moment.

"Let her go," he growled.

"Mr. Dralo," Wynona said in a soft, soothing tone. Dark elves weren't exactly known for being easy to please and the fact that this one was still young wasn't doing her any favors. "I already told you that your girlfriend is working. You are perfectly welcome to see her, but it will have to be after hours. My tea shop isn't a place for you two to meet up or spend time together. It's a place of business and my patrons don't come here for drama."

Wynona ignored the huffs that followed that statement. Elderly creatures who had nothing but time on their hands? Yeah...they definitely enjoyed a bit of drama. *But they'll have to get it at the hair salon like everyone else,* Wynona thought.

Hear, hear, Violet agreed. She came racing across the room, giving the elf a wide margin before scrambling up Wynona's leg and perching on her shoulder. *Let's show him who's boss.*

Wynona let out an internal sigh. Why her familiar was so bloodthirsty, Wynona couldn't figure out, but there would be no fighting on her watch, if at all possible.

Dralo was breathing heavily. "I said...let her go."

"Not until you leave," Wynona said, her voice still calm, though her heart was nearly beating through her rib cage. She knew she had enough magic to teach this boy a lesson, but Wynona hated to use it. Protecting herself was fine, going on the offensive was entirely different.

"You don't have the right to do that," Dralo shouted, pointing back at a still shocked Thallia.

The fairy's wide eyes were going back and forth between her boyfriend and her boss, and her mouth was a perfect "O". She apparently had nothing to say for herself.

"Actually..." Wynona corrected him. "I have every right. You are in my place of business, which is my property. As with all business owners, I have the right to refuse service to any and all who enter my doors and since you aren't here for the services I offer, I'm asking you to leave."

The fine hairs on Wynona's skin began to rise when it looked as if Dralo wouldn't back down.

His nostrils flared and it looked like he was prepping for a fight before he finally calmed down. "Fine," he ground out, looking around the room in apparent disgust. "But don't think for a second that this is over."

If eyes could start fires, Wynona knew she was supposed to have burst into a ball of flame, but luckily not even dark elves had that ability. Though, she couldn't help the protective shield that rose up around her when he stalked past her toward the front door.

"Catch you after work, Thal!" he bellowed from the front door, slamming it behind him.

Wynona let go of Thallia, then rushed to the window to make sure the elf actually left. His motorcycle was loud enough to wake the dead and at complete odds with his worn T-shirt and holey jeans. The bike itself was pristine and from the hearty sound of the engine, was treated with more love than Prim gave her plants.

Guess we know where he spends his money, Violet remarked.

Wynona nodded, but didn't respond. The young man didn't seem like the type of elf who had grown up in a well groomed or mannered household. He was rough and tough...everything Wynona would associate with those raised in the slums of Hex Haven. *But then how could he afford a bike like that?*

Probably stole it.

Wynona rolled her eyes before turning back to her patrons. "The show is over, ladies." She paused while several women groaned. "Thallia, I'd like to speak to you in my office, please."

Without waiting for her sulking employee, Wynona walked down the hall. There was nothing pressing going on at the moment with any of her customers, so now was the perfect time to lay down some rules with the fairy.

Boyfriends were fine and good, but having them show up at work, or interfere with work, or even offer up public displays of affection? No...there was going to have to be some conditions that Thallia either abided by, or the job would be gone. Wynona couldn't afford this kind of confrontation at any time, and especially not since she planned to be gone at times, leaving Thallia in charge. Wynona had to be able to trust her new employee and if she couldn't do that, then Wynona would rather work alone.

"Have a seat," Wynona said to Thallia, after settling herself behind the desk. Wynona waited until the fairy was in the opposite chair. "Now...let's have a chat."

CHAPTER 4

Wynona rubbed her eyes as she got off her Vespa the next morning. She hadn't slept well last night at all. Celia, apparently, hadn't either, since she'd been moving around the cottage, keeping Wynona up. The house was warded, so it wasn't like Celia could do any real damage, but her nighttime habits were seriously messing with Wynona's beauty sleep.

Are you sure she's not part vampire? Violet asked.

Wynona sighed. "Violet," she scolded softly. "She's never lived outside the castle. I'm sure she'll adjust to life in the real world soon."

I'm surprised your parents haven't come after her.

Wynona nodded as she searched through her keys for the right one. "I know. I expected at least Mom to make a fuss about Celia sneaking off."

Yet you still don't think she's in cahoots with them?

Wynona paused in unlocking the door to glare down at the purple mouse. "Cahoots? Really?"

Violet shrugged and washed her whiskers. *It fit the bill.*

Wynona shook her head. "No. I don't think they're in cahoots. I think Celia is just...lost right now." She pushed the door open and walked into the dark kitchen, flipping the light switch as she went.

Wynona paused on the threshold for a moment to appreciate Lusgu's magnificent work. The whole place shined, every pot, every mug, every surface...just like it did every morning. "His gift with a little soap and water is pretty magnificent," she said softly.

A few crumbs left here or there wouldn't be a bad idea, though, Violet grumbled.

Wynona laughed softly. "I think you get fed enough, little one."

Violet continued to mumble her disagreement while Wynona went through into the dining room. A cool breeze lapped her ankles and Wynona froze. "Where's that coming from?"

Violet, who was now on the ground, rose up on her hind legs and sniffed the air. *Something's not right.*

Rascal? Wynona sent off the thought.

What's up?

Something's wrong at the shop.

What do you mean? he asked, his tone suddenly serious.

Wynona crept forward, letting the airflow guide her. She gasped when she reached the entrance to the front entryway. "The door's open!"

Don't move! Rascal shouted in her head.

Violet scrambled up and began sniffing around the doorframe.

"Can you tell what happened?" Wynona whispered. She looked cautiously over her shoulder. What if the creature was still inside? She paused. Was she freaking out over nothing? "Did I simply forget to lock up last night?"

No way, Violet snapped. *You locking up your shop is practically a religion. There's no way you left the door unattended.* Violet's nose wriggled. *Plus, even if it was unlocked...how did it get open?*

Wynona nodded. Her familiar was right. Someone had come inside. The question was...were they still there? Finally realizing she wasn't powerless, Wynona brought her magic to her hand. A purple, sparkling ball floated just above her palm. "I'm going to check the office," she told Violet.

Violet raced across the floor and up her master's leg to rest on Wynona's shoulder. *Okay...let's go.* Her tail wrapped around Wynona's neck and the skin to skin contact helped calm Wynona's heart a little more.

Cautiously, ignoring Rascal's order to stay still, Wynona walked down the hall, listening for any and every sound that might be out of the ordinary. Her office door was slightly ajar and a feeling of dread sank into her stomach.

Careful, Violet said. *Something smells bad.*

Wynona shook her head. "I have a bad feeling about this."

That makes two of us.

Letting her magic grow slightly bigger, Wynona used her free hand to press open the door, finally swinging it wide when nothing seemed to react to her presence. "Oh no," she whispered.

"WY!" Rascal bellowed from the front room.

Wynona dropped her magic and stepped back into the hallway. "The office, Rascal.

His angry face appeared at the entrance to the hall. "I thought I told you to stay put."

Wynona wiggled her fingers, purple sparks dancing among her nails. "I'm not helpless."

He huffed and stormed closer. "What's going on?"

She waved an arm toward the room. "Apparently, I'm a magnet for bad luck."

Rascal walked in the office and growled again. The dead body on the floor was chest down, but there was no mistaking the long black hair and gray skin. Death hadn't changed Dralo's pallor much. "Do you know him?" Rascal asked, bending over to get a better look.

Wynona swallowed hard before squeaking out. "Yes."

Rascal's head jerked up. "And?"

She closed her eyes and took in a deep breath, trying to let it calm her. The bodies were always the hardest part when it came to murder cases. Wynona did *not* have a stomach for blood, and the wound on the back of Dralo's head was supplying her with way too much of it. "He's my new employee's boyfriend."

Rascal huffed and folded his arms over his chest. "Unbelievable." Shaking his head, he pulled out his phone. "Chief?" Rascal held the phone away from his ear while his boss chewed him out for leaving the office without warning.

Wynona pinched her lips between her teeth to keep from laughing. Nothing about this situation was funny, but there was just something about the mental image of a man bursting into a wolf and racing out of the precinct that tickled her funny bone.

"Chief...CHIEF!" Rascal finally shouted. He continued before Chief Ligurio could start talking again. "I've got a body at the tea shop. We have an identification and I can tell you about it when you get here." He paused while Chief Ligurio responded. "I know, but it is what it is." Rascal nodded. "Bring a team. The front door was open, so we need to look for signs of a break-in as well as cause of death... Right...on it." Rascal stuffed the phone back in his pocket. "They'll be here in five."

"Thank you," Wynona said softly. She couldn't seem to take her eyes off the young man. Who would do something like this? Dralo couldn't have been more than twenty or twenty-one. So much life ahead...

Rascal walked over and wrapped his arms around her. "You okay?" he whispered in her ear.

Wynona shook her head. "Nope. But I'll live."

The wolf shifter kissed her temple. "I'm sorry this happened again."

Wynona nodded and buried her face in his chest. "Why does everyone seem to die around me?" Her body shook with his growl.

"Don't even joke about that," he said in a low tone. "I don't know why you've had such an unprecedented record since you left home, but let's just decide that it's because you have such a good eye for detail, huh?"

Wynona huffed out a sarcastic laugh. "Sure...let's go with that." She turned her head and eyed the body again. "His name is Dralo. He came by yesterday and I had to kick him out."

Rascal groaned. "That's not going to look good," he admitted.

"I know," Wynona responded. "But I've got a whole room full of witnesses saying that I didn't hurt him or threaten him in any way." She leaned back. "And Celia was up walking the house practically all night, so she can vouch for my whereabouts."

"I hadn't planned to ask," Rascal said quickly. "I was there most of the evening with you, remember?"

She nodded. "You might not need to ask, but someone else would have." Wynona's shoulders slumped. She had been through this rigmarole before. Until she had an alibi, she'd be a suspect. There was no way around it. *And I was just starting to get on the chief's good side,* she lamented.

Rascal rubbed his large, warm hand up and down her back. "You realize you can't open the shop today?"

Wynona nodded. "Yes." She pursed her lips. "Unfortunately, I remember all too well how this went before."

Rascal gave her a sheepish look. "Sorry. We'll get it cleared up as quickly as we can."

"I know." Wynona stepped out of his hold and pinched the bridge of her nose. "It's not your fault...I'm just extra tired this morning."

Rascal huffed. "I'm guessing Celia's nightlife kept you up as well?"

"You could say that," Wynona muttered. She waved a hand in the air. "But it doesn't matter. We'll get used to each other." Her eyebrows went up. "Especially since it looks like I'm going to have some extra time on my hands."

"Deputy Chief?" came an uncertain voice from the front of the shop.

Rascal stepped out into the hall. "Come on back!" he yelled.

Wynona stepped to the side of the hall, making room for every-one that would be coming in. "Good morning, Chief Ligurio," she said with a rueful smile when he entered the hallway.

"Can't stay out of trouble, can you, Le Doux?" the vampire growled.

Wynona shrugged. "I had nothing to do with it."

The chief stopped in the doorway and eyed the body. He took a long sniff, obviously smelling for any evidence. "When was your of-fice last cleaned?"

Wynona shook her head. "You'll have to ask, Lusgu. He does all of that."

"I smell fairy," the chief argued.

"Ah." Wynona nodded. "I hired a new worker yesterday." She hesitated. "In fact..." Wynona waved a hand toward the body. "This is her boyfriend."

The chief's eyebrows shot up. "And how do you know that?"

Wynona explained once again about the confrontation while the chief listened intently.

"Haskill!"

A pale man, who was more than likely another vampire, sidled up beside Chief Ligurio. "Yes, Chief?"

"I want you to contact the Pearlily family. Bring all of them to the station, but keep the daughter separate from the parents." He looked to Wynona, making sure his information was correct. "She's an adult..."

Wynona nodded.

"So she doesn't have to have them in the room with her."

"On it, Chief," Officer Haskill said curtly. Without another word, he turned and disappeared from the room.

Vampire speed, Violet grumbled. *Can't tell they're there until they're there.*

Wynona made a face. "What?"

Chief Ligurio looked her way. "Excuse me?"

She shook her head and pointed to her shoulder. "Sorry. Violet asked a question."

Liar.

Would you hush? Wynona scolded.

Chief Ligurio folded his arms over his chest. "Skymaw?"

The large black hole was wandering around the body. When he looked up, his eyes were bottomless, giving away the exact reason for the name of his creature. "I can't see anything," he said with a shrug of his large shoulders. "The blunt force trauma on the back of the head is the only thing I can see that's wrong with him."

Chief Ligurio snorted. "There's no magic at all?"

Daemon shook his head. "Nope." He blinked and his eyes went back to normal.

"And just for the record, I do have an alibi," Wynona offered.

Chief Ligurio gave her the side eye. "I didn't ask."

"You didn't have to," she said. "I get it."

Chief Ligurio's sigh was long and beleaguered. "Let Skymaw write it down so we have it all official."

Wynona nodded and stepped back. She'd done all she could at the moment.

Chief Ligurio went to walk farther into the room and paused. "You're not coming?" he asked.

"Am I allowed to?" Wynona countered. "It's not a conflict of interest?"

The chief pinched his lips. "Probably, but I'm making a judgment call. Come see what you can see."

Wynona nodded and followed him inside. She looked around the room, taking in the office for the first time since discovering the body. "Everything was neat when I went home last night," she said to the chief's back. She walked around to her desk and eyed the spread of papers. "It almost looks like someone went through all my stuff." Her lips pulled down in a frown.

"What would they have been looking for?" Rascal asked, coming back into the room at that moment.

Wynona shook her head. "I'm not sure." Her eyes flicked to the body. "If it was Dralo doing the snooping, I can't imagine what he would have thought he could find. He wasn't happy that I wouldn't let him and Thallia hang out yesterday during work, but I didn't get the feeling he was trying to rob me or something."

Daemon tilted his head. "He doesn't look like the most upstanding citizen either," he offered. "Dark elves normally flirt with the legal line...heavily."

Wynona nodded. "So he was here looking for something...and someone interrupted him?" Her head jerked up. "You don't think Lusgu would have done something?"

Are you nuts? Violet screamed in Wynona's head. *Lusgu would have used magic, not a baseball bat.*

Wynona let out a breath. "Good point," she said to her shoulder.

"Care to share with the rest of us?" Chief Ligurio asked wryly.

"Oh, sorry," Wynona responded. Heat flooded her neck and cheeks. She spent so much time talking to creatures in her head at this point that she wasn't always good about remembering that others didn't know what was going on. "Violet pointed out that Lusgu uses magic with everything. He wouldn't have hit someone."

"Could he have used magic to hit the boy?" the chief asked.

"There'd be a residue," Wynona responded. She frowned. "Plus, the hit on Dralo's head looks like it came from above. Lusgu is only as tall as Dralo's hip. He couldn't have done it." Shame began to pool in her stomach. The more she thought about it, the more she knew Lusgu wouldn't have just killed an intruder and the realization that she had so easily suspected one of her friends sent guilt running through her system.

Nope, Rascal sent her way. *Lusgu might play well with you, but he's an unknown in a lot of ways.* Rascal's golden eyes bore into hers. *We have no idea what he's truly capable of, especially if he felt threatened.*

She gave him a weak smile. "But I know him well enough to know he's not a killer," she said softly.

Rascal shook his head. "So you say."

Remind me to apologize later, Wynona said to Violet.

The mouse huffed but agreed.

"Hopefully this was just a robbery gone wrong," Chief Ligurio said. "Take note of what papers are out and my team will gather the rest of the evidence. As soon as the coroner comes to collect the body, we'll head back to the station so we can talk to the Pearlily family and get this settled quickly."

Wynona nodded. That sounded like a good plan, though a stop in the kitchen to apologize to Lusgu would also be on her list. Despite his grumpy demeanor, Wynona felt a sort of kinship with the brownie. He was grouchy, but good at his job and she felt that he desperately needed a friend. He might not be willing to admit it or even take her up on the offer, but Wynona was going to be his friend...no matter what.

CHAPTER 5

Wynona continued walking around the desk, looking for anything else that was amiss, but the room seemed clean other than the body and papers. "Can anyone tell what he was hit with?" she asked. "The only thing I have in here are books, and I don't think that would have killed him."

"If hit right, they could," Daemon murmured, his eyes roaming the room. "But I agree, I don't think the wound looks like a book hit. It had to have been something else."

Rascal was bent over the body. "But what?" he asked. "It must have been heavy, the perp must have been fairly tall, and to catch him on the back of the head means that the victim trusted the other person enough to turn away from them."

Wynona shook her head. "Or he didn't hear them coming." She tapped her fingernails against the desk. "I still think it's possibly a robbery gone wrong, even though I have no idea what they would have wanted to steal."

"Look through your files," Chief Ligurio ordered. "See if anything's missing." He paused. "Do you own this place?"

Wynona shook her head. "No. It belonged to Roderick, remember?" The first case Wynona had ever helped with had started just like this. A dead body in her office. But that time, her landlord had been the one involved and she had helped put him behind bars. "His properties were all turned over to his corporation after he died. I'm currently owned by a board, not a single entity."

Chief Ligurio huffed. "Sounds about right." One black eyebrow rose high. "And you really can't think of anything worth stealing?

What about your antiques? Anything that might have caught some interest there?"

Wynona paused. "I hadn't thought of that, though all the teacups I've bought have been at thrift stores, so it would be odd." She shrugged. "But not impossible." She looked over to Daemon. "Would you come help me see if there's extra magic in anything?"

The large officer nodded and together they walked out of the office and down to the dining room. Wynona led him to the huge cupboard where she kept her collection. "I'll look for anything missing and you look for magic that doesn't belong?"

"Right."

The next few minutes were quiet between them, though the crowd of officers milling about the shop kept up a steady chatter. Once again, however, Wynona came up empty handed. "I don't see any cups that are missing. There are no holes and nothing looks like it's been rearranged to hide a theft."

"Agreed," Daemon said in a serious tone. "All the traces of magic I see are attached to a cup."

Wynona put her hands on her hips. "This is so weird. Why was he here?"

Daemon shook his head. "I'm not sure. But maybe they *thought* there was something here and it wasn't? Maybe your friend was killed over a misunderstanding?"

"He's not really my friend," Wynona corrected. "I don't think he'd count me as one either." She chewed on her bottom lip. "I suppose it's also possible he was just upset about yesterday and trying to cause trouble, but then why the death? Vandalizing the place is one thing. Killing is another."

"Agreed."

Wynona walked back to the office. She swallowed when she got inside and saw the coroner there.

"Blunt force trauma," the red cap said in his nasally tone. He adjusted his hat and pushed his spectacles up his nose. "I'll be able to look better for things like fibers or splinters when I do a full autopsy in the office."

"Any guesses on time of death?" Rascal asked.

The coroner shrugged. "Sometime between eleven and two last night? His body has cooled a decent amount."

Chief Ligurio nodded. "Thank you, Azirad." The chief began taking some notes. "I think our best lead is the girlfriend."

Wynona paused. "What?"

Red eyes turned her way. "Your employee? You mentioned they're dating?"

"Well, yes, but you...you think she killed him?"

The chief stuffed his notes back in his pocket. "It's our most likely story."

"What about a robbery?" Wynona argued back.

"You said there was nothing to steal."

"Maybe not, but that doesn't mean he knew that." She waved at the dead body, which was finally being zipped into a bag. "Why in the world would Thallia kill her boyfriend?"

"Lovers quarrel all the time," Chief Ligurio said casually. "They probably used your office as a meeting place and something got out of hand."

Wynona shook her head. "There's no evidence for that."

"There's no evidence of anything," Rascal muttered. He sniffed. "I don't like it. The robbery and the lover story both lack a foundation. There has to be something we're missing."

Chief Ligurio growled but nodded. "Fine. I sent Haskill to pick up the family. Let's interview them and go from there."

"Did anyone check to see if Dralo had family?"

"He doesn't," came a squeaky voice from the doorway.

Wynona spun. "Prim! What are you doing here?"

Prim was in her fairy form, which was unusual when she was around so many human-sized creatures. She said it made her feel at a disadvantage. But her wide pink eyes and pale skin told Wynona the fairy was in shock. She turned those pink eyes to the chief. "He moved here a few years ago, right out of high school. At least those are the rumors. They say he was a foster creature, so no family that anyone's aware of."

"Still," Chief said, his tone a little softer now. "We'll do some digging, but thank you, Ms. Meadows. That gives us a starting point."

She nodded, her movements slightly jerky.

Daemon shifted, his large body coming to stand a little closer. "Why don't I walk you to the dining room, Primrose?" he asked softly. His black eyes darted to Wynona. "I'm sure Wynona can get you something to help settle your nerves."

Prim started to nod, then stopped herself. "No...wait." She took a deep breath, obviously steadying herself. "He was dating Thallia Pearlily. It was all very..." Prim made a face. "Forbidden, for lack of a better word," she said with an apologetic tone. "Her parents hated that he was from the *other* side of the tracks, if you know what I mean, but Thallia..." Prim shrugged.

Wynona should have known that Prim would know the Pearlily's. It was apparent that Thallia came from money, and that more than likely meant they were a prominent family in the fairy community, of which Prim was a member. Plus, Wynona's pink-headed friend loved a good bit of gossip and forbidden relationships would have been at the top of that list.

"Mr. Pearlily is known for being...very vocal," Prim said carefully about his disdain for Dralo.

Chief Ligurio turned to give the fairy his full attention. "Do you believe him capable of killing, Ms. Meadows?" Ever since Chief LIgurio has accused Prim of murder and then found out she was innocent, he'd been much more formal and polite in how he addressed her. It was, most likely, the only apology Prim was going to get from the vampire.

Wynona was holding back an inappropriate giggle at the way he was speaking. He'd been formal with her for a long time as well, but seeing the vampire speak to a tiny fairy in such a polite way just struck Wynona as a little humorous.

You mean he's getting his just desserts? Violet offered. *Eating humble pie?*

Wynona pressed her lips together. *Not helping, Violet.*

Someone has to call it like it is. She sniffed.

Wynona shook her head and went back to focusing on the situation at hand.

Prim was shaking her own head. "No. I'm not accusing anyone of anything. I'm simply saying there were high tensions among that family and that Dralo wasn't exactly known for being..."

"A law abiding citizen?" Daemon offered.

Prim looked up at him and nodded. "Right."

Wynona studied the pair. It was an interesting comparison. Even for a human, Daemon was tall, coming in several inches over six feet, and his features were dark. His skin was tanned and his hair as black as his eyes. He was handsome and well built, and Wynona adored him as a friend. But her *best* friend, Prim, was exactly the opposite of Daemon's steady and calm nature.

Prim was flighty and easily excitable. She tended toward the dramatic and was always eager to jump in with both feet. Her pink hair and eyes were as bright as her personality. The only things missing were wings. A fluorescent set would have been a perfect match for Prim's demeanor, but just like Wynona had been dealt a raw deal when she was born with bound magic, Prim had been born without wings. It made her an outcast among fairies, but perfect for Wynona.

The fact that the black hole and fairy were beginning to have feelings for each other made Wynona look at the situation with a more critical eye. Could two such opposing personalities work? Would Prim's effervescence eventually drive Daemon crazy? Would his solid foundation make Prim feel like she was being held back?

Why don't you let them figure that out? Rascal teased.

Wynona turned away from the couple and met her soulmate's eyes. *Sorry,* she said sheepishly. *I just can't help but wonder. I love them both, so I want them both to be happy.*

They're both adults, Rascal sent her. *If they want to see if they can find happiness with each other...they'll take care of it themselves.*

Spoilsport, Violet huffed. She twitched her tail. *Love life meddling is a woman's right.*

Rascal rolled his eyes and Wynona shook her head. *I wasn't planning to meddle. I was just curious.*

Tomato, tomahto, Violet sent back.

Hush, Wynona said finally. *This isn't important right now.* She ignored when Violet protested. They needed to work on figuring out Dralo's killer and whether or not it was a violent crime. "Is it at all possible that there was simply an accident?" she asked.

Rascal made a face, then shook his head. "I don't think the crime scene lends itself to an accident. We have no murder weapon, the blood is pooling on the floor and not smeared through the doorway to indicate he was dragged in here from somewhere else, and if it was an accident, I think there would be a bigger mess. Don't you?"

Wynona nodded, knowing he was right, but it didn't mean she had to like it.

"The simple answer is often the right one," Chief LIgurio said softly. "And I think all of us know this isn't an accident. I don't like it any better than you that another body has been found in your office, that your shop will have to be closed or that you're involved in yet another investigation, Ms. Le Doux," the vampire explained. "But there truly is no other explanation for what we're seeing."

"And Thallia?" Wynona pressed. "You really think she's the best suspect?"

Chief Ligurio shrugged. "Either her or her father, it sounds like. We'll have to talk to them to find out their alibis."

Wynona nodded and rubbed her forehead. She was getting really tired of all these dead bodies popping up when her life was so complicated.

Are you seriously asking people to only get murdered when you're bored? Violet asked.

"I didn't say that," Wynona hissed, then paused when she realized she'd said it out loud.

Rascal tried to cough to hide his laughter, but it was no use.

"Sorry," Wynona said sheepishly. She pointed to her shoulder. "Someone's in a mood this morning." Her mental blocks had never gone up so fast when Violet decided to respond to the allegation.

The mouse ran down her shoulder and continued chittering as she marched across the room and ducked under her favorite bookcase.

Prim's eyebrows were nearly to her hairline as she watched the scene. "I think she's mad," she whispered.

Wynona shook her head. "I'll bring her a cookie later. It'll be fine."

Not likely! Violet shouted.

Wynona rolled her eyes. Sometimes her familiar was more work than she was worth.

Prim covered her mouth and laughed softly. "Sorry," she said between giggles. "I think I'm still in shock."

Wynona smiled back. "No. It's fine." She walked over and took Prim's arm. "Let's go get that tea." Before they left, Wynona looked up at Daemon. "Would you come sit with her while I take care of things in the kitchen, please?" It took all she had not to react when Daemon's chest puffed out a little.

"Of course," he said in an official sound tone.

Wynona led the way, bringing Prim with her. "Have a seat here," Wynona said, settling Prim on the couch. "I'll be back in a minute with your drink."

Prim nodded and her eyes fluttered to Daemon as he stood next to the sofa.

"Feel free to have a seat, Officer," Wynona said casually over her shoulder. "I need to talk to Lusgu as well as make the tea, so I might be a couple minutes." Not hearing anything behind her, Wynona paused just inside the kitchen door and peeked back, grinning when she noticed Daemon inching closer and closer to the cushion on Prim's right.

Not a meddler, huh? Rascal teased.

I was simply providing an opportunity, Wynona sent back. She smiled when he laughed at her. Her smile remained while she got the tea ready. Odd as the pair might be, watching to see if something actually developed between the two creatures might be a bright spot in an otherwise stressful time. The idea of keeping her eyes peeled for more than just clues to the case appealed a little too much.

CHAPTER 6

"They've already got the whole family here?" Wynona asked Rascal as they pulled up to the station.

Rascal nodded and put the truck in park. "Yeah. Haskill said they were all home. It was easy to track them down."

Wynona sighed. "I really don't think she did it, Rascal. She's young and eager, but not a killer."

Rascal gave her a pitying look. "While I want to believe you, Wy, I've seen some pretty doe-eyed murderers. You wouldn't believe how dark some creatures are on the inside while looking innocent on the outside."

Wynona turned to look out the window. "Still...I don't think she's involved."

"For your sake, I hope not." He jumped out and walked around.

Wynona waited for him. She was in a skirt today, making it difficult for her to get up and down in the massive truck.

Rascal gripped her waist and helped her to the ground. Once there, however, he didn't let go. His eyes flashed a light golden color and he leaned in for a short but fierce kiss. "There," he said huskily. "That'll tide the wolf over until later."

Wynona smiled and rested her hands against his chest. "Maybe it won't tide me over, though."

He chuckled darkly and did a much more satisfactory job on the next exchange. "Better?" he asked when he finally pulled away.

"Mm-hm," she said, feeling slightly off balance. Whew! Her soulmate knew just how to turn her world upside down...in a good way.

Still smirking, Rascal took her hand and led her inside.

"Amaris!" Wynona called.

The vampire, who had been Wynona's friend since she'd begun working with the police, gave a small wave. Ever since word of Wynona's power had rocked Hex Haven, there were a few creatures that were noticeably afraid of the witch.

It hurt Wynona to see that her friend was one of them, though she couldn't exactly blame Amaris. Especially since Wynona had had so much trouble with her control for a while, and it had been absolutely dangerous to be around her up until very recently. While she still needed some good hard practice, Wynona had come a long way in learning about her powers and how to keep them under wraps when necessary.

Rascal tightened his hold, barely restraining a growl at Amaris's less than enthusiastic response. *Ignore her,* he told Wynona. *She doesn't know what she's missing out on.*

Wynona squeezed back. *She's scared. I understand. I'd be scared of me too.*

She's an idiot, he shot back. *She knows you. The fact that rumor and vague magical impressions are enough to sway her opinion says much more about her than anything else.*

Still...it saddened Wynona. She glanced over her shoulder to see Amaris watching them walk down the hallway. They had had such fun conversations and Wynona missed that. She didn't have a lot of friends to begin with and being the most powerful creature in Hex Haven was only going to make it worse.

Violet poked her nose out of Rascal's pocket. It was her favorite place after Wynona's shoulder. *Now that you two are done with the lovey junk, are we going to talk to some murderers or what?*

Wynona tsked her tongue. "Why are you so bloodthirsty? You shouldn't want people to be guilty of crimes."

Violet grinned. *Someone has to take them down. I'm only here for the glory.*

Rascal chuckled and scratched the mouse's ears. "That's my girl," he teased.

Wynona gave him the stink eye, but he only laughed more. "You two are a dangerous combination," she muttered.

"Le Doux!" Chief Ligurio shouted from farther down the hallway. "Can we get on with this?" He waved toward one of the interrogation rooms.

Wynona nodded. "Sorry, Chief Ligurio." She glared at Rascal again when he coughed. "You're not fooling anyone," she whispered, though she knew the vampire a few feet away heard every word.

"Strongclaw," Chief Ligurio growled.

"We're here," Rascal said good naturedly. He stepped back and let Wynona enter first.

"Ms. Le Doux!" Thallia shouted and raced across the room, throwing herself into Wynona's arms. "They said Dralo's dead," she sobbed into Wynona's neck.

Wynona was stiff for a moment before returning the embrace. Thallia was in her human form, but the hug was still slightly uncomfortable. "I know," she finally said, rubbing Thallia's back. "He was in the shop."

Thallia sniffed and pulled back. Her nose was bright red and her eyes puffy. "The tea shop? What was he doing there?"

"That's what we're trying to figure out," Chief Ligurio said firmly. "If you'll have a seat, please?"

Thallia began to shake. "How did he die?" she whispered thickly.

"Ms. Pearlily," Chief Ligurio said in a tighter tone. "Have a seat."

"Come on, Thallia," Wynona urged. "Sit down and we can figure all this out."

"What's there to figure out?" Thallia asked. "You said he's dead. There's nothing we can do about that."

"Maybe not, but we can figure out who killed him." Chief Ligurio wasn't the least bit moved by the young fairy's hysterics, though Wynona found herself struggling a little.

Thallia was definitely being dramatic, but who wouldn't be if their significant other turned up dead?

"Someone killed him?" Thallia's teal eyes widened. "He was *murdered*?" Her voice rose into a high-pitched squeal and without warning, she poofed back into her fairy form. Her wings were beating frantically and Wynona had to step back to keep from being hit. "Why would someone want to kill him? Why was he at the office? He never hurt anyone!" Thallia cried. "He was misunderstood! That's all! Nobody understands him the way I do!"

Chief Ligurio pinched the bridge of his nose and looked to Wynona. "Got a tea for this?"

Wynona pursed her lips. "I can try."

"Do."

She nodded and tilted her head, studying the fairy. "I think we better go with a strong batch. Mint, chamomile, lavender *and* rose." Wynona shrugged. "It should do the trick, though I'm not sure we'll find them all here."

"Go talk to Nightshade," Chief Ligurio said. "See what she's got in her desk."

Wynona hesitated only a moment before heading out the door. She knew the chief was right. Thallia needed something to help calm her, but would Amaris be willing to answer Wynona's questions? She hadn't spoken to Wynona for several weeks. "Amaris?" Wynona asked softly, coming up to the front desk from behind.

Amaris spun, her mouth gaping open. She pulled back visibly before stopping and stiffening her body. "Can I help you, Ms. Le Doux?"

Wynona felt the sting of tears at the back of her eyes, but she fought them off. They wouldn't help.

I told you...she's an idiot, Rascal growled.

Stop, Wynona gently scolded. *She's scared. There's a difference.*

He huffed, but didn't say more.

"I'm looking for a few ingredients for a tea," Wynona continued. "Do you happen to have any mint, chamomile, lavender or rose?"

Amaris took a moment to respond, but she finally jerked open her desk and presented Wynona with a box of mint tea packets.

"Thank you," Wynona added, very slowly picking up a single envelope. "I really appreciate it." She turned and began to walk away, hating the fact that it felt like she was walking away from any chance of ever being friends with the creature again, but Wynona knew that she couldn't force anything. Amaris would have to choose to be friends or not. Fear didn't just dissipate because a person said they weren't dangerous.

It took her another five minutes of walking around the office before she found the other ingredients, but eventually Wynona was able to make it back to the interrogation room. Thallia had calmed enough to speak to, though her answers were still difficult to understand.

"He's really just a big teddy bear," Thallia blubbered, wiping at her eyes, her hands as fluttery as her wings. "All he wanted was a place to belong."

"And were your parents willing to give him that?" Chief Ligurio asked. He gave Wynona a nod of acknowledgement when she brought the steaming mug to the table.

"Here," Wynona said softly, sliding it Thallia's way. "This will help."

Thallia nodded, her bottom lip still trembling. Her long fingers were shaking as she took the mug and swallowed a healthy gulp. "Hot." The young woman gasped.

Wynona held back an eye roll. "It has to be to steep the leaves," she explained as kindly as she could.

Thallia shrugged and took another deep sip. "Thank you," she said softly. Already the herbs were helping.

Daemon came up behind Wynona. "I can see purple in the steam," he whispered.

Wynona stiffened, then looked over her shoulder. "I didn't try to add anything."

Daemon widened his eyes and shook his head. "Just saying."

We can talk about it later, Rascal ordered. *Right now we need to get all the details out of her before talking to her parents.*

Wynona nodded, though she felt uneasy. She hadn't meant to use any magic and yet Daemon noted it was leaking into her work. Her plan to learn to control her magic shifted a little. She not only needed to learn to control large amounts of it, but apparently tiny amounts as well. It wasn't polite to use magic on creatures without their consent, and Wynona would never do it on purpose.

"Are you ready to talk, Ms. Pearlily?" Chief Ligurio asked, bringing Wynona's attention back to the matter at hand.

The young fairy nodded. "I've already told you everything, though," she said with a sniff. "After work, we met up for dinner, but then he had a meeting. We parted ways at about eight-thirty. I went home and stayed in my room. No one saw me, my parents were busy with other things. Dralo rode off on his motorcycle." She sniffed. "I'm not sure where his meeting was, but I'm sure it couldn't have been at the tea shop." Her wide, teary eyes turned to Wynona. "The first time he'd been at the shop was yesterday when you told us no seeing each other at work. I had to give him directions because he'd never heard of it before." She took another pull of the tea.

"How do your parents feel about your dating a dark elf?" Chief Ligurio pressed again.

Thallia's eyes stayed on her mug and she shrugged. "No one is good enough for my father," she whispered.

Wynona exchanged a look with Rascal. It kept coming back to the father. *But why would the father be the one at the office? If he wanted to meet with Dralo, why wouldn't he have called him to the house or something?*

Rascal shook his head subtly. *I don't know. Motive wise, the father makes sense. Execution wise...* His voice trailed off. No one had a good answer for that one.

"Was your boyfriend involved in any...questionable...activities, Ms. Pearlily?" Chief Ligurio continued.

"Questionable? Like what?"

"You said he rode a motorcycle," Chief Ligurio stated, leaning forward. "What did he do for work?"

"He's a bagger at Haven Grocers."

Wynona's eyebrows went up. "How could he afford that bike?" she blurted before she could think better of it. She pressed her lips together after the words were out and shot Chief Ligurio an apologetic look.

Thallia's eyes fell again. "Uh...well...Dralo was doing the best he could, but...sometimes he struggled to make ends meet."

"What are you implying?" Rascal asked, folding his impressive arms over his chest.

Thallia swallowed hard. "I might have loaned him money once in a while..." She jerked straighter in her seat as if to defend her actions. "My father doesn't know! And if he did, I'd be in so much trouble, but Dra just needed a chance to get on his feet, you know? He needed someone to believe in him!"

"You gave him enough money to buy a Parasuki?" Chief Ligurio said slowly. "How much of his lifestyle did you fund, Ms. Pearlily?"

The fairy shrugged and looked away. "Does it matter?"

"It does."

Thallia scowled. "Why?" She was becoming brave enough to turn her anger on the chief. "He's dead. How much money I gave him in the past is just that...the past."

Chief Ligurio folded his long white fingers together and leaned over the desk. "It matters," he said in a low tone. "Because I need to figure out whether or not you grew tired of funding his lifestyle and tried to break it off." He tilted his head to the side as Thallia's eyes slowly widened in understanding. "And if he refused to let you break it off, just how far were you willing to go to get out of your little...arrangement, Ms. Pearlily?"

"I didn't kill him," she rasped.

"He was killed at your place of work where there was an altercation earlier in the day. You gave him unknown amounts of money, your parents didn't approve of him and you have no witness as to your whereabouts last night." Chief Ligurio leaned back, a smug smile tugging on his lips. "If I were you, Ms. Pearlily, I would find myself a very good lawyer...and fast."

CHAPTER 7

"**Y**ou can't really believe she did it," Wynona said as they all convened in the chief's office after finishing with Thallia.

Chief Ligurio didn't respond and Wynona looked to Rascal. He made a face and shrugged. "I don't know, Wy. There are an awful lot of coincidences, if she's not guilty."

Wynona shook her head. "She's a dramatic young fairy. That doesn't make her a killer."

"Anyone can be a killer, Ms. Le Doux," Chief Ligurio said nonchalantly. "You should know that by now."

She rubbed her aching forehead. "Chief Ligurio, I'm fully aware that creatures make bad choices. I'm fully aware that in the heat of the moment, some even make permanently horrible decisions, but there is nothing about this situation that tells me Thallia would have wanted to kill her boyfriend." Wynona threw her arms into the air. "There was nothing in their body language yesterday that said they were on the outs with each other! He was genuinely upset that I kept them apart. His anger was with me, not with her." She leaned onto the chief's desk. "What about the father? Why aren't you more interested in him?"

"Because he's already lawyered up," Daemon offered from his stance by the door. "And the lawyer already gave us his alibi."

"Which is?"

Daemon gave Wynona a sad smile. "He was with his wife all night, who corroborates the story."

Wynona huffed and slumped into a seat.

"You look awfully upset about this, Ms. Le Doux," Chief Ligurio said with a low chuckle. "Have you decided you're going to join the investigation full time?"

She shook her head. "I think I've got enough on my plate, thank you." Sitting straighter, she pinned the chief with a glare. "But that doesn't mean I'll stand by and let you go after an innocent woman."

The chief leaned in as well. "Then do something about it."

Wynona scowled. "You aren't accusing her because you're trying to get me to work the case, are you? Because that's just low."

Chief Ligurio's eyes shot wide, then he burst out laughing. "Ms. Le Doux...even after a year and several cases together...I never seem to be able to keep up with your mind and where it's going." His amusement pulled back and he leaned into his seat. "With your sister, I always knew what I was getting, but with you..." He slowly shook his head.

Rascal apparently took offense to the words and began to growl in warning, but the chief held up a hand.

"At ease, Strongclaw. There was no disrespect." The chief tilted his head and studied Wynona. "I'm just curious. You think so differently than anyone else I know and yet, it's helpful. Not like some of the crazy paranormals running around this town who have lost all sense of reason."

"Gee," Wynona said, her sarcasm uncontrollable. "Thanks."

A long, white finger pointed at her. "That...was your sister. Clear as day." For a man who had smiled enough to count on one hand since they had met, Chief Ligurio was certainly enjoying this conversation much more than Wynona was.

Taking a deep breath, Wynona tried to pull her emotions back together. She had no desire to be compared with her sister at all, whether for good or bad. "Look, Chief...I'm not trying to cause a fuss or even be your morning entertainment. I simply want you to understand that Thallia is innocent. I know her story is sketchy, but my gut tells me she's not a murderer."

Chief Ligurio had sobered and was nodding. "I understand, and I've been grateful for your intuition, but Ms. Le Doux...I can't fight the evidence. She's got motive, opportunity and no alibi. I can't overlook that."

Wynona fell back in her seat. "The motive is weak. You have no true evidence that she wanted to break up with him."

Chief Ligurio shrugged. "I have no evidence to the contrary either."

"And you think her hysteria a moment ago was nothing but an act?"

Red eyes pinned her in place. "Are you really going to tell me that after all you've seen, a creature can't fake it, Ms. Le Doux?"

Wynona held his gaze for a moment before dropping it. The vampire was right. "No," she admitted. "I can't tell you that." She looked back up. "But I still think you're pulling at thin air. She didn't do it."

"Then I invite you to prove it," Chief Ligurio said. He gathered together some papers and stood up. "I need to talk to the Pearlilys' lawyer. While you're welcome to join me, I doubt he's going to want to have extra parties who aren't involved in the investigation hanging around." Chief Ligurio nodded curtly. "If you'll excuse me."

Wynona watched him go, then slowly stood. "I guess that's my cue." She smiled when Rascal took her hand. "Thanks for letting me sit in on Thallia's interrogation."

Rascal gave her fingers a squeeze. "You sure you don't want to help?"

Wynona shook her head. "Not only is it a conflict of interest, but I think I've got enough taking my time. I'm still trying to work out some kind of peace with Celia, I need to figure out how to get the grimoires and now I need to find another employee." She sighed. "I feel like every time I turn around life just keeps getting harder. Leaving home was supposed to make things easier."

"Welcome to the real world," Rascal teased. He reached into his pocket and pulled out Violet, who didn't appreciate being woken from her nap. "Take the truck," he said, handing Wynona both the keys and the mouse. "You can pick me up after work."

"Not on your life," Wynona said, pushing the keys right back. She had no intention of driving that monstrosity. "I'll call a cab."

Rascal scowled. "I don't want you getting in some stranger's car."

"I'll take her," Daemon said, stepping up to the conversation. "Chief won't care if I take a detour."

Rascal hesitated, then nodded. "Fine. Thank you." He kissed Wynona's cheek. "Save me some dinner?"

"Always." She smiled, watching him saunter away before turning to Daemon. "Ready?"

"If you'll set your googly eyes aside, I'm happy to take you wherever you want to go."

Wynona rolled said eyes. "I don't make googly eyes."

"My own eyes would beg to differ," Daemon said wryly. Waving his arm toward the front, he said, "After you."

Wynona set Violet on her shoulder and began the walk to the front of the building. Amaris ignored them, but Wynona called a goodbye anyway. She hated losing a friend...especially over something Wynona had no true control over. At one point in time, others hadn't wanted to be around her because she was powerless. Now people ran away because she had too much power. There seemed to be no middle ground at all.

"Ignore her," Daemon said as they got outside. "She'll eventually come around. Amaris has always taken longer to come to terms with change than anyone else in the office."

Wynona huffed a soft laugh. "She welcomed me in quickly enough."

"Misery loves company," Daemon said with a smirk. He opened the passenger door of his car. "M'lady?"

"Don't let Rascal hear you say that," Wynona joked. "His wolf might come out to play."

Daemon's dark eyes flashed. "I might show him a thing or two."

Wynona was still laughing when he shut the door and walked around to his side. "So..." Wynona hedged. "Tell me about Prim."

Daemon's head jerked her way so fast, Wynona was afraid he was going to lose control of the car. "What?" he squeaked, then cleared his throat. "I mean...I don't know what you're talking about."

"Riiiight," Wynona said with a slow nod. She turned to the window, giving him a slight reprieve, though she couldn't help the small grin on her face.

Meddler alert! Violet said with a laugh.

Hush, Wynona shot back. Though, the comment did remind her that she should probably back off. *Can I help it if I'm curious?*

Curiosity is what got you hired by the police in the first place, Violet commented. *Are you angling for another job?*

I really think this one is a conflict of interest! Wynona huffed. *Plus, I'm booked full! I hope to be able to help them in the future, but not right now. Not with this one.*

If you don't jump in on this, you might very well see an innocent fairy put behind bars.

Wynona chewed her bottom lip, the scenery flying by without her catching any of it.

"What's that mouse saying that's so interesting?" Daemon asked.

Wynona turned toward him, her eyebrows raised. "What was that?"

"I'm just curious what Violet has to say," Daemon asked again. "You don't look very happy about it."

Wynona cleared her throat as Violet pushed about meddling again. "She's telling me that I should get involved."

"And why won't you?"

Wynona's shoulders slumped. "I've already told you. I think it's a conflict of interest, which won't look good in court. And I'm already dealing with a lot right now. I'm trying to figure out how to live with my sister and still live my life. I'm trying to figure out how to get my Granny's grimoires without my parents knowing about it. And now I have to add trying to figure out how to find a new employee and save my business to the list."

"Solving the case *would* save your business," Daemon said with a smirk.

Wynona rolled her eyes. "You're as bad as Rascal."

"That's not an insult."

She gave him a severe frown, though Wynona couldn't hold it for long. "I'll tell you what," she said, feeling slightly smug. "I'll promise to think about helping if..."

"If...?"

"If you promise to think about asking Prim out."

Daemon grunted. "Too late. I've been thinking about that for ages."

Wynona twisted to sit on her hip, her smile wide. "Then why don't you?"

He gave her a wry look. "Are you serious? If you haven't missed the fact that I like her, then you haven't missed the fact that she wants nothing to do with me."

"Do you know why she's so stand-offish?" Wynona asked. "She hasn't said a word to me about it."

He let out a long, loud sigh. "Yeah..."

"And?"

"She can't seem to forgive me for being the one who was assigned to watch her when she was arrested."

Wynona's jaw dropped. "No," she whispered.

Daemon nodded. "Yeah. And I can't really blame her. I mean...I didn't want her to be guilty, but I also didn't have much choice in the situation." His eyes darted to hers and back to the road. "She's beautiful and full of spunk...but I had to sit there day after day, watching it all drain away because she was innocent and nobody could figure it out." He gave Wynona a sad smile. "Until you came along."

Wynona slumped in her seat. "That's a hard one."

Daemon nodded sagely. "Yep."

The situation churned over and over in Wynona's mind. It made her hurt to think of how her friends were hurting. Wynona was positive that Prim was attracted to Daemon. She didn't think Prim would behave so outrageously around him if she wasn't. But how did she help Prim forgive the very man who stood between her and freedom? It wasn't Daemon's fault Prim had been arrested. He had only been doing his job, but Wynona could see how it would be hard for Prim to look past his part in the situation to be able to enjoy his company.

"No words of wisdom?" Daemon teased as he pulled up next to the tea house.

Wynona made a face and shrugged. "None. Though, I admit I feel bad about it." She tapped her knee in thought. "My best advice would be to just wait it out, if possible. I think she's attracted to you, but only she can decide whether or not to act on it."

Daemon nodded, his eyes on the steering wheel. "Yeah...sometimes I get the feeling she returns my interest and other times I think she's ready to feed me to one of her plants."

Violet snickered.

He straightened. "But you're right. I should just be patient. What she went through couldn't have been easy. If...*when*...she decides I'm not a threat, then we'll see where things take us."

Wynona nodded. "I think that's wise." She grabbed the door handle. "Thanks for the ride."

Daemon tipped his head. "My pleasure. I'm just glad you didn't blow up my car."

Wynona laughed. "Yeah...I think I'm *mostly* past that stage with the magic." She sobered. "Unless I'm doing something really big."

Daemon's face also showed the change in emotion. "I don't know that I ever said it, but I'm sorry about your grandmother."

"Thanks." Wynona knew her smile was as fake as fake got, but it was all she could manage in the moment. "I'm trying to just be grateful for everything she left me."

He snorted. "That list isn't all good."

"I know...but it's what I have."

"Good for you," Daemon said with a nod. "I know a lot of creatures who would use your life as an excuse to go rogue or feral."

Wynona shrugged. "We all make our choices, I guess." She stepped out of the car, then leaned down. "Thanks again. I'll see you later."

Daemon gave her a teasing salute, then drove away after she had closed the door.

Wynona watched for a moment before sighing and turning to the tea house. She actually wasn't quite sure what she was going to do. She couldn't clean up the crime scene, and she couldn't open. "Might as well call our regulars," she muttered. "That's going to be fun."

Better you than me, Violet said. She climbed down Wynona's side and rushed inside, squeezing under the front door without slowing down.

"Guess I need to mouse-proof the shop," Wynona murmured.

Don't you dare!

Wynona laughed. "Don't tempt me." She could hear Violet chittering. As Wynona locked the door behind her, she heard a clash of pots and pans in the kitchen, reminding her that she hadn't spoken to Lusgu yet. He might now know that she'd lost her faith in him for a moment, but it still nagged at Wynona and she wanted to make it right, and he hadn't been around when she was in the kitchen earlier.

She took a fortifying breath. "No time like the present." Squaring her shoulders, she walked toward the noise.

Better watch it, or this'll turn into a double homicide, Violet yelled.

Wynona shook her head. "You're no help."

Nope. Even without seeing Violet's face, Wynona could hear the smug glee.

She pushed open the kitchen door. "Lusgu?"

He grunted an answer.

"I owe you an apology."

CHAPTER 8

Lusgu paused what he was doing and slowly turned, his brows pulled together in question. "What?"

Wynona couldn't hold his gaze. "I...I'm sure you heard there was another murder here last night?"

Lusgu nodded curtly.

"When I was talking to the chief about it, the question came up as to whether you could be involved..." Wynona swallowed hard. "And it took me a minute before I defended you. I just wanted to tell you I was sorry. That I know you well enough to know you wouldn't kill someone like that, and I'm sorry I doubted your character." She straightened her shoulders, preparing herself for his anger. "It's not what friends do."

Lusgu stared for several moments before his thin, dry lips pulled into a grin. He snorted, but instead of his usual disdain, Wynona could almost hear laughter in the noise. "It's apparent, girl, that you don't know me well at all."

Wynona paused. "Excuse me?"

Lusgu shook his head and turned away from her. "If you think I wouldn't kill, then you don't know me well at all."

Wynona fell against the counter top, gripping it hard to hold herself up. "I don't understand."

His black eyes were fairly twinkling when Lusgu glanced her way. "I existed many years before I came here, and odds are I will exist many more after you are gone. Don't assume you can imagine the life I have led, or will yet lead."

Wynona's head was spinning. She had never heard Lusgu speak so much, nor had she ever seen him anything but dour in his expressions. In only the space of a few moments, she realized he was right. She had no idea who this creature truly was.

She knew he was a brownie. She knew that her grandmother had maneuvered the situation so he would be hired by Wynona when the time was right. She knew Lusgu was powerful enough to stop her own magic, and to build himself a portal in the corner, where he disappeared to every night, but Violet was the only other creature who had ever entered that portal with him.

As far as Wynona knew, he never left the shop and didn't have any other friends, though he obviously knew Mama Reyna as they both had made plans with Granny Saffron before her death.

Wynona tilted her head to study him. "Where are you from, Lusgu?"

He grunted. "This isn't the time."

Wynona was undeterred. This morning's shock seemed to have emboldened her. She pushed off the counter and put her hands on her hips. "Then when is the time?"

Lusgu glared.

"I'd really like to know where you're from."

"And I'd really like you to leave me alone," came the waspish reply.

"Hello?"

Wynona turned at the sound of Prim's voice. She sighed. Her conversation with Lusgu would have to be continued another time. Prim had apparently finished talking with the police and Wynona should make sure she was okay. "We're not done here," she said to Lusgu.

He shrugged, not the least bit intimidated by her warning.

Wynona shook her head and walked out. She was starting to have the sense that there was far more to Lusgu than she knew. "Prim?" Wynona walked out into the dining room.

Prim stood near the room entry, still looking far too pale. "Hey."

Wynona gave her a sad smile and walked across the room with her arms wide.

Prim *poofed* into her human size and embraced Wynona. "This is going to cause such a ruckus in the fairy community," she mumbled into Wynona's shoulder.

Wynona rubbed Prim's back. "I'm so sorry."

Sniffing, Prim pulled back and nodded. "I know Dralo wasn't a fairy, but he was dating the daughter of one of our most prominent families. If Thallia's guilty, this won't go over well."

Wynona shook her head. "Thallia isn't guilty, so don't count her out just yet."

Prim's pink eyebrows shot up. "You're sure? She had an alibi?"

"No..." Wynona trailed off. She finally shrugged. "I mostly just have my gut instincts. Unfortunately, Thallia had time, motive and no one to back up her alibi. Chief Ligurio really wants to believe it's her."

Prim folded her arms over her chest, looking angry. "Yeah, well, we know how that goes."

"Be nice," Wynona scolded. She pulled Prim farther into the shop. "Have a seat and I'll get us something to eat."

Prim plopped herself in a chair and put her face in her hands. "You have to help her."

Wynona waited to answer until she had pulled a tray with lavender tea and a plate of pastries on it out to their table. "Help who?" she asked, though Wynona was pretty sure she knew the answer.

"Thallia," Prim said. "You have to help her. I know what it's like to be accused of something you didn't do and to have no evidence to help save you."

Wynona nodded. "I know you do," she said softly. "But I don't think I should get involved."

"Why not?" Prim demanded, setting her cup down a little too hard. "She needs you."

Wynona sighed and leaned back. How many times had she had this argument in the last few hours? "Because it's a conflict of interest," Wynona started with. "And because I'm still dealing with Celia and now I have to figure out how to keep an income coming in while the police solve yet another murder that occurred in my office."

Prim huffed. "It'll get done much faster if you help. That's the best way to save your business."

Wynona shrugged. "The police are plenty competent."

"For the most part," Prim admitted, "they're good people. But some of them need a good kick in the pants."

Who're we kicking and do I get to help? Violet asked as she sauntered out of the kitchen.

"Where have you been?" Wynona asked as her familiar climbed the table leg.

Around.

Wynona rolled her eyes, then turned back to Prim. "Ignore her."

Prim smirked. "I can't hear her. You're the one who has to do the ignoring."

Wynona made a face. "Sorry."

"Although I *am* curious as to what she said that has you all huffy."

"I'm not huffy," Wynona argued. "I just...am tired of everyone saying I should jump into the investigation."

Prim leaned forward. "Why aren't you?" she pressed. "If everyone is after you, it's for good reason. There has to be something else that's keeping you from helping."

Wynona stared at her teacup and twisted it back and forth.

"Nona..." Prim urged. "It's me. You know I won't judge you for anything."

Wynona glanced up from under her eyelashes. "I know," she assured Prim. "It's...it's stupid really, but I just..." She sighed. "Is it so wrong to want to live a normal life? To let the police handle the murders? To only want to run my tea business and learn about my magic like every other creature in Hex Haven? To not want everybody to want something from you or feel like the only people who *don't* want something from you only stay away because they're too afraid to ask for it?"

The table was silent for a few moments other than Violet's muching. She didn't seem the least bit concerned by Wynona's emotional turmoil.

She hadn't really meant to blurt it all out, but sometimes it all felt like too much. First she had no powers and learned to adjust. Now she had too many powers and no idea what to do about it. Meanwhile, she somehow kept getting roped into murder investigations, she fought with her parents, killed her own grandmother, was living with a sister who hated her guts, was desperately trying to learn how to control her rising abilities and had only recently found out that she had special soulmate powers with a wolf shifter. How much was too much before a creature went completely insane?

Prim's lips pressed to the side and her eyes narrowed. "Nona...I don't mean to sound trite about anything, but...maybe you're looking at this all wrong."

"And how is that?" Wynona snapped. She paused. "Sorry. I didn't mean to be rude."

"I know." Prim pushed her cup aside. "You're stressed. I get it." With a flick of her fingers, Prim grew one of the vines from a plant at Wynona's window and had it spreading across the room until it arrived at the table with the women. "You see this?"

Wynona gave Prim a look. "How could I have missed it?"

Prim smirked and waggled her eyebrows. "This is known as a princess of the night."

Wynona leaned back. "Really? That's cool."

Prim nodded slowly, fingering the petals. "That's kind of a blanket term for a plant such as this, but I thought it applied to our situation." Prim turned her bright eyes to Wynona. "It not only blooms at night, but only once a year."

Wynona slumped a little. "It's kind of hard to enjoy it if it only blooms once a year while we're sleeping."

Prim pursed her lips and ticked her head back and forth. "You can say that. Or you can see that by blooming at all, she helps bring beauty to the world and changes us for the better." Cupping the vine in her fingers, Prim stilled and slowly Wynona watched as a bud formed, eventually spreading into a stunning white flower with spikes and petals that sprang in every direction.

"You're obviously trying to teach me a lesson," Wynona said softly, her eyes still on the flower. "But I don't quite understand it."

Prim's eyes were closed and she didn't answer right away. After a moment, she let out a long breath and looked at the flower, only to have it fade right in front of her, finally turning to ash. Prim gently set down the vine and allowed the plant to go back to its original size. Folding her fingers together, she turned to Wynona. "Was it worth seeing the blossom?"

"Of course. It's beautiful," Wynona responded.

"Even though it requires circumstances to be just right in order for it to come out?"

Wynona nodded. "Even then."

Prim leaned in. "You're like that flower, Nona. You required special circumstances in order to bloom. It took so long and was so different from every other path that you're not quite sure what to do with yourself. I understand. My path has been different as well, but that doesn't mean your flower isn't worth blooming. There's a reason the rarest blooming flowers are the most beautiful." Prim winked. "It's because they're the ones worth waiting the most for."

Wynona laughed softly. "Excellent lesson."

Prim preened. "Thank you."

"But I don't completely agree with you."

Prim shrugged. "I knew you wouldn't."

"And it doesn't fix the fact that I'm really busy."

Prim raised an eyebrow. "Do you really think you'll ever *not* be busy?"

Wynona opened her mouth, but paused. There was truth in that statement. Life hadn't been what she planned ever since she escaped the palace. There'd been murders, fighting, loving, learning... Her life had been on the go ever since she'd left home. To believe that it would calm down if she didn't help with the investigation was probably a bit on the naive side.

"You mentioned that everyone either wants something from you or is afraid of you," Prim said softly. "But this time it's my turn to disagree." She gave Wynona a sad smile. "We don't all *want* something from you...we *need* something from you." She leaned in. "And you need something from us."

Wynona took a sip of tea. The heated drink felt good going down her throat as she contemplated what Prim was trying to explain. "And what is that?"

"Support. Acceptance. Friendship." Prim shrugged. "Call it what you will, but the very thing every creature in Hex Haven is looking for is the ability to feel like they belong somewhere and have a purpose. So, yeah, we need that from you." She grinned. "And you seem to have taken on the challenge of accepting all the weirdos, so...congrats on that."

Watch it, Violet muttered.

Wynona absentmindedly scratched behind Violet's ears. She grinned at Prim. "You realize you're talking about yourself, right?"

Prim fluffed her pink hair. "And proud of it." She dropped her hand. "But seriously, the world wouldn't be the same without you, Nona. We need your bloom, not just your plant. And I know you well enough to know that you won't be able to sit by and let Thallia be accused of a crime she didn't commit. It would eat you up inside. So why not just skip all the hullabaloo and jump in with both feet?"

Wynona dropped her friend's eyes and stared at her empty teacup. "What about Celia?"

Prim shrugged. "Celia's here. We don't know how sincere she is yet, but only time will tell us. Meanwhile, working the case will get you out of the house and away from her prying eyes."

"You think she's here for Mom and Dad as well?"

Prim pursed her lips. "I'm not sure. Honestly, as much as I hate to say it, I want to believe her. I want to think she's itching for a change and that your dad's empire is about to be shaken, but she's been with them a long time and I've seen her do some nasty things, so..."

Wynona nodded. "Yeah...I feel the same way. I want to believe her, but I'm not quite sure how."

"So what will you do?"

Wynona pinched her lips together. "I suppose first I ought to make sure Thallia's taken care of."

Prim snorted and grinned.

"Then I should find Granny's grimoires."

Her friend nodded.

"And finally, I should keep an eye on Celia and see what she's up to."

Prim held her teacup in the air. "That's quite the list, but it sounds decent to me."

"Oh," Wynona said wryly. "And all the while I'll work to keep my business from going under, hire a new employee, keep my relationship with Rascal moving forward and learn to control my magic even though no one can help me."

Prim laughed. "Here's to the road less traveled."

Wynona held out her cup and muttered good naturedly, "I'm not even sure this road has been invented."

"If anyone can pave the way, my princess blossom...it's you," Prim said with a wink.

Wynona shook her head. "Don't call me a princess."

Prim's eyes widened. "Why not? Technically it's true."

"Because it's what my parents called Celia all my growing up years and I want nothing to do with that."

"Fair enough." Prim finished her tea. "Now...you have a fairy to save and I have a gossip chain to tap. I'll let you know what I find out." She leapt up from her seat and began to walk away.

"Where are you going?" Wynona asked.

Prim grinned over her shoulder ."The Curl and Die... Where else?"

"Have fun." If anyone would know the secrets of the Pearlily family, it would be the hair and nail salon. Those creatures knew more secrets than an invisible servant.

"Oh, I will!" Prim called out just before she opened the front door. "And I'll check in soon! Love ya! Bye!"

Wynona smiled as the door slammed. "Love you too," she whispered. She was touched by Prim's pep talk. Her little fairy friend truly cared and had also been right. Everyone needed a place to belong.

The tea shop was Wynona's place and she worked hard to make sure it was open to every creature who needed a place. Her community was still pretty small and yes, they might be some of the more unusual citizens of Hex Haven, but Wynona was pretty sure her life wouldn't be the same without them.

"So...now it's your job to protect this place," she told herself, standing up. "And to do that, you have to make sure Thallia is exonerated. Once the true killer is caught, this place can be a sanctuary once more."

She wiggled her fingers and began to clean up the tea mess. It was time to contact Rascal.

CHAPTER 9

Wynona unclipped her helmet and stepped off her Vespa. "Don't say it," she warned Rascal, who was waiting by his truck.

The wolf shifter put his hands in the air. "I didn't say anything."

Wynona sniffed as she walked past him. "You didn't need to."

He chuckled, low and delicious behind her, and Wynona had to pinch her lips to keep her smile in check. She loved that wolf a little too much.

There's no such thing as too much, he teased.

"Get out of my head," Wynona hissed.

Then close it up!

Wynona sent up her mental block so fast that Rascal actually winced.

"Point taken," he said, rubbing his temple.

Wynona's eyes grew wide. "Did that actually hurt? Like, for real?"

Rascal pressed circles against his head. "Surprisingly enough...it sort of did. Like someone closed a door too fast inside my brain."

"I'm so sorry," Wynona gushed, rushing back to him. She checked him over as if touching him would assure her he was alright. "I didn't know that was even possible! How could I hurt you?"

"Wy," Rascal said, grabbing her wandering hands and smiling. "I'm fine. I guess we're both still learning about this soulmate thing, huh? I didn't know it was possible either."

Wynona shook her head. "That's twice I've hurt you," she whispered thickly. How was it that the person she adored most in the world was the one who always seemed to be caught in the middle of her mistakes?

"And that's twice I've moved on without even thinking about it." He kissed the tip of her nose and spun her around. "Now come on, Detective. We have a house to look through."

Still feeling heavy with guilt, Wynona looked at the apartment door in front of her. "What did Thallia say he did for a living?" she asked.

"Grocery store bagger."

Wynona looked over her shoulder. "I'm guessing she paid for more than his motorcycle."

Rascal nodded. "Guess the elf had a sugar fairy... Must be nice." He laughed when Wynona elbowed him gently. "That's one way you can't hurt me, babe."

"I don't want to hurt you."

Rascal winked. "I know. And I fully plan to use that to my advantage."

Wynona rolled her eyes. He was ridiculous...and wonderful. "Let's go inside."

Rascal handed her a key and Wynona let them in. Just as they walked inside, another set of tires pulled into the driveway of the condo and Wynona turned around. "Oh good, Daemon's here."

"Speaking of," Rascal hedged, "don't think I didn't hear you interrogating him yesterday."

"Ugh." Wynona groaned. "I wasn't meddling."

Bright gold eyes gave her a disbelieving look.

"I was trying to help!" Wynona threw her arms to the side. "Someone has to break the ice between them!"

"Pretty sure I can handle that myself," Daemon said gruffly as he walked inside. "Sorry I'm late, Deputy Chief. Got stuck in traffic."

"We have sirens for that kind of thing," Rascal said wryly.

"Some of us don't get away with fudging the law as much as others," Daemon shot right back.

Rascal snorted. "Just don't get caught."

Wynona shook her head. "You're incorrigible."

"Thank you."

Sighing and turning to Daemon, Wynona asked, "Can you turn on your sight? I think we need to keep an eye out for magic from the get go."

Daemon's eyes immediately went solid black. He slowly turned around the room. "There are traces of red everywhere."

Wynona nodded. "I'll bet that's Thallia's color."

"Her wings are sort of blue," Rascal pointed out.

"Their wings are parts of their body," Wynona responded. "Not magic .So they don't necessarily have anything to do with each other. Just like her hair and eyes. They're all teal. My magic is purple, but my eyes and hair are black."

Grumbling under his breath, Rascal walked farther inside. "She might have paid for everything, but this definitely looks more like Dralo's decorating than Ms. Pearlily's," he murmured.

Wynona had to agree. The condo was dark. Very dark. One wall was painted completely black and the furniture blended right in. A rug with bright red accents sent a shot of color through the room, matching the throw pillows scattered through the sitting area. "I don't think he did much of the decorating, though," she said after a moment.

"He's a dark elf," Rascal argued. "Thallia doesn't strike me as the type to like such masculine surroundings."

Wynona shrugged. "And yet, how many men do you know who worry about matching their throw pillows to their rugs?"

Rascal frowned. "If I didn't have sisters, I wouldn't even know what a throw pillow was."

"Exactly my point," Wynona said. "Look." She pointed to the rug, the pillows and then a large piece of art. "Either this place came furnished, or Thallia had a say in what she bought."

"She didn't influence his groceries much," Daemon called from the kitchen.

Wynona and Rascal headed that direction.

Daemon smirked as he opened a couple more cupboards. Canned soup, chips and bottles of soda were the main ingredients in each and every one.

Wynona laughed softly. "Good thing I didn't bring Violet. She would have had something to say about Mr. Ziumar's palate."

Rascal snorted. He opened and shut a few cupboards. "I'm not seeing anything out of the ordinary here."

"Can we look in the bedroom?" Wynona asked. "If he was a thief of some kind, I'm guessing he has to have a safe space where he stored the stolen property until he could sell it."

Rascal led the way down the hall. More artwork hung on either side of them.

"You don't think he stole art, do you?" Daemon asked from behind Wynona.

"He doesn't seem the type," Wynona murmured, her eyes wandering to every nook and cranny. "But sometimes looks can be deceiving." Just as they reached the bedroom, her phone buzzed. Grabbing it out of her pocket, Wynona was surprised to see a note from Prim.

Salon sisters are quiet, but they'll keep their ears to the ground. What are you doing now?

Deciding not to waste the time typing it all out, she pressed the call button.

"Whatcha got, hot mama?" Prim asked.

Wynona grinned. "Hey, Prim." She didn't miss Daemon's head jerk. "We're at Dralo's house looking for clues." Wynona hesitated only a moment before asking, "Did you want to help?"

Rascal scowled and Wynona ignored him.

"Really? Let me lock the greenhouse and I'll be right over."

She was gone before Wynona could share the address. "I'm gonna guess she already knows it," Rascal said, giving Wynona a look.

She winced. *Sorry, but she's been feeling left out. If it's a big deal, I'll call it off.*

He sighed and pinched the bridge of his nose. *You promise this isn't about setting them up?*

Wynona shook her head. *Promise.*

He made a face that said he'd capitulated and Wynona gave him a sweet smile. Finally, she took the time to go over her surroundings. "Whoa..."

Daemon nodded. "Yeah. Whoa."

Dralo's bed looked like it hadn't been made in six months. Whoever helped keep the front part of the house clean never ventured to the bedroom area. His sheets were wadded up and covers flung in a chair in the corner.

A pile of dirty clothes sat on the floor next to the full laundry basket.

"I'm guessing Ms. Pearlily didn't pay for a maid," Daemon said with a snort.

"Is there magic in here, Daemon?" Wynona asked.

He paused, his head slowly swiveling. "Nothing more than what I saw out front. Hints of red, but it's all just dustings."

"Fairy dust?" Rascal tried to hide his laughter behind a cough, but as usual, he wasn't fooling anyone.

"Do fairies actually leave dust?" Daemon asked in seriousness. "I'm not sure I've ever actually thought about it."

Wynona shook her head. "Not that I know of. None of the books I read growing up said they did." She put her hands on her hips and pursed her lips. "I'm guessing the light color is simply because Thallia didn't do direct magic on any of it." She paused. "Come to think of it, I'm not sure exactly what type of magic Thallia can do."

"She works with fire."

All the heads whipped toward the doorway where Prim stood. Her bright pink hair looked awful against the black and red decorations.

"Fire?" Wynona asked, her jaw agape. "How do you know that?"

One pink eyebrow shot up. "She's a Pearlily."

"Does the whole family work with that element?" Rascal asked, his laughter gone.

Prim nodded. "As far as I know. The parents had an arranged marriage and Thallia is their only daughter. If any of them have other gifts, they aren't strong enough to be talked about."

Rascal nodded. "Thank you, Prim."

Prim gave him a grin and tilted her head. "Glad I could be of help, Detective Strongclaw."

He chuckled. "Come on in and see what you can see, huh?" He dropped his voice. "Just don't tell the chief. He'd have my hide."

"Literally," Daemon snorted.

"So what are we looking for?" Prim asked, daintily stepping through the messy room.

"Anything out of the ordinary," Wynona said. She began walking along the walls. "If Dralo was trying to steal something at the shop, odds are he's stolen before."

"So he probably has a place he stores his goods, right?" Prim asked.

Wynona smiled at her friend. "Exactly."

Prim's pink eyes flared. "Has anyone looked for a secret room? Or maybe a hidden safe?"

Daemon chuckled softly. "There's plenty of artwork. Why don't you have a look?"

Prim bounced on her toes and began rushing from one picture to the other. For the next half hour the entire group searched the house up and down, but the only thing they found was more expensive furnishings, expensive dirty clothes and a garbage can in desperate need of being dumped.

Prim's bottom lip poked out as they reconvened in the front room. She put her hands on her hips. "This is way more boring than I thought it would be."

Wynona laughed. "What did you think would happen? We would just find evidence lying around in the middle of the room?"

"Something like that." Prim tapped her lips. "There has to be something here, though, right? I mean...he was killed. Shouldn't there be something that hints at what was going on in his life?"

Rascal shrugged and rested a hand on Wynona's lower back. "Not necessarily. He was the victim, but we're not sure exactly *why* he was the victim. It could be for any number of reasons, and that means his normal life could be exactly that...normal."

"Booooring." Prim groaned, throwing back her head.

Wynona shook her head. "Where to next?" she asked Rascal.

Prim huffed. "You guys are going to keep going? Stink. I have to get back. I have a bride coming in to look at flowers."

"I'll catch you up on whatever we find," Wynona assured her.

"I'll walk you out," Daemon offered quickly. His look at Rascal's snort told Wynona she and Rascal had better back off.

Prim hesitated, then shrugged. "Whatever. It's not like I could stop you anyway."

Rascal shook his head slowly back and forth as the two walked out the door. "She likes him, doesn't she?"

"I think she does," Wynona whispered with a smile. "But she's...hesitant."

"Do we know why?"

"Daemon said it's because he was the guard in charge of her at the prison."

"Huh." Rascal scratched the back of his head. "I can see how that would be a little awkward."

"Remember," Wynona teased, "no meddling."

Rascal rolled his eyes. "Yes, ma'am. Now come on. I say we talk to the Pearlilys next."

"Won't they want their lawyer there?"

Rascal's smile was full of mischief. "I'm hoping they'll talk to you at home without worrying about it. You tend to put people at ease."

"Sneaky," Wynona muttered.

"I prefer the word genius."

"I'll bet you would."

Rascal laughed as he set her helmet on her head. "I hate that you're not riding with me."

"I know, but I don't want to leave the Vespa here."

"How about we stop at the shop and you can leave it there?"

"That's the complete opposite direction!" Wynona said in exasperation.

"So?"

Her shoulders fell and she huffed a laugh. "Fine. If that's what you want."

"It's what I want." He left a quick kiss on her cheek. "Meet you there."

Wynona started the scooter and took off. Prim was already gone and she knew Rascal would be right behind her, with Daemon probably right behind him. They'd make a nice line-up headed back toward town.

Violet?

A loud yawn came through their mental link. *Yeah? Did you find anything at Elf Boy's house?*

No. The place was definitely a bachelor pad, but nothing that would hint at an illegal operation.

Figures, Violet murmured. *Glad I stayed behind.*

We're heading to the Pearlilys to see if they'll talk to us without their lawyer. I'm stopping by the shop first. Did you want to come this time?

How long until you get here?

Maybe ten minutes? Wynona guessed.

Yeah...Lusgu's sweeping for the tenth time and there are no crumbs left anywhere. Might as well do something else.

Wynona smiled. *I'll see you in a few.*

CHAPTER 10

"Wow," Wynona said as she and Rascal pulled into the Pearlilys' driveway. "Prim was right. They're definitely at the top of the fairy food chain."

"But not the witch food chain?" Rascal asked.

Wynona shrugged and looked over at him. "They obviously have money, which means they have some power, but their magic isn't enough to compete with the witches. That's probably why I never saw them running in my family's inner circle."

"I hate politics," Rascal grumbled.

Hear, hear! Violet shouted.

"I'm not overly fond of them myself," Wynona commiserated. "Which is why I wasn't interested in Granny's suggestion that I take over Hex Haven."

"Thank goodness for that." Rascal hopped out of the truck and walked around to help Wynona get down.

"I think maybe we should install a ladder for whenever I ride with you," Wynona said with a laugh when he lifted her to the ground. Her skirts were often an impediment when it came to getting in and out of the monstrous vehicle.

"What? And lose a chance to hold you close?" Rascal winked. "Never."

Wynona slapped his chest. "So that's how it is? This was all pre-planned?"

He shrugged.

"Should I ask how many other girls you've done this with?"

He leaned over and kissed her cheek. "Just you, beautiful. So put your claws back in."

Wynona gave him a look, but she couldn't help but be pleased at the answer. She had assumed he'd had girlfriends before they'd met. It would be only natural and she hadn't planned on being jealous of any of them, but after the tease had come out, she had to admit that something decidedly possessive had started to unfurl in her belly. Rascal's answer put it all to rest, however, for which she was grateful.

"Ready?" he asked, his hand in the air above the door.

"Should we wait for Daemon?"

Rascal shook his head. "He's here."

Wynona frowned and turned. Daemon was just pulling into the driveway. "How did you know that?"

Rascal tapped his ear. "Maybe you need hearing aids?"

Her glare only made him laugh.

Without waiting for Daemon to get out of his car, Rascal knocked.

It only took seconds for the door to be opened. "May I help you?" a woman asked, her voice soft and inviting. Wynona knew instantly it had to be Thallia's mother. The fairy had the same teal wings and they fluttered incessantly. Her hair was lighter than Thallia's, almost transparent, with blue ends. Her eyes, however, were dark, a near black that contrasted against the bright pastels found elsewhere.

"I'm Deputy Chief Strongclaw from the Hex Haven Police Department," Rascal said in an authoritative tone.

The woman shrank back. "We've already spoken to the police."

Wynona stepped up. This was exactly why Rascal had wanted her here. "We know," she said politely. "But we were hoping you wouldn't mind answering just a few more questions for us."

The fairy paused and narrowed her eyes. "You look familiar..."

Wynona kept her smile in place, though she wanted to drop it. She knew her resemblance to her mother would be considered by most a wonderful gift, but Wynona could have done without the connection, thank you very much. "I'm Wynona Le Doux. I'm an independent consultant for the police."

The woman's eyes widened and her wing speed picked up. "Oh my goodness. Oh my goodness!" The door flew open. "President Le Doux's daughter. Right here on my front porch!" Gone was the shy, quiet creature and in her place was a gushing fan. "Come in, please. Come in."

Can't say they never gave you anything, Rascal said.

I think I could manage without it, thanks. Wynona forced her lips to stay in a wide smile as she, Rascal and Daemon were brought inside. Any fan of her father's was not someone Wynona wanted to spend time with.

"I'll bring tea," the fairy stammered. "Do you like tea? Would tea be alright?"

At this point, Wynona was starting to feel sorry for Thallia's mother. She was obviously a nervous woman and having a Le Doux in her house was pulling her apart at the seams. "Tea would be lovely, thank you..." Wynona trailed off, waiting for confirmation that this woman was who she thought she was.

The fairy slapped her forehead. "Oh, my goodness! I'm so ridiculous!" She straightened. "Sequoia Pearlily. Wife to Florian Pearlily." She smiled proudly, as if that should mean something to Wynona.

Wynona had no idea who Florian Pearlily was, but from Prim's chatter and the way Sequoia introduced herself, Wynona guessed she was supposed to be impressed. "So nice to meet you," Wynona said, holding out her hand.

Sequoia's wings were almost frantic by the time their handshake was over. "Sit, sit," she said quickly. By this point she was hovering off the ground. "Let me heat the water and I'll be right back. Our butler has the day off, so I'm afraid I'm on my own."

Wynona exchanged a look with her two companions when Mrs. Pearlily disappeared from the sitting room.

"Wow," Daemon mouthed, making an incredulous face. "She was...something."

Wynona nodded. "A little bit excitable, I think," she whispered very softly.

Rascal's face said that was an understatement.

She plum loco, Violet said with a snort.

Hush, Wynona scolded. *We can't all be purple mice.*

Idiots. Violet sniffed.

Wynona shook her head and took the time to look around the room. Color was everywhere. The walls of the space were white, but bright flowers, draperies and artwork covered almost every inch of it. The hardwood floors had multiple rugs and the couches were each a different style and color. With reds, blues, greens, the room looked like a box of crayons had been dumped upside down and left behind.

"Interesting style," Rascal murmured, his eyes roaming the room just like Wynona's.

"Maybe it's a fairy thing?" she whispered.

Rascal shrugged and shook his head.

"I don't care who they are!" a loud voice boomed. "Get them out of my house!"

Wynona turned to Rascal. "Uh-oh."

I think we're about to meet Mr. Pearlily, Violet said wryly. *And I'm guessing we'll understand why Mrs. Pearlily is so nervous all the time.*

Wynona could only nod before a great bear of a man stormed through the threshold of the sitting room. He was obviously in his human form as there were no wings to speak of, but even for a human, Mr. Pearlily's size was impressive. He stood well over six feet with a barrel chest and a wide, square jaw. His green hair was the only part of him that told a passerby he wasn't a human body builder.

"We already spoke to the police!" he boomed as soon as he walked in the room. "If you want more information, you'll have to talk to our lawyer."

Wynona took a breath for courage and stepped forward. "Hello, Mr. Pearlily. My name is Wynon—"

"I don't care!" he shouted, getting in Wynona's face.

Rascal was immediately beside her, growling a harsh warning. "Sir, you need to calm down and back off." The words were slightly garbled since Rascal's teeth had elongated.

Shaking his head, Mr. Pearlily turned his glare onto the wolf. "You think a wolf can stop me?" He snapped his fingers, and flames danced across his palm. Mr. Pearlily sneered. "How'd you like to see what your coat looks like in leather?"

Wynona held still and worked to keep her magic under control. Mr. Pearlily was a bully. Plain and simple. She'd dealt with bullies before and trying to bully back wasn't the way to do it. She needed to be strong, but not aggressive. "Mr. Pearlily, if you would just listen for a moment."

"I SAID, GET OUT!" he bellowed.

Wynona's magic surged to the forefront in an effort to protect her, and Wynona couldn't quite stop it in time. A purple wall sprang up between the fairy and Wynona's group just as Mr. Pearlily's flame went out.

The large creature stared at his fingers. "What? What's going on?" he muttered. He snapped his fingers several times, his eyes going between the purple wall and his hand. Finally he turned back to Wynona. "Did you do this?"

Wynona shook her head and calmly turned to look at Daemon, whose eyes were just as she suspected.

Although not quite as wide, Daemon was just as tall, and when his eyes went black, just as intimidating.

Mr. Pearlily's shoulders slumped. "Should have known you would have a black hole." He glared at Daemon. "Your kind is rarer than a three-horned unicorn."

Daemon held his ground.

"But what's this?" Mr. Pearlily asked, poking the wall. Sparks shot out and he yelped.

"That..." Wynona said clearly, "is my contribution." *Violet? A little help here?* Her magic was raging and Wynona knew she'd have trouble convincing it the danger was over. While she was grateful for the instinct to protect, Wynona wished she felt like she had more control.

Violet grumbled, but wrapped her tail about the back of Wynona's neck. *Alright...give it a go.*

Rascal reached over and took her hand and Wynona practically sighed at the contact. Between her familiar and her soulmate, she was able to force the magic to back down and the wall slowly dissipated.

Mr. Pearlily was still glaring, but his demeanor was much more intrigued than before. "Who are you people?"

"Oh dear," Mrs. Pearlily said from the doorway. "I'm so sorry. I—"

"Stop talking, Sequoia," Mr. Pearlily snapped.

Wynona's magic flared again, but Rascal squeezed her hand tighter. "My name is Wynona Le Doux," she said tightly.

Unfortunately, or fortunately, depending on how it was looked at, Mr. Pearlily's face paled. Wynona knew he recognized her just as much as his wife had.

"I'm working with the police on an independent consulting basis and wasn't present when you and your lawyer spoke to Chief Ligurio." Wynona raised an eyebrow. "I came today hoping you would grant me a few minutes of your time so I could ask questions about Dralo Ziumar's death."

Mr. Pearlily looked much more cooperative now, but there was a definite wariness in his eyes. "You're the president's daughter?"

Wynona nodded.

"Are you the oldest?"

Wynona nodded again.

Hazel eyes narrowed. "I thought the oldest was a magic dud."

Rascal growled and Mrs. Pearlily tugged on her husband's shirt sleeve.

It took a moment for him to acknowledge her, but finally, he turned back and her wings fluttered until she rose off the ground and was able to whisper in his ear. Whatever she said had to have been good because his skin paled even farther. When Mr. Pearlily turned to Wynona again, he wasn't wary...he was scared. "That magic a few weeks back. That was yours?"

Wynona hesitated only momentarily before nodding again. "It was. I was cursed at birth and that spell you felt was the curse breaking."

Mr. Pearlily swallowed audibly before straightening himself to his full height. "Still doesn't excuse you barging in here like you own the place," he said darkly, though the bite was gone. "But we don't cause trouble with the president. Sit down."

Wynona's jaw was beginning to ache from how tightly she had it clenched. This was a legacy she would never thank her father for.

Granny asked you to end his reign.

I'm NOT waging war against my dad, Wynona said, hoping that would be the end of the subject. She walked over and sat on the edge of a couch. "Thank you for your time, Mr. Pearlily. I'm sure you want to see Dralo's killer caught just as much as we do."

The large man snorted and dropped into a club chair across from the couch. His green hair complemented the red fabric. "I don't care a bit that the kid's gone. Never was any good for my bubble-headed daughter."

Wynona's jaw tightened. "I'm sure you already told the police where you were that night, but would you mind catching me up?" she asked.

"Here. Home."

Mrs. Pearlily fluttered back in, setting a tray down on the coffee table and with shaking fingers, dunking a tea bag in the water before handing it to Wynona.

"Thank you," Wynona said softly, giving the battered woman a soft smile. She had a feeling Mrs. Pearlily needed all the friends she could get.

Not to mention a divorce, Violet snapped.

Wynona completely agreed, but kept her thoughts to herself. She knew all too well how the magical community worked. If she still lived under her father's thumb, he would never have let someone like Rascal near the house, let alone let Wynona and him date.

"And your witness?" Wynona asked cooly.

"My wife," Mr. Pearlily ground out. "We were together all night." He smirked. "Find it hard to believe?"

"Not at all," Wynona said. "Just covering all my bases. After all, it's clear you didn't like your daughter's boyfriend."

"Boyfriend." He huffed. "More like troublemaker. Thallia has a thing for taking in strays. It was a phase. Once he showed signs of actually growing up, she'd have become bored and moved on."

Wynona tucked that thought away. Much as she hated to admit it, he might have a point. "Do you know anyone who *would* have wanted to kill him? Or perhaps he had friends who might have seemed shady?"

Mr. Pearlily sat back, crossing a leg over the other knee. "I don't know anything about him other than that he's not good enough for Thallia." He chuckled. "She thinks I don't know about her sneaking out to see him, but nothing gets by me. Nothing at all." He sighed. "But like I said, she would have eventually moved on. Meanwhile, I would have found her a suitable match."

"And did you have someone in mind?"

He hesitated. "Nothing I can speak of. Talks had only just begun."

"And will they continue now that the boyfriend is dead?" Wynona knew she was pressing, but she really didn't like this guy and now that he was afraid of her, she wanted to use it a little to her advantage.

"Probably." Mr. Pearlily shrugged. "It'll probably even be easier now. I won't have to get the kid out of the way."

"What do you do for a living, Mr. Pearlily?" Wynona asked.

He scowled. "What's that got to do with anything?"

Wynona shrugged and sipped her tea. "Just curious. You must be good at it since you have such a beautiful home." She ignored the twin snorts of Rascal and Violet in her head. Decorating aside, it was a large, nice home. Just because Mrs. Pearlily had no sense when it came to combining colors didn't mean there was something wrong with it.

"I'm an investor."

"Oh? What kind?"

"Real estate. I own the apartments in downtown Hex Haven."

Wynona paused. "The condos? White with gray trim?"

"That's right. That complex is part of my portfolio." He turned away, obviously bored with the conversation.

Wynona, however, set the information in her "keep" pile. Mr. Pearlily, it would seem, owned the very condo that Dralo was living in. But did Mr. Pearlily know? And how could the fairy have used that to his advantage?

CHAPTER 11

"Celia?" Wynona called out as she walked inside her cottage. There was no answer. "Violet? Is she here?"

Violet scrambled down from Wynona's shoulder and disappeared. Wynona could hear her scuttling around the place until she finally came back to the front door. *No Celia. Thank goodness.*

Wynona frowned. "Be nice."

Her first.

Wynona sighed. "Come on. Let's fix dinner." *Rascal? Are you coming to eat tonight?*

I'll be running late. Keep a plate warm for me?

Always. Wynona headed to the kitchen. The interview at the Pearlilys had been interesting, but ultimately they had gained very little knowledge. Mr. Pearlily owned the condo Dralo had been renting. He was also a bully, while Mrs. Pearlily was a nervous woman who was so overpowered by her husband she barely knew how to breathe. It was an interesting dynamic and Wynona had to wonder how they had stayed married for so long.

It would be easy to assume that fire talents meant a temper and for Mr. Pearlily, that was definitely the case. But Mrs. Pearlily and Thallia were more fluff than substance. "Must run in the family," Wynona murmured to herself.

She stirred the pot on the stove. The herby aroma tickled her nose and she almost missed it when the hairs on the back of her neck rose. Wynona spun and blinked her ghost vision to her eyes. "Who's there?" she asked, her fingers tingling with sparks.

"It's just me," Celia said with a huff.

"What?" Wynona blinked her sight back to normal and watched Celia stumble into the kitchen. The feeling on the back of her neck persisted, but she hadn't been able to see anything.

Violet? Do you sense any animals?

The only time Wynona hadn't been able to see a ghost in its invisible form had been when she'd dealt with a bunch of ghost cats. Her belief was that animals were on a different plane than her sight allowed her to see, though it was only a guess at this point.

No, Violet said. *No animals, but something feels...off.*

Celia huffed and dumped her load on the table. "You could have helped, you know." She sat down and wiped her forehead. Her hair was in a messy bun and she was still makeup free. Dark circles hung under Celia's eyes, and Wynona immediately felt bad.

"Sorry, I was...caught off guard."

Celia snorted. "Whatever." She shoved the box, but it didn't move. "There."

"There, what?" Wynona walked over and opened the lid. She gasped and the feeling against her skin grew stronger. "The grimoires..."

Celia nodded, then hung her head back and closed her eyes.

"How did you get them?" Wynona lifted the top one, then immediately dropped it. The magical buzz was almost painful against her skin. "Are these all Granny's?"

Celia never bothered to open her eyes. "No, I took them all."

Wynona studied her sister more closely. Celia didn't just look tired, she looked exhausted and...dirty. She was wearing all black and there were dirt smudges on her knees and all down the front of her shirt. "What did you do?" she asked softly.

Celia cracked open one eye. "You probably don't want to know. Your boyfriend might take offense."

"I might take offense!" Wynona cried. She backed away from the box, suddenly fearful of what she might find. "But seriously, Celia. What did you do?"

Celia rolled her eyes and stood up. She wobbled slightly and Wynona reached out, but Celia brushed her off. "I did what I needed to do," Celia said quietly, but coolly. Brushing herself off, she began to walk away. "I'm going to take a shower."

"Celia?" Wynona called after her. "One question."

Celia paused but didn't turn around.

"Did anyone get hurt?"

Celia's shoulders fell. "No one of consequence."

Wynona stepped forward. "Where are you hurt?"

Those slumped shoulders tightened, rising almost to Celia's ears. "I *said*, no one of consequence."

"And I asked where you were hurt." Wynona hated confrontation, but in this she was holding her ground. Granny had given her a charge and Wynona would fulfill this one. She couldn't save all of Hex Haven—that would have to fall on someone else—but her sister? Wynona wasn't going to let her fall through the cracks, especially if Celia was trying to change.

Celia turned and sneered. "I don't need your help," she said icily.

Wynona walked to the pantry she kept her herbs in and began to pull things down. "Is it a cut? A scrape? A bruise?" When Celia didn't answer, Wynona turned and tilted her head, using her tea skills to pinpoint what was going on. Her eyes widened. "You're bleeding?"

Celia jerked back. "How did you know that?"

Wynona shook her head. "You need bacoba and black pepper," she explained, quickly grabbing the jars she needed. "They both promote an increase in blood." Wynona looked back. "Where?"

Celia sighed and slumped back into the dining chair. "I think there's a cut on my back."

"Turn and lift your shirt."

"Wynona..." Celia moaned.

"Turn and lift your shirt!"

Heal her, Violet said softly.

Wynona paused. "What?"

Violet rolled her eyes. *I said...HEAL her. You've learned how to heal with your magic, not just your tea. Remember?*

"Oh my gosh, I'm an idiot," Wynona murmured.

"What?" Celia asked over her shoulder. She had pulled her shirt up just enough to show a nasty gash on her lower back.

"Celia," Wynona admonished. "That's bad." She went over and looked it over. "It's all jagged. Whatever cut you must have been harsh."

"It certainly didn't feel good," Celia snapped. "Are you going to do something or not?"

"Yeah. Sorry." Wynona put out her hand and brought her magic up. Purple danced on her palm and Wynona gently sent it over to her sister's back.

Celia hissed as the cut closed up.

"Am I hurting you?" Wynona asked through a clenched jaw. She was trying to keep the magic as gentle as possible, but it still felt like she was holding back a tornado at times. She'd gotten used to it when using it for simple jobs like lifting trays or making teas, but healing was still a new skill.

"No," Celia ground out, just as tightly. "I'm fine."

"All done." Wynona straightened. "You still need that tea, though. It'll help the rest of you heal."

"Fine." Celia sat down, straightening her clothes.

"You're really not going to tell me what happened?" Wynona asked.

Celia laid her head down. "I'm really not going to tell you," she mumbled.

Dishing up a bowl of rice and putting the chicken and herbs on top, Wynona brought it over. "Here. This'll help." She pointed toward her tea set. "And the tea'll be ready in five minutes."

"Thanks." Celia took the spoon and began to poke at her food. She nodded toward the box. "Are you going to read them?"

Wynona hesitated. "Maybe."

Celia's eyebrows went up. "I thought you wanted them."

"I'm not sure some of them are meant to be read." Wynona could still feel the presence of the grimoires and it unsettled her. She had expected them to simply be books, but there was obviously power in those pages and Wynona couldn't quite be sure what kind of power it was.

"Whatever." Celia slumped over her food, stirring it again.

"You really should eat," Wynona said. "You obviously expended a lot of energy tonight." Her eyes went back to the box. She was torn. She wanted to know what they said...but she was scared as well. There was something in those books...but was it safe to find out what?

Celia made a noncommittal noise and continued stirring.

Wynona sat down next to her sister.

"Isn't your wolfy pet coming over?"

Wynona bit back a retort. She knew baiting when she heard it. "What's wrong, Celia? What happened when you got the books?"

Celia didn't respond.

"Celia," Wynona said softly. She dared to reach out and touch her sister's shoulder. "What happened?"

Celia sniffed. "It doesn't matter."

"It does," Wynona insisted. "*It* matters and *you* matter."

The laugh coming out of Celia's mouth could have belonged to a two hundred year old witch. The dry, cackling sound held no trace of humor and a slight bit of insanity. "It matters? I matter?" She shook her head and slowly sat up. "*Nothing* matters. Do you hear me? NOTHING MATTERS!" she screamed.

Wynona jerked back at the anger in her sister's tone.

"You sit there with powers oozing from every pore and you don't care!" Celia waved her hand and her bowl of soup flew across the room, smashing into the wall. "You never cared about powers. You never even wanted them and now you have more than anyone in the history of our family and you don't even care!" Celia began to pace the room. "Granny gave you everything! She helped you get away and left me there to rot!" Celia faced her sister, pounding her own chest. "NOBODY CARED! I've been a pawn in our father's schemes and the peasant for our mother's whims, but nobody cared!" She cackled again, the tone becoming more insane by the moment, as if Celia had finally snapped. "You had no idea what Dad has made me do over the years. Absolutely no idea. And now you want to make me think you care? You want me to think that I matter?" Celia shook her head, her messy hair flying all over her face. "I've never mattered," she said hoarsely.

Wynona couldn't stop the tears from trailing down her face. She had no idea that Celia had felt so used. While Granny's actions had suggested that Celia was a pawn, Wynona hadn't truly understood. But the street also went both ways.

"You're right," Wynona said, not trying to hide her emotions. "I don't understand." Slowly, she rose to her feet, facing her raging sister. "But neither do you."

Celia scoffed and folded her arms over her chest.

"You have no idea what it's like to be so ignored by your family that you want to not exist any longer," Wynona said calmly.

Celia's expression fell.

"You have no idea what it's like to be disowned over and over again by the two people who were meant to love you most in the world." Wynona took a step forward, hesitating only slightly when

Violet raced up her leg. "You don't know what it's like to be seen as an abomination, a cur, as something so broken even your own parents think you're worthless."

"Being worth something to them wasn't a picnic either." Celia sneered, though her voice held less vitriol than before.

"So why don't we just agree that our parents are horrible and that we're going to choose to live our lives without them?" Wynona stopped moving just a few feet from Celia.

Celia shrugged, looking as if she carried the weight of the world on her shoulders. "Is that even a choice?" she asked in a low tone.

Feeling as if words wouldn't be enough, Wynona reached out and pulled Celia into a hug. At first it was like hugging an ice statue, but after a few seconds, Celia collapsed against Wynona.

Tears continued to trickle down Wynona's face and for the first time in a long time, Violet wasn't blasting her brain with sarcastic retorts. "I'm so sorry. I didn't know."

Celia's shoulders began to shake and her hands gripped Wynona's back. "I never meant to do all those horrible things. I never wanted to push you away."

Wynona wasn't sure how to answer. Celia's actions *hurt*. A lot. If she wasn't careful, Wynona still sometimes found herself drowning in a rabbit hole of despair, but she worked hard to overcome it. Her friends, her soulmate, her work at the tea shop, they were all wonderful medicine for helping her step from the dark into the light, but they didn't make the dark hurt any less.

Celia pulled back, sniffling and rubbing at her red face. "Is there any chance we can start over?"

Wynona wanted to say yes. She absolutely did, but it was so *hard!* It seemed her family was fighting her at every turn and no matter how hard Wynona tried to do what was right, another Le Doux was blocking her. How was it possible to ache for forgiveness as much as she ached from the original hurt?

If anyone can forgive...it's you, sweetheart.

Wynona felt her muscles begin to relax. There was absolutely a reason that Rascal had been chosen as her soulmate. *How did I get so blessed to have you in my life?* she sent back.

Eh. Just lucky, I guess.

Shaking her head at his ego, Wynona found herself smiling at Celia. "I'd like that."

"Really?" Celia rasped. "You don't want to simply zap me with your magic and be done with it?"

Wynona shook her head. "I won't deny that we've got a long road to climb. Neither of us were treated right and that led to us treating each other badly, but...as long as you're willing to change, so am I." Her smile grew rueful. "I think it's what Granny wanted."

Celia slumped back into her seat, looking like a limp dishrag. "What do you mean?"

Wynona took the seat across from her sister. "She wanted me to save you."

Celia's eyes widened and she jerked back. "What? That makes no sense. Granny never spent any time with me."

Wynona sighed. "She was training me to be ready to eventually take over Hex Haven, with the intent that I would save you in the process." She managed to look up at Celia's confused face. "The day I...killed Granny?" Wynona swallowed hard as Celia nodded. "Do you recall what she said when she was being pulled into the portal?"

Celia looked away, obviously trying to recall the situation, but she finally shook her head. "No. I was too busy trying to hold on."

"She said, 'You're the one,'" Wynona explained. "I knew then that Granny had planned it all. She had planned to raise me so I could save you."

"And all of Hex Haven," Celia added.

Wynona nodded.

"And you're going to do that, how?"

Wynona shook her head and stood up, going back to the stove. "I'm not," she answered. "Granny wanted me to challenge our father, but I have no desire to do that at all." When Celia was quiet, Wynona turned around from dishing up her soup. "What?"

Celia's head jerked up. "Nothing," she said too quickly. "Just thinking."

Wynona came back to the table. "Why don't we eat and let the rest take care of itself, huh? I think we could both use a good night's rest."

Celia nodded. "Sounds good."

I'll catch you another time, Rascal said in a low silky tone that gave Wynona goosebumps. *I love you, but your sister needs you more right now.*

I love you too, Wynona sent back. She loved Rascal more than anything, but never had those words been truer than they were in that moment. She finally had a little hope that everything was going to turn out alright. As long as she had the right people by her side.

CHAPTER 12

Rascal yawned, his jaw cracking when Wynona climbed into the truck the next morning.

"Late night?" she said with a soft laugh.

Rascal grunted. "You could say that."

She handed over a travel cup full of matcha. "Here. This ought to help."

Rascal took a drink, then winced. "Hot," he rasped.

"Sorry!" Wynona pushed across the bench seat and touched his cheek, immediately healing his burnt tongue.

Rascal sighed. "I think I like this new power." He gave her a quick kiss, then put the truck in drive. "And I'm glad to see you're turning to your powers more."

Wynona slumped. "Don't scare me like that and then pretend that nothing happened!" She slapped his arm. "You scared me!"

Rascal chuckled and grabbed her arm before she could move back to her side of the cab. "Where are you going?"

"To my side, to buckle up."

The wolf shook his head. "I don't think so. You can buckle up right here."

Wynona rolled her eyes. "I'm not sitting in the middle of the truck, Rascal. It's not seemly."

"What's unseemly is how much time you spend too far away from me." He gave her one more kiss, then pressed the gas pedal.

Wynona scrambled to grab the lap belt. "Bully," she muttered.

"Boyfriend," he shot back with a wink. "It's my job to drive you crazy."

"Well, at least you're honest about it."

Violet snickered and burrowed deeper into Wynona's hair. She hadn't been thrilled about getting up this morning. The night had been a late one and Violet would have preferred to sleep in, but she also refused to miss out on any details about the murder. *Next time, you and Celia need to have a break down at noon, not midnight.*

Rascal snorted and glanced over. "How did things go with the sister? I cut out after I realized what was happening."

"You shouldn't have been in there in the first place," Wynona teased, laying her head against his shoulder. "But I was glad for your support," she said softly.

Rascal squeezed her knee.

"We're...starting over, I suppose," Wynona answered. "I'm not really sure what that's going to mean. She wasn't awake when I got up this morning, but I healed her last night, and now I have a room full of grimoires that I don't know who they belong to and I think Celia stole them, and I can tell some have magic I don't really want to mess with."

Rascal whistled low under his breath. "That's...a lot."

Wynona only nodded.

"But for your sake, I hope things with Celia work out."

"Me too."

They were silent the rest of the way to the station, but Wynona's mind wouldn't stop churning. She really didn't know how things would go with Celia. Better? Worse? Would Wynona regret sharing so much? Had she shared enough?

"Time to find a murderer," Rascal said as he parked the truck.

Wynona made a face. "I suppose that's a little more important, huh?"

Rascal shook his head. "Nah. There's no 'more important' or 'less important'. Just what matters in the moment." He hopped down and reached out his arms for her.

Wynona gave him a look.

Rascal grinned, completely unperturbed by her surliness. "Don't deny me my rights to hold you whenever possible."

Sighing, but secretly loving it, Wynona scooted over and he helped her down. "Sometimes I think you're like a little boy who never grew up."

"Glad you finally figured it out," he teased, pulling open the precinct door for her. "Chief's waiting for us in his office."

Wynona nodded and they walked through the front lobby. She gave a small wave to Amaris, who pretended not to see her, adding yet another layer of hurt to their already strained relationship.

Rascal growled quietly.

Let it go, Wynona said with a sigh. *She'll have to decide one way or another soon enough.*

It just means I get more of you to myself, he sent back. *Best choice she could have made.*

Wynona squeezed his hand. He was too good for her. She knocked on the chief's door. "Chief Ligurio?"

The vampire was on the phone when she poked her head through the door, but he waved them inside. His eyes went back to the wall while he focused on his conversation. "Yes, sir. I understand, sir. You know I work by the book, Judge Tolarus. I won't push unless there's cause for it." There was a pause and then Chief Ligurio made a noncommittal noise. "I understand. Thank you." He hung up the phone, then growled. "Money," the vampire said through clenched teeth. His incisors had elongated, showing just how frustrated he was. "Why does money always think it's more important than the law?"

Wynona sat down on the edge of one of the chairs. "It's not money," she said softly. She had seen this far too many times in the family she grew up in. "Money is just a piece of paper or coin. It's the importance we give to it that matters." She shifted a little as all the men in the room watched her.

Violet's tail curled comfortingly around her neck and Wynona reached up to scratch behind the mouse's ears.

"To most creatures, money means power, so they hoard it as if their life depends on it. Then when they gain power, they convince everyone else that their money is worth something and that it can change their lives as well."

Chief Ligurio leaned back, his teeth shortening, and his red eyes searching. "Should we add philosopher to your resume, Ms. Le Doux?"

Wynona laughed uncomfortably. "Please, don't."

Rascal squeezed her shoulder. "Well said, sweetheart."

"Still..." Chief Ligurio leaned forward, folding his long fingers together. "It doesn't change the fact that those with that money seem to think they're above the law."

"What's going on?" Rascal asked.

"What's going on is that Mr. Pearlily complained to the right people that we were harassing his family," Chief Ligurio said tightly. "I've been informed that if I cross that line again, I'll lose my position."

Wynona blanched. "I'm so sorry," she said softly. "That's my fault."

"No, it's not," Rascal growled. "It's mine. I was hoping Wynona's influence would help bring down their walls so we could get a few more answers. I take full responsibility."

Wynona reached up and took her soulmate's hand. "What can we do to fix it?"

Chief Ligurio rolled his eyes and shook his head. "Next time, don't get caught."

Wynona's jaw gaped while Rascal chuckled.

"The idea had merit," Chief Ligurios said. "When people lawyer up, we often miss half the story, so trying to get around the barrier wasn't bad at all." He raised a black eyebrow at Rascal. "But maybe don't be so blatant about it?"

Rascal nodded. "Consider it done."

"Now that that's out of the way..." Chief Ligurio pulled open a file folder from the side of his desk. "I'm afraid to say it, Ms. Le Doux, because I feel like I know what your response will be, but we can't find anything on this case that doesn't come back around to your Ms. Thallia."

Wynona sighed. "Everything you have is circumstantial."

"And yet all the circumstantial evidence points to her."

"But you can't build a court case on that," Wynona pointed out.

Chief Ligurio tilted his head. "Why are you so determined to defend her?"

"Why are you so determined to accuse her?"

"Because she's a spoiled young creature who's never heard the word no," Chief Ligurio said. "She's flighty and has grown up with a bully for a father and spends her time trying to rehabilitate ex-cons." The vampire snorted. "Why do you think it's out of her wheelhouse to kill someone?"

Wynona pinched her lips together. "I don't quite know," she admitted. "You're right. She is spoiled, and she doesn't know how to deal with real life. While she was the best option I had for hiring an employee, she had a lot to learn." Wynona shrugged. "But everyone needs a chance and I was trying to give her one. She's young. She'll learn how to work, if she's willing. Yes, she lied and yes, she has a penchant for bad boys, but that doesn't make her a killer."

Chief Ligurio sighed. "Without other evidence, I've got nowhere else to turn my attention."

"And you're sure the father is innocent?" Wynona pressed. "His temper was...volatile."

Chief Ligurio shook his head. "Unless he or his wife change their stories, I can't do anything about him. They're backing each other and I have no other evidence to suggest he's lying."

Wynona jerked upright. "What about the landlord angle?" She turned to look at Rascal. "What did you find out about that? You were looking into it last night, right?"

Rascal nodded. "We did, but it was a dead end." He made an apologetic face. "The condo was actually leased to Thallia."

"So she was letting him stay there?" Wynona asked. "While she lived at home?"

"It appears that way."

She gave the chief a look. "And you don't think her father knew that? Why would his daughter lease a condo from him, but still live at home?"

"According to the property management company, she kept the condo as a place to hang out with her friends." Rascal shrugged. "They didn't realize someone was actually living there full-time."

Wynona blew out a breath. "That just seems suspicious. Don't you think?"

"So your bet is on the father?" Chief Ligurio clarified.

Wynona shrugged. "I'm not sure. All I know is that of all the Pearlilys, he seems the most likely to have killed someone in anger." She tapped her fingernails on her knee. "But truth be told, if I had to pick a story, I'm still curious about a theft gone wrong."

"I thought you said nothing was missing," Daemon said by way of announcing his arrival.

"Nothing *was* missing," Wynona admitted. "But that doesn't mean they knew there wouldn't be anything worth stealing when they came. Maybe the partner got angry when there was no money or magical objects and took it out on Dralo."

Chief Ligurio pursed his lips. "I'll give you twenty four hours to look into that, but otherwise, I'm focusing back on Thallia. Her story just doesn't add up."

Frustration seeped into Wynona's chest, but she pushed it back and stood up. "Fair enough." Turning, she raised her eyebrows to Rascal. "Coming?"

He grinned, his predator coming out just a little. "Wouldn't miss it."

"Tone it down, Deputy Chief." Daemon groaned. "Because I'm coming too."

Wynona laughed softly when Violet grumbled her agreement with the officer. "Okay. Can I see Dralo's wallet? Was it found at the crime scene?"

"Evidence locker it is," Rascal said, taking Wynona's hand. "Nothing like a visit to the dank basement to cheer your spirits."

"At least I'll get to say hello to Yetu," she replied with a smile.

Rascal grinned. "He'll be happy to see you."

Wynona looked over her shoulder. "Daemon? Did you look at the evidence for magic?"

He nodded. "Yeah. There was a light dusting on his wallet, but it was nearly black, the same color as the leather. I'm guessing since Dralo was a dark elf, it was more than likely his."

Wynona nodded. That made sense. "He could have put a non-theft spell on it."

"That's what I assumed, though I can't tell for sure."

Rascal pulled open the door to the basement and they all marched down the concrete steps.

Upon reaching the bottom, Wynona couldn't help but laugh lightly. Heavy snoring, loud enough to shake the concrete walls, reverberated throughout the room.

Rascal rolled his eyes. "Trolls," he grumbled. He marched up to the window and banged against it. "Yetu!"

A loud snort shook the bars at the window and Yetu snuffled a little before the snoring picked up again into its regular rhythm.

Wynona covered her mouth to hold in her laughter, but it bubbled through anyway. "Sorry," she said to Rascal. Clearing her throat, she clasped her hands at her waist and schooled her features. "I think he must be tired."

Mountain trolls were notorious for being deep sleepers, and Yetu had been living under the station for more years than Wynona had been alive, but he also prided himself on being alert and the evidence locker being the safest place on earth, so it tickled Wynona that the elderly troll obviously took naps on the job.

Rascal grumbled, then banged against the window harder. "YETU! AVALANCHE!"

The snoring instantly stopped and the room grew quiet.

Wynona backed up when a heavy stomping started their way. "Who called avalanche? There's no avalanche!"

Rascal stood with his hands on his hips, not the least bit concerned that a giant mountain troll was bearing down on him.

Yetu hesitated when he saw who was waiting. "Oh, hello, Deputy Chief." His slate gray eyes wandered to Daemon and then Wynona. "Ms. Le Doux!" the troll rasped in his gravelly tone. He came up to the window. "I was hoping I would see you again someday."

Wynona smiled and walked up. "Hello, Yetu. How are you doing?"

Yetu glanced at Rascal and scratched under his rock chin. "Doing alright, thank you. I, uh...didn't sleep well last night." His massive shoulders shrugged.

Wynona waved away his worries. "It happens to all of us," she assured him.

The troll smiled. "Did you come to chat? Or did you need to see something?"

Wynona stepped closer, pressing up against the still glowering Rascal. "We'd like to see the evidence from the Ziumar case," she said politely. "But getting to see you was definitely a bonus."

His smile widening, Yetu leaned in. "How about you leave the wolf for a man like me?" he teased. "I can crush wolves with my fist."

Wynona laughed as Rascal growled even more. Daemon tried to hide his laughter, but was only able to get it under control when Rascal turned his bright golden glare in the black hole's direction. "As tempting as that is," she began, taking Rascal's hand, "I'm afraid my heart is already taken."

Yetu put a hand to his heart and sighed. "A troll can only dream," he said. "Let me get you your bag." He shuffled off and Wynona heard the banging of lockers and more stomping before the troll reappeared. "Here it is," he said, handing over the plastic bag. "Very little in it."

Wynona nodded. "That's alright. Thank you!" She blew the troll a kiss as they walked back up the stairs and enjoyed watching a bit of pink climb into Yetu's granite cheeks.

"Come back anytime!" Yetu yelled, shaking the walls with his enthusiasm.

"Flirt," Rascal teased her as they emerged.

Wynona grinned. Payback was fun sometimes. "Girlfriend," she whispered. "It's my job to drive you crazy."

Rascal didn't speak out loud, but the flare of light in his eyes said it all.

Wynona swallowed hard. "Daemon!" she said a little louder than she needed to. Wynona cleared her throat. "Let's get this wallet out and you can take another look at the lingering magic."

Daemon nodded, though the stiffness to his shoulders said he hadn't missed the exchange between Rascal and Wynona.

We need to stop, Wynona scolded Rascal. *We're going to give Daemon a coronary.*

No way. It'll give him ideas on how to get Prim's attention.

Wynona closed her eyes and shook her head. "Time to catch a killer," she reminded him. *Not play matchmaker.*

Meddling, Violet reminded her. *It's called meddling and who'd have thought the wolf was so good at it?*

Rascal chuckled as he let them all into his office. "Work now," he said as she passed. "Play later."

It's a date.

CHAPTER 13

"I don't understand why I'm here," Daemon muttered, his eyes darting over the full shelves in Wynona's greenhouse. It wasn't anywhere close to the same size as Prim's, but Wynona was proud of it just the same.

She grew most of her own herbs and with the way the greenhouse backed up to the Grove of Secrets, she knew there was probably a little something *extra* that inhibited the plants.

"We're at a sticking point with the case," Wynona reminded him, the wallet search having gone nowhere. "So I thought now would be a good time to think about something else. You know...in order to clear our heads."

Rascal snorted and settled himself in a chair in the corner.

"And what does that have to do with your plants?" Daemon asked, waving at the shelves to emphasize his point.

Wynona reached under the center table and pulled a large cardboard box up and into her arms. The tingle was immediate and Daemon winced.

"What. Are. Those." He pointed to the box and his eyes looked wary.

Wynona set the box down and stepped back, brushing off her shirt. "Grimoires. Specifically, my family's grimoires."

Daemon's brown eyebrows shot up. "Okay?"

"I'd like to look through some," she said. "And possibly try some of the spells."

Daemon sighed and pinched the bridge of his nose. "Let me guess. I'm insurance?"

Rascal tapped the side of his nose. "Bingo."

Daemon glared at his boss. "I don't think this was in the job description."

Wynona poked out her bottom lip. "I thought it was in the friend description."

Rascal chuckled as Daemon sighed. "Live and learn, Skymaw. Live and learn."

"Rascal," Wynona scolded. "Leave him alone. I've caused a lot of trouble in the past, so don't blame him for being scared."

"I'm not scared," Daemon said tightly.

Violet snickered, then innocently began to clean her face when everyone in the room turned toward her.

"I'm not," Daemon defended. "I just know how many things that can go wrong. It's not bad to have a bit of common sense."

Wynona nodded. "I know," she assured him. "I wasn't trying to insult you, but I can understand why you're worried." She rested her hands on the box, doing her best to ignore the jump in magic. "I'm hoping my granny's grimoires will be able to teach me better how to use my magic. Celia wasn't able to pick out just Granny's, so I have the whole family instead." Wynona's eyebrows pulled together. "I don't have anyone left to teach me," she said more softly.

"Unless you want to talk to your father," Daemon asid, nodding understandingly. "I get it." Another sigh escaped the large man. "Okay. I get it. Let's do it."

Wynona held back from hugging the black hole. Rascal probably wouldn't appreciate it and neither would Prim, whether she was there or not. "Great! Thank you!" She lifted the first book out of the box and tried to look at the author's name. "I don't see who wrote this one," Wynona murmured.

Rascal came up behind her. "Magira Thidaran." He pointed to a small bit of scrawling on the corner.

Wynona set it aside. The humming magic from that particular book was weak and it wasn't a name she recognized. "Next," she muttered. Her hand grabbed another book and she immediately threw it to the table. A shiver rocked her spine and Wynona was grateful when Rascal's hands landed on her hips.

"What is it?" he asked.

"Don't touch that one again," Daemon said, his voice low and harsh.

Wynona looked up to see his eyes fully black. She wiped her hands on her pants. "Don't worry. I don't have a desire to."

Rascal's head jerked back and forth. "Will someone tell me what's going on?"

Wynona pointed to the innocent-looking book. "I think the owner of that one wasn't a good person."

Rascal's hands flexed. "How are you going to get through this box if there's evil information in there?"

Daemon shifted his weight. "I got it. Go ahead."

Wynona nodded her thanks. She was feeling a little more cautious now that she'd felt first-hand that some of her ancestors chose a darker path.

Shouldn't surprise you. All that power goes to people's heads, Violet snapped. *Think of your parents.*

Wynona nodded again, understanding what her familiar was saying. She would have to be careful that she didn't end up the same way. The next three books still weren't Granny's but weren't nearly as repulsive as the previous one.

"Are Granny's even in here?" she grumbled, pulling a handful of slim ones out of the box.

"Is there anything you can do magic-wise that would help you find it?" Rascal asked.

Wynona paused. "I hadn't thought of that." She turned to Violet and raised her eyebrows in question. "Any ideas?"

Violet's nose twitched. *I don't know. It wouldn't hurt, I suppose.*

Wynona glanced up at Daemon. "You ready?"

Daemon's put upon look was plain to read, but he nodded. "Okay. Go ahead."

Wynona closed her eyes and put her hand over the box. She really didn't know what she was planning to do, but surely there had to be a better way to sort things than to touch it all. She put a picture of Granny in her mind's eye and then swished her fingers, moving the books around.

She could hear Rascal's intake of breath and Wynona had to assume the books were moving like she hoped they would. Her hair began to shift and Wynona realized she'd created another one of her wind tunnels, just like when she read tea leaves.

Just admit it, Violet snorted. *You're a dramatic magic user.*

Let me focus and then we'll discuss it, Wynona sent back.

Violet climbed Wynona's arm and wrapped her tail around Wynona's neck. The touch helped ground Wynona as she felt her magic try to flood the room.

Daemon grunted and Wynona pressed down harder to keep the magic under control. "Saffron Le Doux," she whispered through clenched teeth. "Saffron Le Doux."

Open your eyes, Violet ordered.

Wynona bent her knees slightly in order to stabilize herself better before chancing opening her eyes. About ten books of various sizes swirled in the air around her head. "Are they all hers?" Wynona asked.

I can't tell, Violet responded. *But it's better than it was.*

Wynona tried one last time. "Saffron Le Doux," she said firmly. One more book fell to the table. "Okay." Wynona's hand was trembling by now, but she stiffened her muscles and brought the books into a neat pile on the table.

By the time she was able to let go of her magic, she was overly hot and her clothes were stuck to her skin. She stared at the pile for a moment, breathing heavily. "Time to see if it worked," she said breathlessly.

Reaching out her still shaking hand, Wynona took the top book. She frowned. "It says Daegal Le Doux." Her eyes shot open. "Oh my gosh. That's my grandfather!" Grandfather Le Doux had died before Wynona had been born, though she had heard stories about him.

"Your dad's dad?" Rascal asked. "Was he dark?"

Wynona shook her head. "I don't really know. The stories about him vary wildly and Granny didn't talk about him a lot."

"What kind of stories?" Daemon asked, stepping up close to the table. He looked slightly flushed, but otherwise alright from the show of magic.

Wynona shrugged. "Anything from he fought feral dragons to save Hex Haven to the idea that he was the first person to use a petris luminis."

"What's wrong with that?" Rascal asked.

Wynona gave him a look. "The story goes that he used the lightning to punish anyone who didn't pay their taxes."

Daemon sucked in a breath. "That can't be true. I've never heard of that."

Wynona flipped through the pages. "One of the gifts of certain witch families is the ability to live a long time."

"How old was he when he died?"

Wynona paused in her browsing. "Uh...I think he was over three hundred years old."

Rascal choked. "How old was Granny?"

"About the same, I think."

"And your parents?" Daemon pressed.

"They're both over a hundred," Wynona said easily. She went back to flipping pages, letting the men overcome their shock. "Ah!" She paused and pressed the book open. "Look."

"Looks like your spell wasn't quite as specific as it needed to be," Daemon said with a chuckle.

"So this pile has books with Granny's name in them," Wynona mused. "But hopefully that just means hers are in the pile as well." She set aside her grandfather's book, not really interested in reading it at the moment. It was unusual for a warlock to keep a grimoire, so it might be worth a look later, if only to dispel all the crazy stories about him. She paused before grabbing the next book. "How old is Chief Ligurio?"

Rascal frowned. "I have no idea."

"I wonder if he knew my grandfather?"

Daemon shook his head. "No clue. But he was there long before I came along."

"Who was?"

All the heads jerked toward the greenhouse entrance where Prim was standing with her hands on her hips.

"Why wasn't I invited to the party?" she demanded.

"Come on in, Prim," Wynona said. "I'm trying to find Granny's grimoires."

Prim gasped and rushed over, poofing into her human form so she was tall enough to see the top of the table. "You got them?"

"Celia did."

Prim huffed. "What have you found?"

"Dark magic," Wynona said, pointing to the book she'd touched in the beginning. "And then I used a spell to try and separate the books, but it looks like I got anything that had Granny's name in it."

Prim reached out to pick up a book.

"STOP!" Daemon shouted, holding out his hand.

Prim jerked back. "What?" she yelled back.

"You have no idea what kind of magic is in those books," he growled, stepping forward. "Why would you touch something when you don't know what it is?"

Prim's pink eyebrows pulled together and she scowled at the large creature. "First of all, I can touch whatever I want. Second, who do you think you are telling me what to do? You have no control over me." She folded her arms over her chest in defiance.

Wynona stepped back at the returning glower on Daemon's face. She sought out Rascal, who looked like he was enjoying the little argument. *Rascal,* she scolded. *This isn't a soap opera. These are our friends.*

Yep. Isn't it great?

They're fighting? What's good about it?

Rascal gave her a look and subtly shook his head. *Sweetheart, there's so much tension between these two. It'll be a miracle if it doesn't explode and knock us through the glass walls.*

Wynona's eyes bugged out. *But...they're FIGHTING.*

Yep. That's what couples do before they figure out other ways to get rid of their attraction. Once he finally mans up and asks her out, it'll all calm down.

Wynona tried to look at the argument with new eyes, but as someone who hated conflict with a passion, she just struggled to understand it the same way Rascal did.

Prim and Daemon were now toe to toe. "You. Have. No. Say." Prim poked his chest with each word.

"Maybe not," Daemon said, his voice starting to come back down. "But the fact that you have people who care about you should be enough to make you think twice."

Prim opened her mouth, then shut it again and stepped back a little. "If you'll notice, Wynona didn't try to stop me," she said, her tone hesitant, as if testing his answer.

Daemon's nostrils flared, but he kept his voice calm again. "She's not the only one who cares."

Prim's breathing grew ragged. "You only cared about putting me in jail," she whispered.

"I knew you were innocent."

"Then why didn't you do anything?" Prim pleaded.

Wynona stepped back even farther and began to move toward the door. She was thrilled this conversation was finally happening, but she probably shouldn't be privy to it. *Rascal. Let's go.*

Spoil sport, Violet grumbled.

Wynona ignored her. Prim would tell Wynona what was happening later. She had just about reached the door when one of the books began to tremble, shaking the table.

All conversation, mental or otherwise, stopped and turned toward the noise.

"Uh-oh," Wynona whispered.

The book lifted from the table and stood upright. It paused for just a split second before shooting through the air straight toward Wynona. She squealed and put her hands up to keep from being smacked in the face, but the book never made it.

Falling to the floor with a thud, the book skidded a few feet, stopping near enough that Wynona picked it up. "It's the one," she said softly, slightly shaken from the encounter. "It's Granny's last grimoire." The dates on the front went right up until the day before Granny died. Wynona looked up at her friends. "Sorry. I didn't mean to ruin the moment."

Daemon's hand was still in the air and his fist closed with a snap of his muscles.

"Oh." Wynona realized why the book had stopped. "Thank you, Daemon."

Prim's face completely changed. "Did you do that? Protect Nona?" she asked.

Daemon straightened, dropped his hand and took a deep breath. "Yeah." He shrugged. "It wasn't a big deal."

Prim marched up and grabbed his uniform collar, yanking him down closer to her level. With one swift moment that caught them all off guard, she kissed him right on the lips. "Maybe we should work all this out over dinner?" she asked in a low tone.

Wynona rubbed her eyes. What the heck was happening? She knew her mouth was open like a codfish, but she couldn't help it as she turned to look at Rascal. His eyes were glowing and he looked like he was trying to hold back laughter. Wynona scowled and smacked his shoulder.

What? Skymaw looks shell shocked. It's great.

Wynona sighed and turned back. Daemon and Prim were back to talking, but it was much calmer at this point. "Come on," she said, grabbing his hand. "Time to read a book."

"Only if I get to cuddle," Rascal whispered in her ear.

Wynona grinned. "I can get behind that."

"Then let's get going!"

CHAPTER 14

Wynona sighed in contentment as she settled into Rascal's open arms on the couch. She held the grimoire in front of her, slightly nervous about opening it. "What do you think is going to be inside?" she whispered.

Rascal shrugged against her back. "I don't know. But you aren't throwing it across the room like that other one, so I'm hoping that means your granny didn't use dark magic."

Wynona turned the slim volume around, studying the leather cover. "I'm guessing there are more of these."

"Maybe they were in the rest of the pile."

"That's possible." Her fingers began to tremble a little. There could be some very important answers for her in this book...or there could be more devastating revelations like Granny had dropped when she'd come back as a ghost.

Like a Band-Aid, Violet encouraged. *Just rip it off.*

Taking a deep breath, Wynona opened the first page. Granny had written it more like a journal and Wynona found herself relaxing when the first page spoke of taking care of her tea plants.

"You're a lot like her, you know," Rascal said softly against her ear.

Wynona huffed. "I don't think I would have the courage to curse someone," she admitted. "Even if I thought it was for the greater good."

"I don't know..." Rascal hedged. "I think you've already proven that you'll go pretty far to save those you love. Your grandmother's methods might have been extreme, but she wasn't just trying to save you. She was trying to save an entire town."

"I suppose you're right."

"Eh? What?" Rascal leaned forward. "Could you say that again? I didn't quite catch it."

Wynona rolled her eyes and glanced over her shoulder. "You have paranormal hearing. I think you heard just fine."

He put a finger in his ear and wiggled it around. "I must have had a piece of ear wax stuck or something."

"You. Were. Right," Wynona enunciated very carefully.

Rascal's chest puffed out and the triumphant smile on his face would have been cute if she hadn't been the one it was aimed toward. "I'm filing that one away for a rainy day. Let it be noted that us men aren't always wrong."

"You're not a man," Wynona teased sweetly. "You're a wolf."

Rascal growled and wrapped his arms around her tightly. "Predators are awfully good at catching their prey," he said huskily against her ear.

"I know we said we were starting over, but please...don't make me watch this," Celia drawled as she sauntered past the couple and into the kitchen.

Rascal's growl went from playful to angry. "No one is asking you to watch," he snapped.

"You're out in the middle of the house," Celia shot back. "It's asking for an audience."

When is she moving out? Rascal asked mentally. Even his inner voice was tighter than a piano string.

I know it's hard, but please try to get along. Rascal had been so sweet about Celia last night, but apparently that courtesy didn't extend into the daytime.

Her first, Violet sniffed.

"It's my house," Wynona said softly to Celia. "I understand that living together in a small space is different from what you're used to, but we're all adjusting here. We'll all do better if we choose to get along rather than bicker over little things."

I'm sorry, Rascal said, squeezing her a little tighter.

Wynona rubbed the arm wrapped around her. She knew he wasn't trying to cause problems. But she also knew he couldn't handle someone disparaging her. The alpha in him didn't like that.

Celia rolled her eyes. "We're not just magically going to be some big, happy family," she argued.

Wynona's eyebrows shot up. "There's a spell for that? Let's give it a try."

Celia's lips quirked before she frowned again. "Are you reading Gram's grimoire?"

Wynona looked at the book, then back up. "Yeah. I found this one in the box."

"And?"

Wynona shrugged. "And nothing. I only started reading the first entry when you came in."

Celia pursed her lips.

"Are Mom and Dad going to be coming after these?" Wynona asked. She hadn't thought about it before, but if Celia stole these, then there was every chance that her parents would come hunt them down. "Where exactly were they in the house? The library?"

Celia's eyes dropped to the floor and she shifted her weight. "In Mom's lab."

Wynona jerked upright. "All of them?" she rasped.

Celia nodded, looking up from under her eyelashes.

Wynona rubbed her forehead. "Oh my gosh, Celia. No wonder you had to do crazy stuff to get them." She looked at the book with new eyes. "She's gonna be so mad."

Celia nodded again.

"I don't understand," Rascal spoke up. "What's your mom's lab?"

"Mom has a spell room under the library," Wynona explained, her mind racing with ways of protecting the books. "As little girls, we always called it Mom's lab because it was where she did her experiments." She turned to her soulmate. "Sometimes noises would leak out of there and..." Wynona shook her head.

"I'm guessing your mom's grimoire would be one of the ones Skymaw doesn't like."

Wynona nodded. "I'm guessing so."

He shook his head and ran a hand through his hair. "What needs to be done? Should we put them in the evidence vault?"

"I don't think a mountain troll will stop her if Mom realizes they're gone," Wynona murmured. "She'd take the whole building down if they're important enough."

"How do we know if they're important enough?"

Wynona turned to Celia and raised her eyebrows. "Did Mom use them? Do you know?"

Celia shrugged. "I don't know for sure, but if I were you, I would figure something out. She'll notice sooner or later and I have no idea how she'll react."

"Helpful," Wynona said sarcastically.

"What do you want from me?" Celia threw her hands out to the side. "I got you the books. My job is done."

Wynona closed her eyes. "It doesn't matter." She stood up. "It is what it is. I'll just have to read fast and hope Granny has a good cloaking spell or something in here." She walked to the kitchen, feeling hungry, when her phone buzzed.

Wynona changed her trajectory to grab the device off the side table and glanced at the screen. She paused when the text was from a number she didn't recognize.

I can prove Thallia's innocent.

Wynona's eyes bulged and her entire body stiffened. Glancing up, she noticed that no one was paying attention to her. For some reason, the message felt...secretive and she wasn't sure anyone else should know yet.

Who is this? Wynona texted back.

Who this is doesn't matter. You can't tell anyone or people might get hurt. Meet me at your shop at midnight.

Wynona immediately texted several more times, but there was no response. What was she supposed to do? Did she take something like this seriously? Or was it a trap to hurt her?

You can't go, Violet said.

Wynona immediately threw up her mental barriers. Did Rascal already catch what was going on? Had he read the messages through her?

She looked up. Rascal was hunting through his own phone, answering messages, and Wynona breathed a sigh of relief.

I mean it, Wynona. It sounds like a trap.

Wynona looked at her familiar, who was standing on her back legs on the coffee table. Very carefully, she let her thoughts through to the mouse, but not Rascal. *What if it's real? Thallia still doesn't have an alibi and if we don't find one soon, Chief Ligurio will accuse her officially.*

It's not worth your life, Violet argued.

You would let a young woman rot in jail for a crime she didn't commit? Wynona gave her mouse a look. Even blood-thirsty Violet couldn't be that heartless.

Are you really that sure she didn't commit it? Violet's nose twitched. *They might not have concrete evidence she did, but you also don't have concrete evidence she didn't.*

She's not a killer, Wynona argued stubbornly. *Tell me you really think she would kill that boy.*

Violet sighed and scrubbed her face. *You're right. I don't think she did it. But I'm also not letting you go alone tonight. If you won't take the wolf, at least take me and promise to have your magic ready.*

"Wy?"

Wynona's head jerked up and she did her best to look innocent.

Rascal was looking between Wynona and Violet. "Everything okay?"

Wynona nodded. "Yep. Just peachy." *Thank you,* she whispered to Violet.

I better at least get cookies out of this, Violet grumbled before scrambling down the table leg and disappearing into the kitchen.

"What's nipping her tail?" Rascal asked, coming up to stand near Wynona.

She tried to keep her heart rate under control, knowing Rascal would be able to hear it. "Hungry!" Wynona said a little too loudly. She cleared her throat. "And so am I." Walking toward the kitchen, Wynona looked over her shoulder. "Want something?"

Rascal was standing with his arms folded over his chest and a narrowed gaze. "I'm always hungry," he said in careful tones.

Wynona turned away. *He suspects something.*

Of course he does, Violet snapped. *You're acting like a weirdo.*

Well, excuse me for not being good at subterfuge, Wynona retorted. She paused and pinched the bridge of her nose. "I've got leftover chicken," she finally called out.

"That'll be great. Thanks."

The door from the greenhouse opened and Daemon and Prim walked in, both looking at ease and content.

Wynona studied them. Was Prim's hair a little...disheveled?

"Got enough to share?" Prim asked. "I'm starving."

A loud growling sound caught their attention and all eyes turned to Daemon, whose face was bright red all the way up to the tips of his ears. "Sorry," he grumbled.

Celia snorted. "I don't think leftovers are going to cut it." She took a vicious bite of her sandwich and began to walk out of the room. Apparently she wasn't keen on making nice with a large group full of people.

Wynona dug through the freezer. "I've got lasagna." She faced the group. "If I use magic, it should be done in just a few minutes."

"Sounds good to me," Rascal said. The suspicion in his voice was lighter, but Wynona knew he wouldn't have let go of the situation yet. He was a wolf. He'd hold the trail until he figured out what was going on.

Hopefully that'll be AFTER the meeting.

"Do you have any greens?" Prim asked, walking toward the fridge. "I can make a salad."

"Oh. Yeah." Wynona slapped her forehead. "Sorry. I forgot you don't eat meat."

*Like I said...*Violet said with a laugh. *You're acting weird.*

Prim's vegetarianism would normally have been something Wynona remembered easily. Today she was so flustered over the text that she wasn't thinking straight. Yeah...Rascal had good reason to be suspicious.

"The crisper drawer is full of greens. Help yourself."

Prim began pulling things out and chopping veggies while Wynona put her hand over the lasagna. Within two minutes the whole room began to smell like melted cheese and cooked meat. Her own stomach began to complain. Working all that magic this morning had made her hungry and a carby-cheesy plateful of pasta sounded like just the thing she needed.

"Rascal, if you wouldn't mind getting down plates?" Wynona asked, her eyes still on the pan. She didn't want to overcook it and if she got distracted, her magic tended to go a bit overboard.

"On it."

Within another five minutes, the whole group was seated at the table loading their plates. Conversation was almost nonexistent as they all filled their empty bellies.

A door down the hall creaked open and Wynona looked up to see Celia cautiously walking their way. "Is there enough for me?" she asked tentatively.

"Of course," Wynona said. She jumped up to grab another chair for her small table, but Rascal put his hand on her arm.

"Let me," he said softly. Walking into the greenhouse, he came back with a stool, then proceeded to give Celia his chair and sit on the hard stool himself.

Wynona could tell Celia was staring just as much as she was, but there was nothing for it. She loved this creature so much. She knew without a shadow of a doubt that this was his peace offering and it warmed Wynona's heart.

I love you, she sent to him.

Rascal grinned and winked. *I know.*

Wynona grinned back. *So this was all for brownie points?*

Rascal shrugged. *I'll claim my reward when the time is right.*

She rolled her eyes, but smiled and went back to eating.

"So..." Celia began. "Tell me about this murder."

Wynona jolted and began to choke on a bite. It took several sips of water and a couple of minutes to clear her airways enough to breathe normally.

Celia watched her with a frown. "Why didn't you just heal yourself?"

Wynona paused. "Uh...habit?"

Celia shook her head. "Whatever." She stuffed a large bite in her mouth. "Who died again? Some punk?"

Wynona sighed as the table broke out in arguments and conversation. She leaned back, listening to her friends and family argue and explain their points of view in the case. It was exhausting to listen to them...and yet, Wynona wasn't sure she would have it any other way.

Her life wasn't nearly as easy as she had hoped it would be after escaping, but there were some parts that made the uphill battle all worthwhile.

Let's just hope you live long enough to see those, Violet said wryly.

Wynona pressed her lips together to hold back her defense. Violet was right. Going tonight would be dangerous, but Thallia deserved the chance for a life just as much as Wynona did. *It's worth fighting for,* she finally sent to Violet. *Freedom will always be worth fighting for.*

CHAPTER 15

The day seemed to pass at a snail's pace as Wynona waited for night to arrive. She read through Granny's grimoire, marked the spells she wanted to try and took notes on the techniques Granny mentioned. She also cleaned her house, played referee between Rascal and Celia and generally watched the minutes tick by.

"I'll see you in the morning," Rascal murmured, giving her a sweet kiss. With a wink, he disappeared into the dark.

Wynona waited at the door for his massive truck to roar down the driveway. She sighed and leaned her head against the doorframe. *I love you.*

Love you too. Tomorrow we'll catch a killer together.

Wynona huffed a soft laugh. *Perfect.* She shook her head and closed the door. She had no idea how she had managed to get him off without Rascal knowing she was keeping a secret, but Wynona wasn't going to look a gift horse in the mouth. "Now to figure out how to slip out without Celia knowing."

"Without my knowing what?"

Wynona mentally cursed. She didn't use naughty words very often, but this seemed like the right time for it. "I was contemplating how to keep the two of you from fighting like cats and dogs." She closed her eyes as soon as the words were out. The unintended pun was a little too on the nose.

Celia snickered. "Nice one. Has he heard it yet? I might have to steal it."

Wynona sighed. "What's your problem with him, Celia? Rascal is the best thing that ever happened to me and I'm tired of being a go-between with you two."

Celia studied her nails.

Wynona shook her head. "Whatever. But you'll have to get used to him. Rascal is it for me."

Celia rolled her eyes. "Why would I care?"

Wynona closed her eyes for a moment. "If you don't care, then why do you go so far out of your way to make things difficult?"

Celia smirked. "I'm your sister. Isn't it my job?"

Wynona smirked back. "You know something? If you'd calm down around him, you and Rascal would probably get along just fine. He's always saying that as my boyfriend it's his job to drive me crazy."

Celia tapped her bottom lip. "Hmm...maybe he's more worthy than I thought." She tilted her head and narrowed her gaze. "I do have a question, though..."

Wynona stiffened. Celia's tone was a bit ominous.

"Your relationship seems...closer than a normal couple." Celia dropped her hand and clasped them behind her, taking a step forward. "In fact, I could swear there are times when you seem to be talking to each other in your minds."

Wynona's heart was pounding so hard she was sure it was visible from outside her chest. Her family didn't know that Rascal was her soulmate. Only a select few knew that and Wynona wasn't quite sure how much of that she was willing to share. It worried her that it was something that could be used against her, especially by her parents. "What are you implying?" Wynona asked, her voice tighter than she would have wished.

Celia paused in her approach. "I'm not sure, but something seems a little off."

Wynona forced a shrug. "That's fine. You don't have to understand us."

Celia leaned forward a little. "You're keeping something from me, Wynona. And I realize we've never been close, but something about this feels big and I plan to figure it out."

"Good luck," Wynona said with a curt nod. She was done with this conversation. They could definitely start their relationship over–Wynona was all too happy to allow Celia the opportunity to try again–but that didn't mean Wynona would simply forget all the times her sister had betrayed her trust. The ability to share secrets would have to be earned, and it definitely hadn't happened yet.

She headed to the hallway. "I'm bushed. I'll see you in the morning." Pausing at the hallway's entrance, she looked over her shoulder. "I'll be working on the case again tomorrow, so if you sleep in, I might already be gone."

Celia spun on her heel. "Have fun."

Wynona headed to her bedroom. The closer she got, the more her elevated heart rate had nothing to do with Celia's nosiness. In just a few short hours, she would be sneaking out to meet an unknown person in order to gain an alibi for Thallia.

When you put it like that, it sounds even more stupid.

Wynona looked to Violet, who was settled on her pillow in the corner of the bedroom. "You don't have to come."

Someone needs to keep you from getting yourself killed.

"I have my magic now," Wynona argued. "I can protect myself."

You also hardly rely on your magic. You're still too used to going without.

Wynona plopped on a chair. "I know," she said softly. "But what if the person runs when I bring Rascal along? What if they refuse to help?"

What if they don't know he's there, Violet shot back. *You really think a wolf can't stay hidden if he wants to?*

Wynona scrubbed her hands over her face. "I'm afraid to risk it. Thallia's innocent. What if this is the evidence we need to get her off the suspect list once and for all?

And what if this has nothing to do with Thallia, but is an opportunity for your parents to grab you? Or even kill you? I hate to break it to you, but you've probably earned a few enemies along the way this last year.

Wynona nodded. "I know," she whispered. "I've thought of that."

Then why are you going?

"Because I have to take the chance."

Violet snorted and curled back up. *Wake me before we go.*

Wynona leaned back. Violet might be able to sleep, but Wynona knew she never could. She was nervous about tonight, she was anxious about getting out of the house undetected and she was terrified of finding herself in a trap. "Thallia needs you," Wynona whispered to herself. "She's innocent." Nodding firmly, Wynona grabbed a book and settled back in her chair. She would do her best to keep her mind off the meeting until it was time to leave.

The seconds ticked by steadily, but not fast enough for Wynona's anxiety. A few minutes before she planned to leave, she dressed herself in all black, hoping to blend into the night as much as possible.

Violet wrapped her tail around Wynona's neck. *How are you going to avoid Celia?*

Wynona put her ear to the door. "Is she awake?"

Hang on. Violet skittered down and ran under the door.

Wynona could hear the mouse scurrying down the hallway, but the noise disappeared the farther she went. Taking deep breaths, Wynona forced herself to wait. It would be so much easier if Celia was in bed, and so Violet's information would be very helpful.

She's eating the last of the cookies, Violet said in disgust as she arrived back in the room.

Wynona nodded, her lips pursed. "I thought they were disappearing a little too quickly."

If there are no crumbs left, I'm staging a revolt.

"We'll make more." Wynona spun once Violet was in position and eyed her window.

I hate to say it, but that might be the best way.

Wynona nodded and walked over. The screeching sound from lifting the pane was enough to wake the dead and Wynona had to pause to make sure Celia wasn't coming down the hall to see what creature was tearing down the house. She didn't hear anything and Wynona nearly collapsed in relief.

"Geez," she grumbled as she lifted one leg extra high to get out. "I need to up the yoga practice." Wynona quickly blocked her inner hearing when Violet tried to offer her own snarky retort. She didn't need that kind of negativity in her life.

It took several moments of careful maneuvering, but eventually Wynona fell to the grass just outside her house.

She stood, rubbing her sore knee and looking around for anything out of place. Celia was either completely deaf or she simply didn't care that Wynona was making weird noises.

Probably the latter.

Wynona nodded, then walked to the back of the house where she was sure no one would see her.

Where are you going? The garage is the other way.

Wynona shook her head, still watching the area around her. The Grove of Secrets wasn't that far and Wynona felt as if there were eyes watching her. "Do you feel that?" she whispered to Violet.

I think it's time to grab the Vespa and run. Violet shivered and tightened her hold on Wynona's neck.

"They can't hurt us as long as we don't cross the boundaries," Wynona murmured, doing her best to keep her own shiver in check.

So you say. Violet sniffed. *Again...where are you going?*

"I'm going to port us to the shop," Wynona whispered. She winced and blocked out Violet's diatribe. Wynona had known from the start that taking the Vespa wasn't an option. There was no way someone wouldn't notice her. But porting? That could be done silently and with no one the wise.

Why did we bother to come outside if you were just porting?

"Because I didn't want to ruin my room if something goes wrong," Wynona explained.

Violet grumbled but left it at that.

"I ported my whole family home after the encounter with the cats," Wynona continued. "Surely I can do one person."

We can only hope. And don't forget to take a mouse along.

"Right." Wynona rubbed her sweaty palms on her jeans. She could still feel the eerie vibes from the forest, but she did her best to ignore them. Closing her eyes, Wynona allowed her magic to soar to the tips of her fingers, consuming her whole body. "The tea shop," she chanted over and over again.

She'd never ported on purpose before, so Wynona wasn't quite sure how to initiate such a spell, but she figured it had to start with knowing where she was going.

Try picturing the dining room, Violet suggested.

Wynona wiggled her fingers and let her mind's eyes create the tables, chairs, couches and antique teacup display she kept in the back. The tingling of magic began to prick her skin from head to toe. It was almost painful, but Wyonna held firm. "The tea shop, the tea shop," she said, her voice getting tighter as her body began to feel like it was being pulled in all directions.

You better know what you're doing! Violet screeched, her tail nearly choking Wynona's airway.

Wynona ignored the panic rising in her throat like bile and Violet's question. Her skin was being flayed from her body, Wynona was sure of it. She cracked one eye open and nearly fainted when she saw that her house was gone and she was in some kind of multicolored tunnel. The colors were so bright she could barely keep an eye open and she felt as if every direction was tugging on her to follow. What was she supposed to do now? Was this how it worked? Had she sent herself to another dimension and would now be lost forever?

You have to keep going, Violet ordered. *The tea shop!*

Wynona squeezed her eyes again. "The tea shop, the tea shop," she said more firmly. With one last wave of pain, which caused Wynona to cry out and drop to her knees, the rush and pressure finally ended. Hard flooring dug into Wynona's knees and when she leaned forward to catch her breath, she breathed easier when she recognized the hardwood under her palms. "Oh my gosh," she panted. "We did it."

There was no answer.

"Violet?"

The space was still dark and too quiet.

Wynona forced herself onto shaky legs. *VIOLET!* she screamed internally.

I'm here! A scuttling noise cut into the dark and Wynona finally blew out her breath when she felt the familiar tugging on her pants, climbing all the way up to her neck.

Wynona reached up and lifted Violet from her shoulder, cuddling her close. "What happened?"

I ended up in the office, Violet grumbled. She was shaking, which undermined her snarky tone. *Apparently you need to work on that before I join you again.*

Wynona kissed the soft head and put her familiar back on her shoulder. "I promise we'll get it figured out."

So...is your informant still here? Violet asked. *You shouted loud enough to bring those ghost cats back from the beyond.*

Wynona huffed. "Sorry for being worried about you."

Violet chittered.

"I guess we'll find out, huh?" Wynona said, coming back to Violet's original question. She was also worried about it, but Wynona had timed her arrival to be early enough she hoped she would beat her informant. According to her cell phone, it was still fifteen minutes to midnight.

Feeling her way to a wall, Wynona was proud of herself for only stumbling over chairs twice before reaching a light switch. She blinked rapidly when the light came on. "Gosh, that's bright."

Tell me about it. Violet rubbed her eyes and sighed. *Now what?*

Wynona shook her head. "Now we wait, I guess."

Well, I want a cookie.

"I don't think I have any," Wynona admitted. "But last I knew, there were a couple of Danishes. Will that do?"

I suppose, Violet said on a sigh.

Wynona smiled despite the fear churning in her belly. She wished she knew what to expect this evening. Was the informant going to knock on the door? Would they get into the shop somehow? Were they someone who could also port?

Not knowing what else to do in the meantime, Wynona began to walk across the dining room toward the kitchen, only to come to a screeching halt.

You've got to be kidding me, Violet snapped. *Again?*

Wynona's heart fell to her stomach. "I thought we were early, but I'm guessing we were too late."

Really? Whatever gave you that idea?

Wynona closed her eyes and tried to hold back tears. This was *not* how tonight was supposed to go. *Rascal?*

Yeah?

I need you and the team at the tea shop.

Open the door.

Instead of being surprised, Wynona simply walked stiff-legged to the front entrance. She unlocked it and pulled it open.

"We can discuss you keeping this from me later," Rascal growled, stepping inside. "What's going on?"

Wynona waved toward the dining room. "The body is that way."

Rascal pinched the bridge of his nose. "Unbelievable." He grabbed his phone and began to walk farther inside. "Chief? We've got an emergency at the tea shop."

CHAPTER 16

"Do you know who she is?" Rascal asked when Wynona walked up behind him.

Wynona shook her head. "No. I've never seen her before."

The shifter squatted down and studied the body without touching it. "She's very pale," he noted. "Could mean a couple different things."

"When was the last walk-through of the shop?" Wynona asked, once again cuddling Violet to her chest. She never did enjoy seeing the bodies. Solving the cases intrigued her, but death, no matter how many times Wynona came in contact with it, was hard for her to stomach.

Rascal glanced at his watch. "Would have been about two hours ago. They're due any minute."

As if his words were a premonition, there were footsteps in the front entryway. "Deputy Chief?" one voice asked tentatively. "You in here?"

"Keep coming, Aldor," Rascal said, rising to his feet. He wasn't in his uniform since he'd had the day off, but he still looked every inch the officer in charge.

An older man with long, white hair peered around the corner, his baton in hand. When he spotted Rascal and Wynona, he sighed in relief and put the weapon away. "I thought that was your truck out front, but with the open door I was worried."

Rascal nodded. "I've called the chief. We're going to be overrun in the next few minutes."

"Chief?" The officer's white eyebrows shot up. "Why?"

Rascal stepped to the side.

The officer's green eyes dropped to the ground. "Oh." He made a face. "I didn't see that coming." Those same eyes came up to meet Wynona's. "I don't think we've met, but everyone at the precinct talks about you." He stepped forward, hand outstretched. "Officer Aldor."

Wynona shook his hand. "Wynona Le Doux," she said softly. "Nice to meet you."

"Likewise." The officer took a deep breath and put his hands on his hips. "Guess I'll start taping it off, though the whole building has been kept trespasser free anyway."

"Not completely," Rascal muttered.

"Looks like she might have been here awhile," Officer Aldor said. "She's pretty pale. Body looks cold."

Rascal began to nod, but Wynona jumped in.

"Actually, I think she's a vampire."

Rascal turned to her with raised eyebrows. "How can you tell?"

"Come stand over here," Wynona directed, moving to the side.

Rascal came back and stood in the exact spot.

"Now look at her mouth."

"Ah," he said in understanding. "Good call, sweetheart." The tiniest tips of the girl's fangs were poking through her lips, though they wouldn't have been seen from any other angle. "Well, that makes things harder." He rubbed the back of his neck.

"How so?" Wynona asked.

"Vampires are already cold," Officer Aldor answered. "So the coroner can't use body temp to figure out the time of death."

"And the paleness of our skin means physical signs are useless as well," Chief Ligurio finished as he walked through the dining room door. He paused and grunted in disgust. "Who is it this time, Ms. Le Doux?"

Wynona shook her head. "I'm sorry. I've never seen her before."

"Then why was she here?"

Rascal folded his arms over his chest. "I'd like to know that myself."

Wynona felt her cheeks heat and she suddenly wanted to be anywhere but where she was.

Told you, Violet sang.

Not helpful, Wynona sent back. Realizing there would be no use in dilly-dallying, Wynona straightened her shoulders and looked the chief in the eye. "I got a text earlier today." She pulled her phone out of her back pocket and found the texting thread before handing it to the chief.

"You can't have been that stupid, Ms. Le Doux." Chief Ligurio snorted. "Why would you agree to meet someone, a complete unknown, at midnight in your shop?"

Wynona couldn't look Rascal in the eye. She could feel his anger. It penetrated through her shield and was consuming her, making it hard to breathe. She tried to shrug, but it felt stiff and fake. "I was willing to risk it for Thallia."

"You barely know her," Rascal said in a low tone. There was a slight lisp to his words, telling Wynona without looking that his teeth were closer to those of a wolf than a man. "You were willing to risk your life for a fairy you only met a few days ago?"

Wynona finally turned to look at him. "No," she said, shaking her head slowly. "I was willing to risk my life for the truth. No one should be accused or locked up when they're innocent. And I was afraid that if I contacted you or the rest of the squad, the informant wouldn't show."

Rascal pushed a hand through his hair, causing it to stand up on end, and stormed away from her.

Wynona began to go after him, but Chief Ligurio, clearing his throat, stopped her.

"I have a few more questions, Ms. Le Doux," he said in a clipped tone. Apparently, he wasn't very happy with her either. "I need to know exactly what happened when you got here. All of it."

Wynona nodded and gave him the story. The longer she talked, the more her legs began to shake. Her adrenaline was dying off and the excess use of magic tonight had her ready for bed.

Somehow I don't see that happening any time soon, Violet said nonchalantly.

Again...not helping!

Violet began scrubbing her face. She clearly wasn't the least bit concerned with whatever punishment Wynona was about to receive.

The chief got back on his phone. "Bring in the Pearlily girl," he snapped. "Yes, bring the lawyer if you must, but get them to the office. We have a body to identify and an alibi to collect." He shoved the phone back in his pocket and crooked his finger at Wynona. "You're coming to the precinct. I want this figured out tonight."

Wynona took in a deep breath. "I understand," she said softly. She turned over her shoulder to see Rascal shouting orders at a few other officers. It wasn't like him to be so grumpy. His normally care-free attitude made him a wonderful police deputy chief, but tonight, he sounded ready to tear everyone's throats out.

Wynona waited several minutes, but Rascal didn't even look her way. Finally, she went and sat on the couch. When the chief left for the office, she would find a way to get there. Even if she had to port again.

Over my dead body, Violet argued.

We need to practice, Wynona sent back.

Once a night is enough.

Sighing, Wynona leaned back, then stood up again. She was too tired. If she sat down, she was going to fall asleep. Instead, she walked over to the body and forced herself to look for clues. "Any idea on what may have killed her?" she asked softly.

The coroner looked up. "I'm guessing it was this." He held up a large butcher knife.

Wynona's eyes widened. "I didn't see that!"

The red cap huffed. "She fell on it. Which didn't help the situation at all."

Wynona frowned and looked around. "Chief? Is Daemon here?"

Chief Ligurio shook his head. "No." He walked over. "Why?"

Wynona pointed to the weapon. "The killer used a butcher knife. I thought Daemon could look for magic."

The chief rubbed his chin. "Careful with it, Azirad."

The red cap glared. "I've been doing this job for fifty years and you think I'm going to screw up now? Really?"

His unhappy tone made Wynona realize she hadn't seen Lusgu since arriving. Gasping, she raced to the kitchen. "Lusgu! Lusgu!"

Violet scurried down Wynona's arm and disappeared into the portal in the corner.

Wynona's heart was still beating like a racing hippocampus. When Lusgu's scowling face appeared through the wall, she put a hand on her heart and took a deep breath. "Oh, thank goodness."

"What's going on?" he growled.

Violet sat primly on Lusgu's shoulder. *Do you want to tell him? Or should I?*

Wynona was ready to port Violet back to the house. The little rodent was being far from helpful, even if Wynona knew she deserved some of her disdain. "There's been another death," Wynona said. She held up her hands. "Before you say anything, no. I'm not here to accuse you and it never even occurred to me you were involved." She dropped her hands to her side. "I actually ran in here to make sure you were okay."

Lusgu's frown deepened. "Why wouldn't I be?"

Wynona shrugged. "You're always here. I don't know how much you can hear when you're in your home or anything, so..."

Those black, beady eyes rolled toward the ceiling. "My home isn't here. I only come for work." He shook his head and began shuffling toward the dining room. "Who was it this time? And why does everyone die in the tea house? Don't they know how hard it is to get clean?" He grunted. "Unsanitary buggers."

Wynona hadn't felt like smiling since she'd arrived that night, but Lusgu's complete disregard for someone's death and the police roaming around struck her as inappropriately funny and she had to fight to keep from laughing.

Violet turned backward on Lusgu's shoulder and gave Wynona a look, but Wynona could only shrug. Shaking her head, Violet turned around and the pair disappeared into the dining room.

Wynona waited a few moments before following. This evening had not gone anything like she had planned and now she had to deal with another death on top of it all. Questions were mixed with the shame she was struggling with at the moment. Who was the girl? What did she know that should help keep Thallia out of jail? Why hadn't Thallia talked about the girl if they really had an alibi together?

Knowing she wouldn't find any answers in the kitchen, Wynona stepped back out, only to stop in the doorway. Her eyes were caught on an empty space in a wooden block. "Lusgu?" Wynona asked, not taking her eyes off the spot.

He grunted.

"Do we normally have a full knife block?"

There was a general pause in the dining room as every paranormal paused what they were doing.

"Ms. Le Doux?" Chief Ligurio asked. "Are you saying you think the knife is yours?"

Wynona waited, glancing quickly to Lusgu. Now that she hired out the cooking, she rarely used the kitchen except to heat water and mix tinctures. None of which required her to use the utensils. Lusgu, however, used the kitchen not only to help her, but also for his own use. If anyone knew if a knife was missing, he would.

Lusgu shuffled over and peered into the kitchen. His black eyes narrowed. "It's ours," he affirmed.

Rascal growled again.

"ALDOR!" Chief Ligurio shouted.

The white-haired officer from earlier rushed to his boss. "Yeah, Chief?"

"Bag the block," Chief Ligurio said curtly. "And anything else that looks suspicious."

Wynona stepped aside and allowed the officer past her. "I'm totally replacing those knives," she murmured. There was no way she would ever use any of those knives again. The idea made her sick to her stomach.

"Come on," Rascal said gruffly. He'd snuck up behind her when Wynona wasn't looking.

Wynona jumped a little. "Where are we going?"

"I'm driving over to the station," he said. "Chief will follow soon and then we'll talk to Thallia and her lawyer."

Wynona hesitated and Rascal noticed.

"I'm not going to tear your head off," he said in that same exasperated tone.

"I know that," she whispered. There were so many paranormal ears listening in on their conversation and she didn't want anyone else involved at the moment. *I'm not afraid you're going to hurt me,* she assured him. *But I don't like having you mad at me either. It hurts to be close to you when you're like this.*

Rascal stared at her, his lips squishing from one side to the next with his emotions. *Why don't we talk in the truck?* he finally asked.

Wynona nodded. She still preferred speaking out loud, but that would keep them from having an audience.

Rascal took her hand and led her outside.

Wynona was surprised, but grateful for the touch. They'd never had a fight like this and she wasn't quite sure how to handle it. He ushered her quickly into the vehicle and walked around to his side.

After jamming the key in the ignition and merging onto the road, Rascal spoke up. "How did you get to the shop?"

Wynona clasped her hands in her lap. "I ported."

His head jerked her way before going back to the road. "Please tell me that's new. Or did you simply keep that skill to yourself?"

Pain hit Wynona in the chest and Rascal sighed.

"I'm sorry," he said, his voice finally losing some of its edge. "That was uncalled for." He blew out a harsh breath. "I'm fighting the alpha at the moment who wants you to understand exactly how he feels, yet my human side wants to understand why you felt like it was a good idea to risk yourself in such a way when you know there are creatures who love and depend on you."

Put that way, Wynona's shame only grew hotter. "I'm sorry," she whispered thickly. "I didn't think about the outside repercussions. All I was worried about was helping Thallia and I didn't take into account how my being hurt would affect you or Violet."

"Speaking of...why did Violet know?"

"She heard me read the text in my head before I was able to throw up my mental wall."

Rascal nodded. He pushed a hand through his hair. "I gotta be honest, Wy. It scared me to death to know you were throwing yourself into something so risky. I understand your desire to help people. It's one of the things I love about you." He parked and turned off the engine before turning to face her, his arm resting on the steering wheel. "But I thought we'd reached a point in our relationship where our decisions weren't just about ourselves anymore."

Tears trickled down Wynona's cheeks. "I'm so sorry. I thought my magic would be enough to protect me and didn't think about anything else. Violet was there to help and I thought we'd be able to get in and out quickly. Unless..."

His eyebrows went up. "Unless?"

Wynona shrugged. "The only scenario I could think of that I would struggle to handle would be if it was my parents setting a trap."

Rascal closed his eyes and hung his head. "I hadn't even thought of that one," he growled.

Wynona hesitated only a moment before reaching over and cupping his cheek.

Rascal's already glowing eyes became brighter, his wolf just under his skin.

"You're right," she whispered. "I have more than myself to think about and I promise to do a better job of thinking things through next time."

He shook his head. "There's not supposed to be a next time."

"I can't guarantee that," Wynona admitted. "But I won't keep it from you. Is that enough?"

He nodded. "For now. But I'm starting to think we should simply lock you in your greenhouse and hide you from the world."

Wynona laughed through her tears and wiped her cheeks. "As long as you were with me, I don't think that sounds too bad."

Rascal leaned in and kissed her cheek. "Come on, beautiful. Let's go save your friend."

"She's not even a friend," Wynona added. "But she's innocent. And that's enough."

CHAPTER 17

"Thank you," Thallia said thickly. Her bottom lip was still quivering even as she tried to get a hold of her emotions. Her face was bright red and her nose was running. "I just can't believe she's gone," she murmured. Shaking her head, more tears poured down the fairy's cheeks.

"I'm very sorry for your loss," Wynona said softly. "But Thallia, we need to know why your friend was there to begin with."

Thallia sniffed, wiped her nose and nodded. "I know... I just... I never expected her to be killed. I told her not to talk to you, but she hated that I was under suspicion for Dralo's murder." Her face crumpled. "Two of my friends. Gone. Why is all this happening?"

"How about we start with her name?" Chief Ligurio said. His tone was firm, but not unkind. There didn't seem to be anything fake about the young woman's emotions and every officer in the room seemed slightly uncomfortable with the hysterics.

"Edana Lycoris," Thallia managed to get out between her sobs. "She was my best friend. Other than Dralo, of course."

Wynona nodded. "And she was a vampire?"

Thallia's eyebrows pulled together. "Yes. How did you know?"

"Her teeth were out," Wynona explained.

"Oh." Thallia nodded, still frowning.

"Thallia?" Wynona pressed. The fairy was thinking about something.

Thallia pursed her lips and shook her head. "Sorry. She just usually kept them hidden, like most vampires, so it seems odd that they were out."

Most likely because she was fighting off her killer, Rascal supplied.

Wynona nodded. That was a very logical explanation. "Why was she at my shop, Thallia? This is very important."

Thallia kept her head ducked, refusing to meet anyone's eyes. "I told you. She hated that I was being accused of murder and she had the ability to help."

"Thallia," Wynona snapped, growing frustrated. "What alibi did Edana supposedly have?"

Thalia sighed and turned away. The fact that she was barely out of her teenage years was becoming more and more prevalent. "I spent the night at Edana's the night that Dralo was killed."

"I don't understand why that's a big deal," Wynona responded, leaning back in her seat.

Another long sigh escaped the fairy. "Because there's this creature...a raccoon shifter whom I used to be friends with." Thallia's bottom lip quivered again. "But when he started getting...weird, I had to stop being his friend."

"Interrogating my client, Chief Ligurio?" a man asked as he slipped into the room. The lawyer was in fairy form and was hovering above the ground, his wings creating a frenzy. He glanced around the room. "Elian Musgaver. The Pearlily family lawyer."

"I'm not doing anything she hasn't consented to," Chief Ligurio growled back. "Would you put those wings away?"

The lawyer landed on the floor and wiped his hands down the front of his suit coat. "My client isn't old enough to know the law."

"She's an adult," Chief Ligurio said wryly. "Any judge will see it my way."

"Oh, it's okay," Thallia said hurriedly. "I don't have anything to hide."

The lawyer's face turned red and he marched over to sit next to her. "Everyone has something to hide, Ms. Pearlily, and it's time you learned how to keep your mouth shut." Facing the crowd, the lawyer stuck his nose in the air. "Moving forward, you are not to speak to her unless I am present. Is that clear?"

"Again," Chief Ligurio said, one black eyebrow raised high. "She's an adult. If she agrees to speak to us, she has the right to do so."

"Her parents say otherwise."

"If she was a minor, that would apply, but no dice."

The fairy's jaw clenched and he finally took his demand to Thallia. "Never again, Ms. Pearlily. Is that understood? You don't talk to any of them without my presence."

She shrugged. "What if you're not available?"

Wynona bit her lips between her teeth to keep from laughing as the lawyer's jaw dropped. *I don't think Thallia understands the seriousness of the situation.*

Lucky for us, Rascal sent back, clearing his throat a couple of times.

"Ms. Pearlily," the lawyer said in a strained, patient voice. "Please simply follow the suggestion. I can't do my job otherwise."

Thallia pouted. "Fine." She folded her arms over her chest and looked back at Wynona. "Apparently, my lawyer is here. Should we continue?"

"No, we should not," Mr. Muskgaver said curtly. "We need time to talk before this continues."

Thallia's lips pinched. "Syn has been stalking me," she burst out.

Wynona's eyes widened. "What?"

Chief Ligurio leaned over the desk. "If you're being stalked, why haven't I heard this before? And why is there no record of any complaints in your file?"

"Ms. Pearlily," her lawyer warned.

"Because my parents don't know," Thallia snapped, glaring at Mr. Muskgaver. She turned to the chief. "He's been in love with me for months, but I was with Dralo. Syn started saying weird things and was telling people things that weren't true about us, so I finally had to break up with him." She shrugged. "As friends, I mean. We never dated."

"And you think he killed Ms. Lycoris?" Chief Ligurio clarified.

Mr. Muskgaver cleared his throat pointedly, but Thallia continued to ignore him. "Could be, but I don't really know. He hated that I spent time with anyone else, and ever since I stopped talking to him, he's been popping up in odd places."

Chief Ligurio began typing on his computer. "I need a full rundown of what he's done, Ms. Pearlily. Showing up in weird places isn't enough."

"Ms. Pearlily!"

Thallia once again ignored the lawyer, whose face was growing redder by the moment. "Sometimes he'll be standing across the street when I come out of a shop," she said. "Other friends have said he's talked to them. Says I'm still his." She shivered delicately. "A raccoon shifter. Can you imagine?"

Wynona listened carefully. Why hadn't Thallia mentioned any of this before? "How would this shifter know that Edana was at the shop?"

The room quieted at the question and Thallia looked like a fairy caught in the headlights. She slowly shook her head. "I don't know. Maybe he followed her? I told you that he was jealous of the people I spent my time with."

"And you say you were at Ms. Lycoris's the night Dralo was killed?"

Thallia nodded, her eyes filling with tears once more.

Wynona tilted her head. "If..Syn...was in love with you, why was he upset you were at your friend's house? Wouldn't he be more upset if you were with Dralo?"

Thallia nodded. "Oh yeah, that drove him crazy. He once got in a shouting match with Dralo."

"But why Edana?"

Thallia grew more pale and slightly more subdued. "Dralo and I..." She swallowed audibly. "We were having problems."

"And?" Wynona pressed.

"Ms. Pearlily," her lawyer tried to get in while things were quieter, but it still didn't work.

"Edana was helping me come up with a way to make Dralo jealous."

"Jealous," Wynona clarified.

Thallia nodded and began twisting a piece of hair around her finger.

Wynona was starting to feel like she was in the middle of a teenage drama. Suddenly, she was very grateful she never went to public high school. "Was Dralo breaking up with you?"

"No!" Thallia shouted. "I loved him! He would never break up with me!" Her wings began to flutter and she rose a few inches off her chair.

"Ms. Pearlily!" Mr. Muskgaver shouted, holding up a hand to keep her wings from whacking him in the face. "If you please!"

"Thallia," Wynona said tightly. "Sit down, please. We need to know what's going on and we need all the details."

Thallia thumped down and folded her arms again, pouting like a champ. "Dralo had mentioned he might be looking to move on," she whined. "I didn't want to leave the mansion yet, so I couldn't go with him."

"Why didn't you want to leave?"

Thallia rolled her eyes. "Because as long as I live at home, Daddy pays for everything."

Chief Ligurio frowned. "But you have a job."

She straightened. "My father says it's real world experience." Her smile widened. "Plus, I'm working with Wynona Le Doux! Do you have any idea how the tabloids will pay for any stories?"

Wynona jerked back, not even recognizing Rascal's growling as it reverberated through the room.

"Ms. Pearlily," her lawyer whispered, eyeing the shifter warily. "I don't think that's a good plan."

Thallia smiled at Wynona. "But you're so sweet, I doubt I'll even have anything to sell."

She's lost her mind, Wynona sent to Rascal. *How can she not see how horrible that plan is?*

When her dad said 'real world' experience, I think he meant it. Ms. Pearlily does NOT live in the real world at all.

"You do realize that Ms. Le Doux, the very one you want to sell gossip about, is the only person in this room who thinks you're innocent?" Chief Ligurio said coldly.

Thallia's jaw snapped shut.

"And I will let you know here and now," Chief continued, his voice growing dark. "I will consider it a personal insult if anything...untoward...begins to show up in the rag columns." He flashed a sharp smile. "Anything."

"But what if I didn't do it?" Thallia squeaked.

"You'll still be the first person I come to."

What little blood that was left in Thallia's head drained and she swayed a little from side to side.

"Come, Ms. Pearlily," her lawyer said wearily. "I think it's time we retired." The fairy paused. "Unless you're charging her with something?"

"Not tonight," Chief Ligurio said pleasantly. "But you'll be hearing from us soon."

Thallia followed numbly behind her lawyer, pausing at the door. "You know I adore you, right, Wynona? I've wanted in with the presidential family for so long!"

Wynona didn't answer, simply watched. She felt bad for the young woman. She had absolutely no concept of how her actions affected others. Her spoiled, rich world had been a curse rather than a blessing and Wynona had seen it all before. If Wynona had been born with her magic, she might very well have been in the same position.

Your parents would have used and abused you, but even Celia knows more than Thallia.

Wynona nodded gently, not realizing Thallia would take it as an answer.

Thallia relaxed and blew out a breath. "Oh, good. I was worried for a moment that I wouldn't be able to keep working for you." Her hand fluttered to her chest. "I mean...it is kind of awkward that my friend and boyfriend were killed there, after all."

"We're leaving," Mr. Muskgaver said sharply, taking Thallia's upper arm and pulling her out into the hallway.

The room sat in stunned silence for several long heartbeats after the two fairies disappeared.

"I'm starting to think we need a psych eval." Chief Ligurio groaned, pinching the bridge of his nose.

Wynona barely glanced at him before being hit with an answer. "Blood and ginger root," she said automatically.

Chief Ligurio gave her a look.

Wynona shrugged. "Sorry. When I'm upset my magic is close to the surface."

"And what does it tell you about Ms. Pearlily?"

Wynona slumped in her seat. "I still believe she's innocent. But I'm starting to truly feel sorry for her. Her father is more than just a bully. He's crippled her for life."

"Maybe that was her mother?" Rascal offered. "Did she work too hard to protect her baby?"

Wynona shrugged. "Possible. But somehow I doubt dear old Dad let Mom get away with much. If Thallia's using Daddy's money, then it doesn't sound like she's hiding behind her mother."

Chief Ligurio sighed and leaned back in his seat. "My money is still on Thallia."

"I think we need to check out this Syn guy," Wynona argued. She held up a hand to stave off the argument. "I know. It looks terrible. And Thallia has shown us that she's a little unhinged. But being naive and a product of a digital age isn't a crime. Half the teenagers we meet on the street are the same way."

Chief Ligurio snorted and Rascal huffed.

"But we have an alibi now."

"That can't be corroborated," Chief Ligurio pointed out. "How do we know Ms. Pearlily didn't set up the meeting, then kill Ms. Lycoris to keep her from spilling the truth?"

"The truth being?"

"That Ms. Pearlily has no alibi because she was the one at the shop," Rascal finished.

Wynona looked over her shoulder at him. "You're right," she admitted. "It all looks horrible. But I still don't think she's a killer. I think she needs help. I still just don't think she'd kill to get her way. That thought doesn't feel right."

"Someone did. Twice."

"Do we know it's the same person?" Wynona pressed. "And Thallia has given us another person of interest. Shouldn't we, out of duty to the public, check the shifter out before pinning it all on Thallia's shoulders?"

Chief Ligurio shook his head, gathering his computer and papers. "You and Strongclaw take care of it. I need sleep if I'm going to deal with this circus."

Wynona stood and walked with Rascal back the way they had come. They went straight to his truck, where he bundled her in and pulled onto a nearly empty street.

"You're still sure she's innocent?" Rascal asked.

Wynona nodded. "Yes."

"And you're still willing to investigate?"

"Yes," she responded again.

"Okay." Rascal nodded curtly. "I'll pick you up at nine."

Wynona smiled. "I love you," she whispered, knowing he'd easily hear it.

Rascal's gold eyes flashed her way before going back to the road. "I know," he teased, though it wasn't as playful as normal.

Still...it was a start and Wynona was grateful for it. Even with their argument and her unpopular opinion, Rascal was by her side, right where he was supposed to be.

CHAPTER 18

Wynona leaned forward, eying the rundown apartment building in front of the truck. "Well...Thallia certainly doesn't take care of her stalkers the way she takes care of her boyfriends."

Rascal snorted. "I think you spend too much time with Violet."

Wynona grinned.

"Speaking of..." Rascal frowned. "Where is she this morning?"

"Sleeping," Wynona said with a laugh. "She's tired of running around, apparently."

Rascal shrugged. "Glad someone is getting beauty rest." He opened his door. "Hang on, I'll come let you out."

Wynona smiled to herself as her handsome wolf walked around. She loved how he took care of her. Whoever said gentlemen didn't exist anymore had never met *her* gentleman. "Thank you," she murmured as she slid from the high bench. Taking a deep breath, she looked into his eyes. "Ready?"

"As I'll ever be." He glanced farther down the parking lot. "Skymaw's here somewhere. He'll meet us inside."

Wynona nodded. "We need to get this case wrapped up. My shop has been closed too long."

"Agreed." Rascal led her up the stairs to a dark brown hallway with peeling wallpaper.

Wynona ran her fingertips along the ripped edges. "It wouldn't take much magic to fix this."

Rascal grabbed her hand. "And yet it's not going to be your magic. Let the owner handle it, huh?"

Wynona grinned. "Afraid I'll blow something up?"

Rascal chuckled, but shook his head. "Nope. I'm afraid whatever drug they're smoking in here will get in your system."

Wynona tripped. "What? Drugs? Are you serious?"

"He is," Daemon said, jogging to catch up with them. He slowed down once he was right behind the couple. "Can't you smell that sickly sweet scent?"

Wynona took a tentative sniff. "Yeah. I mean...I guess I figured it was something herbal."

Rascal's chuckling grew. "You could call it that if you want."

Wynona rolled her eyes. "Okay. So Syn lives in a terrible building. Let's get this interview over with so we can all get out to the fresh air." *Boy am I glad Violet's not here.* Wynona was positive that the mouse's tiny body wouldn't be able to handle the smoke as well as the larger creatures could.

"Yes, ma'am," Daemon said. He stepped around her and banged his fist against a door. "Syn Ringer? This is the Hex Haven Police. Open the door."

Wynona stayed in the back. She'd watched the officers deal with this kind of thing before, but never in a place quite so run down. For the first time since she'd started working with them, Wynona was positive that the blunt way of handling things would be useful. Who knew what kind of creature Syn was if this type of environment didn't bother him.

Slowly, the door cracked open. "Let me see some identification," came the raspy voice.

Daemon pulled out his badge and shoved it at the doorway. "Officer Skymaw." Tucking the badge back in his pocket, he jammed a thumb over his shoulder. "This is Deputy Chief Strongclaw and Ms. Wynona Le Doux, independent consultant. We have some questions for you."

The door opened farther and a young man with a wild crop of black hair appeared. His skin was lightly tanned and dark rings lay under his eyes, though from the alert look she was being given, Wynona wasn't sure if the rings were from sleep deprivation or a gift from his shifter creature.

"What do you want?" the young man asked, his voice still coarse. It appeared that was simply how he spoke and Wynona was intrigued by the tone of it. Especially for one so young, the voice didn't seem to fit.

"We'd like to ask you some questions," Daemon said firmly. "Will you let us in?"

Gray eyes narrowed, but finally Syn stepped back. "This is about Edana, isn't it? It was all over the news this morning."

Wynona gave him a small smile of sympathy as they walked inside the small apartment. She was thrilled to detect that the drug smell didn't continue into the young man's apartment. That was definitely something in his favor. But the way he was eyeing Rascal and Daemon said he'd had encounters with the law before. "It is," Wynona responded. "Did you know her well?"

Syn snorted and shut the door before walking around the room and throwing himself in an old, ratty recliner. "She was my girlfriend's best friend. I suppose I knew her."

Wynona exchanged a glance with Rascal. "Your girlfriend? Who might that be?" he asked.

Syn's eyes fluttered as he rolled them. "It's not public knowledge, of course, but Thallia Pearlily and I were a pair for a while." His gaze dropped to the armrest where he picked at a loose thread. "It couldn't last. Not when she was dating Dralo at the time." Syn glanced up from under his brows. "Dralo would have killed me."

Wynona frowned. "You dated Thallia?"

Syn straightened up as if offended. "Of course. We were crazy about each other."

"While she was dating Dralo?"

Syn nodded. "Look, do you have questions about Edana, or what? I hung out with her whenever I was with Thallia, but that's about it. I knew she was a vampire, I knew she hated her job as a waitress at the Weeping Widow, and I knew her and Thallia were close, but that was about it. Edana and I would never have been friends without Thallia being in the middle."

"Thallia told us that you never dated."

Syn blew out a raspberry. "Of course she didn't. Even with Dralo dead, if her father ever caught wind that she'd dated a raccoon, and a poor raccoon at that...well..." Syn smirked and shook his head. "It wouldn't have ended any better for me than it did for Dralo."

"Mr. Ringer," Wynona said carefully.

"Syn," he corrected, winking. "I'm too young to be a mister."

Wynona gave him a placating smile. "Syn." She ignored Rascal's mental growl. "Do you mind if I sit down?"

Syn waved toward the couch.

Wynona wanted to put herself on his level and make the raccoon feel comfortable, but she was partly afraid that the couch would give her some kind of disease if she came in contact with too much of it. In order to meet in the middle, she perched right on the edge. The men chose to stand behind. "Can we start from the beginning? I'm afraid much of what you're sharing with us doesn't match up with the other stories we've been told."

Syn huffed, but didn't respond.

"Let's start with where you were last night...somewhere between eight and midnight."

Syn frowned. "You think I killed Edana?" He pushed a hand through his hair, showing just how he'd gotten it to stand up in such a wild pattern. "Why the heck would I do that? I told you, I barely knew her."

"I haven't accused you of anything," Wynona assured him. "But we've had your name mentioned in conjunction with Ms. Lycoris and we needed to see what your relationship with her was."

Nicely done, Rascal sent to her. *You'll be a full blown detective yet.*

Wynona kept her grin to herself. She was going to have to get better about hiding her emotions if she continued helping the police handle murder cases.

Syn sighed, long and weary. He slumped in his seat. "I already told you. I didn't have a relationship with her. I was dating Thallia."

"But where were you last night?" Wynona persisted.

Syn gave her a look. "I was here. At my apartment. Having dinner by myself."

"So there's no one who can corroborate that story?" Rascal inserted.

Syn gave the officer a look. "My neighbors. Old lady Hilaran down the hall knows when everybody leaves or comes. She can tell you I came in around six and never left."

Rascal pulled out his phone and punched the notes tab. "What room is she in?"

"Really?" Syn drawled. "You're that desperate for my alibi?"

"We're looking at everyone's alibi," Wynona assured him.

Syn huffed in disbelief, but didn't argue with her.

"Can you think of anyone who would have wanted to kill Ms. Lycoris?" Wynona asked. "Or Mr. Ziumar?"

"I don't know anything about Edana," Syn said quickly. He leaned forward. "But who wouldn't have wanted to hurt the dark elf? He was creepy and Thallia was afraid to leave him."

Wynona could hear the men shuffling behind her. This was the complete opposite of what Thallia had said...but who was telling the truth? The dramatic young fairy who was raised in a rich bubble? Or the poverty stricken shifter who obviously had feelings for the fairy? Either one of them could have gained from Dralo's death, depending on whose story was right, yet Wynona still felt like Thallia didn't have it in her to kill. Syn...she wasn't as sure about. He didn't *look* like a killer, but half the people Wynona had helped put behind bars didn't look the part.

If Wynona had learned anything along this journey, it was that the brightest smiles often hid the darkest minds.

"Did Thallia tell you she wanted to leave him?" Daemon asked, finally stepping into the conversation.

Syn leaned back, smug in his confidence. "Not outright. But she used to tell me stories about how he treated her. She gave him everything and he just wanted more."

"And how did you feel?" Rascal asked. "Not only were you the hidden boyfriend, but she didn't seem to lavish her money on you at all. Weren't you jealous?"

Syn's gray eyes turned hard. "I had her heart. That's all I needed."

Wynona took a slow breath. He truly seemed to believe what he was saying. But how could she be sure? "Can you tell us about any of the incidents you're referring to? What did Thallia tell you about Dralo?"

Syn shrugged, shifting his weight as if slightly uncomfortable. "She said he hated when she was late. That she always had to tell him where she was and he was constantly texting her if she wasn't where she was supposed to be."

"Was she often where she wasn't supposed to be?"

Syn's eyes narrowed. "She was where she wanted to be. That should be enough."

"But you just told us that she was cheating on Dralo," Rascal pressed. "Don't you think that would make an elf suspicious? He obviously had good reason to be."

Syn slapped his hands on the armrests, anger written plainly on his face. "Dralo didn't know anything! He was a meathead who used his fists when he should have used his brain."

"How long were you and Thallia together?" Wynona asked, her voice slightly raised. She was a little worried one of the men would continue to pick a fight. There were times when an angry suspect was useful, but Wynona much prefered to be at the station to handle any outbursts. This place wasn't safe...at all.

Syn slumped down again, looking surly. He folded his arms over his chest. "Six months."

"And when did you break up?"

He laughed harshly. "You mean when did she break it off? That's what you mean, right?" His eyes suddenly looked misty. "I'd have married her if given half a chance." He shook his head, one side of his lip curling. "But Thallia wasn't ready to let go of Daddy's money yet."

At least that one we know is true.

Rascal snorted, drawing another glare.

"When was it?" Wynona asked again.

Syn sighed. "About two months ago."

"And have you been following Ms. Pearlily around since then?"

Syn looked genuinely confused. "What?"

"Did you follow Thallia around? Or start rumors that you two were still dating?"

He shook his head. "Why the heck would I do that? Then everyone would know we'd been dating. That was the last thing she wanted."

"And yet you're telling us now," Daemon pointed out.

Syn laughed in that same harsh tone. "What does it matter now?" he asked, holding up his hands. "She's dumped me and now she's lost everything. Her abusive boyfriend and her best friend. If she decides to come back, it'll be public. If she doesn't, then I don't really care if her old man finds out. Maybe he'll finally cut her off the way she deserves."

Wynona stood, trying to resist the impulse to brush off the back of her skirt. "Thank you for your time," she said politely. "If we have more questions, is it alright with you if we come by again?"

Those gray eyes regarded her warily.

Wynona could practically see the intelligence swimming in them. Raccoons weren't dumb animals and it appeared that neither were the shifters. Syn might be bitter and dirt poor, but his mind churned with more thoughts than most. He knew exactly what she was doing. "It's not like I can legally stop you," he finally said.

Wynona nodded and clasped her hands in front of her. "Do you mind telling us where you work?"

It was amazing the shifter could see at all, considering how tightly his eyes were narrowed. "Why does it matter?"

"You said you got home around six," Wynona clarified. "I assumed it was from a job."

One black eyebrow shot up. "Ah. You're trying to figure out my character. You want to know if I'm a chronic liar." He chuckled darkly. "I'm a janitor with Coffee Haven. Go ahead. Check me out." He leaned forward and dropped his voice. "Then I'll let your pretty little head figure out who's telling the truth."

Wynona nodded once more and turned to leave. The creepy factor of the apartment just shot up a little too high for her. She was so grateful she wasn't by herself as Rascal and Daemon flanked either side of her.

"Should we check with the neighbor?" she asked once they were all safely in the hall. Well...safe was probably a little premature. But at least they were out of Syn's place. Wynona felt like the young shifter saw too much and his passionate emotions were a roller coaster to keep up with. She was exhausted just from listening to him.

"Yeah, but stay close," Rascal said. His jaw was clenched and he didn't look like he wanted to stick around, but the room number they were looking for was only two doors down.

Ten minutes later they were finally out in the fresh air and settled around Rascal's truck.

"So, at least according to the neighbor, he really did get home at six." Wynona pinched her lips. "I'm not quite sure who to believe here."

"His story is more believable than hers," Rascal pointed out. "We already know Thallia isn't quite right in the head."

"No. We know that Thallia has been too protected in her life," Wynona shot back. "But we don't know enough about Mr. Ringer to know if he's a liar or not."

Rascal sighed. "Wy. I know you don't want it to be Thallia, but you can't keep fighting the mounting evidence."

"Do you have anything concrete enough to charge her?" Wynona argued.

Rascal's shoulders fell. "No."

She nodded. "Then I have a little more time." Her eyes went up to the third story window that belonged to Mr. Ringer. "I don't know who's telling the truth, but there's got to be a way to find out. And that's what we're going to do next."

CHAPTER 19

"**P**romise you won't do anything without me," Rascal ordered as he dropped her off back at the house.

Wynona gave him a patient look. "I promise not to do anything dangerous," she clarified. "But I'm not going to sit around and twiddle my thumbs for the rest of the day."

Rascal made a face but nodded. "Fine. But no more meeting strangers."

She put up her hands. "I already told you I've learned my lesson. It wasn't a good idea and I won't do it again."

He grinned. "Thank you. And my heart thanks you as well." Grabbing her waist, Rascal pulled Wynona in for a sweet, lingering kiss. "Save me some dinner tonight?" he asked once pulling back.

"Of course." She ran her fingers through his hair, loving the silky strands as they brushed across her skin. "What kind of girlfriend would I be if I didn't keep my wolf happy?"

He growled playfully at her, his gold eyes flashing, before stepping back and leaping into the truck. "See you tonight." Rascal winked, his favorite way of communication, and sped off.

Wynona stood in her driveway, watching him leave. She felt slightly cold inside as her soulmate drove out of sight. It was amazing to her how much her life had changed in one short year. She'd been lonely yet determined when leaving her parents' castle and now she had good friends, a job, and a soulmate. Never in a million years would Wynona have dreamed of so much good, and now it was all so normal that she couldn't imagine her life without it. It was odd how a creature could adjust to something new so quickly.

Turning around, Wynona headed inside. Her mind went back to the meeting they'd had with Syn that morning. In truth, all it had done was cause more confusion in the case, which hadn't been helpful at all. While Wynona would like to say she knew that Thallia was the one being honest in her stories, the truth was...Wynona *wasn't* sure.

Thallia had changed her words enough times to make Wynona believe there were lies mixed in with her words, but how to tell the truth? And if Syn's stories were true, that made Thallia look even worse.

"How do we prove it?" Wynona murmured as she reached for the front door handle. Before she could open it, a small purple body squeezed beneath it.

Quick. Let's get out of here.

Wynona made a face and waited while Violet scrambled up her leg and arm. "What're you talking about?"

Sissy poo is cleaning. CLEANING!

"Violet. I clean all the time."

Yeah...but she's got magic running amuck and it makes my fur stand on end.

Wynona frowned and ignored her familiar, heading inside. What she saw had her pausing in her tracks. Celia wasn't just cleaning, she was completely changing the cottage. When Wynona had moved in, she had surrounded herself by the kitchy and cute. Vases of flowers and books filled every shelf, with soft, pleasing colors that felt warm and welcoming. It had been the exact opposite of the castle, which was stark and contemporary, feeling more museum-like rather than a home.

Apparently, Celia missed where she'd grown up because the house reeked of magic and looked completely different from the place Wynona had left this morning.

Reacting on instinct, Wynona put up her hands and shouted, "STOP!"

All the silver sparks flying through the air came to a grinding halt and the house fell oddly silent.

Celia spun, her hands still in the air. "What are you doing?"

Wynona's eyebrows shot up. "What am *I* doing? What are you doing?"

Celia dropped her hands to her hips. "What does it look like? I'm redecorating."

Wynona looked around and shook her head. "Celia. I don't want things redecorated. I had my house exactly like I wanted it."

Celia scoffed. "You can't mean that. We used to live in the lap of luxury and this place was..." She made a face. "Well...far from that. Just because you have no money doesn't mean you can't make it look nicer."

Wynona closed her eyes and pressed her fingers into them.

Told you, Violet sang. *She's a menace.*

I think she's actually trying to be nice, but she has a strange way of going about it.

Unlikely, Violet countered. *I think she's trying to upset you on purpose.*

And what would she gain from that?

"Hello?" Celia called out, waving a hand in the air. "I'm over here."

Wynona sighed. "Sorry. I was caught up..." She pinched her lips together.

"Talking with your familiar?" Celia smirked. "Yeah. Caught that." She frowned. "Plus, I think Mom mentioned it once." Celia's eyes narrowed as she stared at Violet, who grew very still on Wynona's shoulder. "A mouse is a really unusual familiar, you know."

"I've never seen you with one," Wynona retorted before she could think better of it.

Celia stiffened. "Yeah, well, not all of us are lucky enough to find ours. It's more rare than you think."

Wynona's brows pulled together. She might still be learning some aspects of the witch world, but in a book she had read while living with her parents, Wynona remembered seeing a passage that declared every witch had a familiar. How was it that after all this time, Celia didn't have hers? Shaking her head, Wynona moved on. "Celia. I want the cottage back the way it was."

Celia scoffed. "What? Do you know how long it took to turn that couch of yours into real leather? The spell was incredibly intricate."

"While I appreciate you trying to upgrade our living situation, I don't want leather. I want warm and comfortable and that's what I had." Wynona tilted her head to the side. "I left because I didn't want to live like that anymore. In every way possible."

Celia paused, her mouth opening and closing a few times. "You *like* this?"

Wynona nodded. Her phone buzzed and she flipped it over to see who had texted.

I thought I might visit the Pearlilys...want to come?

Prim's invitation was followed by a winky face, letting Wynona know that her fairy best friend had decided to poke her nose into the investigation. Prim had mentioned in previous cases that she wouldn't mind helping out, but this was the first time she'd made a real move.

Is this because it's about the fairy community? Or because tall, dark and handsome is finally taking her out? Violet asked with a laugh.

Does it matter? Wynona sent back. *We can't let her go over there by herself. Especially after the threat to Chief's job.*

Celia snorted. "Are you ever going to remember I'm here?"

Wynona blinked and brought herself out of the present. "Sorry," she said. "I just got a text about the case and I need to go." Wynona turned to head to the garage where her Vespa was parked. "Celia, I'm sorry you don't like my decorating, but I have to put down my foot. Please put the house back the way it was by the time I get back."

Celia huffed. "I'm living here too, you know."

Wynona stopped and turned around. "I know," she said softly. "But the house belongs to me. You may feel free to decorate your room however you feel fit, but the rest of the house is to stay the way I had it."

Celia folded her arms over her chest. "So this is how it's going to be living together? I get no say?"

I don't need this.

I told you not to let her live here.

Wynona gave her familiar a scolding look.

Celia growled and began to stomp away.

"Celia...stop," Wynona called out.

Celia's movement stopped, but she didn't turn around. "It's fine," she said, though it was clearly not. Her hand came up. "I can read between the lines."

Wynona closed her eyes and rubbed her suddenly aching forehead. This was ridiculous. "Look, I'm not trying to make you feel unwelcome. But I've worked hard to build my life the way I want it." Wynona swallowed hard, knowing the next few words might be a bad idea. "I think it would be a good idea to help you build the life you want as well."

Celia spun, her eyebrows furrowed. "How?"

Wynona threw her hands to the side. "Have you ever thought about getting a job?"

Celia wrinkled her nose. "You can't be serious."

Wynona walked forward a couple of steps. "I'm working on a case with a girl who's under suspicion for murder, Celia. Do you want to know what I think the biggest crime is in the situation?"

Celia raised one eyebrow.

"The fact that she has no idea how to handle living in the real world. She worked only a few days for me before her boyfriend was killed. He was killed in. My. Shop. The boyfriend was on the wrong side of the law, yet the girl was convinced she could save him. And how did she try to save him? By throwing money at him. This punk had a fancy motorcycle and a nice townhouse in a part of town where he stood out like a sore thumb."

"What does all this have to do with me?" Celia asked.

Wynona shook her head. "Let me keep going. This girl doesn't know how to take care of herself. She refuses to leave home because she wants to spend Daddy's money. She lies and tells tales that we have no way of proving." Wynona blew out a breath. "And she has no idea just how far away from normal she is."

Celia's shoulders drooped. "What do you want from me, Wynona? We said we would let go of the past and move forward, but I don't know what's expected of me. I don't know what you're hoping to accomplish..." She trailed off as if unsure what to say next.

"And you don't know what you want for yourself," Wynona finished for her.

Celia sniffed and her gaze dropped to the floor.

"I understand," Wynona continued. "I didn't know who I was either when I first got out here. But give it time. You have a safe place to live and don't have to worry about where your next meal is coming from. Breathe. Take time to figure out who you are. What have you always wanted to do that Mom and Dad never let you explore? What magic do you have that comes easier than anything else?" Wynona's voice dropped. "Who do you *want* to be? Because for the first time in your life, you have the ability to choose." She waved her hand around the room. "I chose this, but that doesn't mean it's right for you. You're welcome to stay as long as you want, but I'm asking you not to try and change who I've chosen to become."

Celia nodded and wiped at her eyes. "I know I'm a little hard to live with," she began.

Violet snorted.

Hush, Wynona scolded.

"But I'm..." Celia shrugged, still not looking Wynona in the eye. "I'm lost."

"Then take your time," Wynona insisted. "Just don't do it with my furniture." She smiled to soften her words.

Celia laughed through her tears. "Thanks," she hiccuped.

Wynona nodded. "That's what sisters are for."

Celia hesitated, then responded, "I'll work on that."

With one last smile, Wynona headed to the garage to grab her Vespa. She wasn't quite ready to port during the day yet. It was a skill that might need to stay a bit of a secret until she had worked on it a little more.

You should call Rascal, Violet reminded.

Wynona nodded as she strapped on her helmet. "I'll text him when I get there."

He's not gonna be happy.

Wynona sighed. "I promised I wouldn't do anything dangerous. In fact, in this case, I'm keeping Prim from doing something dangerous."

Giant Man isn't going to like it either.

"Which is why I'm not letting Prim go alone." Wynona turned the key and pushed back the kickstand. "I promise I'll let them know. But I have to catch Prim first." With a rush of the engine, Wynona jerked forward and began cruising down the long road to town. She had no idea what Prim thought she was going to accomplish by speaking to the Pearlilys but Wynona was going to be there to help. Or protect. Whichever one came first.

CHAPTER 20

"You shouldn't be doing this, you know," Wynona said as she pulled up next to Prim's tiny car. It was built for fairies and was definitely one of the smallest contraptions on the road.

Prim shrugged. "Yeah, well...how often do I do what I'm supposed to?"

"This time we're talking about the law," Wynona pointed out as she hung her helmet on her steering wheel.

Prim grinned. "We've got an inner connection," she said. "We'll be fine."

Wynona shook her head. "Rascal and Daemon won't like it."

"Then don't tell them."

Wynona gave Prim a look. "I'll just flat out say that's not happening." She put her hands on her hips and stared at the large house. "So...what exactly are you planning to accomplish here?"

Prim pursed her lips. "Since I'm part of the fairy community, I thought maybe I could chat...see if there was something I'd understand that the rest of you didn't."

"Hmm..."

What's going on? Rascal asked, intruding on her conversation.

Prim and I are at the Pearlilys, Wynona responded. *Prim was coming and I met her to try and keep her from doing something stupid.*

Being there is stupid, Rascal retorted. *Go home.*

"He's trying to talk you out of it, isn't he?" Prim said with a smirk.

Wynona raised an eyebrow. "That obvious, huh?"

Prim snickered. "You're not exactly a master of keeping your face neutral. Never play poker."

"So noted," Wynona responded. "Can't say it was ever in the plans anyway."

Thank goodness, Violet muttered.

Wy. I mean it. Go home.

"Okay...here we go," Prim said, sounding like she was psyching herself up.

"Maybe we should think about it," Wynona offered, following Prim up the front steps. "We don't want to interfere with the investigation. What if the Pearlilys file a complaint?"

Prim grinned over her shoulder, a look purely full of fairy mischief. "Why do you think I texted you? You're my failsafe."

Wynona stopped in her tracks. "What?"

Prim chose not to answer, knocking on the door instead.

Wynona clenched her jaw, frustrated with Prim's lack of propriety, and marched up the rest of the steps.

Easy, witch girl. She's never been good at paying attention to consequences.

I know that, Wynona said, her anger starting to deflate. *But this isn't a game, even if she is attracted to an officer. I'm afraid she's going to get hurt.*

Then make sure she doesn't, Violet stated curtly.

Rascal sighed long and loud in Wynona's brain. *I'm on my way. Keep her out of trouble.*

Wynona closed her eyes, only to pop them open when she heard the front door open.

"May I help you?" the butler asked with a heavy look of disdain.

Prim clasped her hands in front of her, bouncing lightly on her toes, and gave the stoic creature her best smile. "Hello. I'm Primrose Meadows. I'd like to speak with Mrs. Pearlily, please."

Good to know she can be polite when she wants to be, Violet said with a snort.

Hush, Wynona responded. She smiled tightly behind Prim. "I'm Wynona Le Doux."

"I see," the butler drawled. He closed the door and his footsteps clicked on the floor as he walked away.

"Do you think he's getting her? Or did we just get rejected?" Prim asked, not seeming worried either way.

"I would guess he'll ask if she's willing to see us," Wynona said. She wrung her hands together. If Chief Ligurio got fired over this, Wynona wasn't sure what she would do. Their relationship might be somewhat akin to a rollercoaster, but Wynona cherished it nonetheless and she didn't want anything to happen to the surly vampire.

Prim sniffed. "Seems to be taking his time about it."

"Prim, I really don't think we should—" Wynona cut off when the butler opened the door again.

"Mrs. Pearlily will see you." He stepped back, and slightly bent his head.

Deciding there was nothing to do but pretend she wanted to be there, Wynona threw back her shoulders, gave a polite nod to the butler and walked inside as if she belonged there. Mrs. Pearlily had been thrilled to have someone of the royal family in her house before. Hopefully that welcome still stood.

"Ms. Le Doux!" Mrs. Pearlily gushed. Her wings fluttered, holding her just off the floor even in her human form. "I'm so glad you came back!" She flew across the room and wrapped Wynona in a tight hug.

Wynona stiffened immediately. She had hoped she'd be welcome, but this was a little much. Fighting her shock, she wrapped her arms around Mrs. Pearlily and gave her a hug in return. "Thank you so much for having us," Wynona said.

Mrs. Pearlily pulled back, her face flushed and her hands clasped tightly at her chest. "Us?" Her eyes were wide as she turned and realized that Wynona wasn't alone. "Oh! Oh my." Her wing movement picked up in her distress. "And who might you be?" She held out her hand.

"Primrose Meadows," Prim replied.

"Meadows?" Mrs. Pearlily blinked several times. "Meadows..." Her eyebrows shot up. "The Meadows of Flicker Valley?"

Prim nodded, relaxing a little that her family name had been recognized. It was clear to Wynona that Prim had been counting on that. "I'm the youngest of the brood."

Mrs. Pearlily nodded, her face deflating as she studied Prim. "The one without wings," the older fairy whispered, as if there was something dirty about it.

Prim's face reddened and for the first time, Wynona understood a little of what Prim had been facing her whole life. When they'd first met, after Wynona's escape from her family, both women had had to fight and struggle for every step they'd taken in their adult lives, but Prim was way ahead of Wynona. She had already had her shop and a wonderful reputation among the flower community by the time Wynona had arrived on the scene.

"Yes," Prim said in a snippy tone. "No wings...but plenty of other gifts." She snapped her fingers and the orchid in the corner window suddenly came back to life.

Mrs. Pearlily gasped, her hands coming up to cover her cheeks.

"Orchids don't like the amount of heat that comes from west-facing windows," Prim said, one eyebrow perched high on her forehead. "South is better and will give plenty of light for the plant."

Mrs. Pearlily's hair shook as she nodded vigorously. "I'm sure your parents are so proud."

Prim snorted, then flounced to a sofa and sat down. "Mrs. Pearlily...I'd like to ask you a few questions."

"Oh, yes." Mrs. Pearlily rushed to the opposite side and sat primly on the edge. She reached to the coffee table and rang a bell. "Dupe. A tea platter, please."

The butler turned to leave.

"Oh, and Dupe?"

"Ma'am?"

Mrs. Pearlily smiled. "Do not make Mr. Pearlily aware of our guests."

The butler hesitated only slightly before nodding.

Wynona walked warily over to Prim's side. "Will our visit cause trouble, Mrs. Pearlily? We would never want to do that."

Mrs. Pearlily waved an unconcerned hand in the air. "Goodness, no. He just prefers to keep to himself. I wouldn't want him to feel obligated to come say hello." She tilted her head and smiled. "I'm sure you understand. He's such a busy man."

"Of course," Wynona said hurriedly. Truth was, she wasn't upset she wouldn't see the angry fairy. If she had to pick a suspect to go to the top of the list, she would definitely pick Mr. Pearlily. Men like him, who were so quick to anger and bullied their associates, could easily hurt someone when they didn't get their way. Wynona had no problem imagining Mr. Pearlily getting angry that Dralo refused to stop seeing his daughter and had simply taken matters into his own hand.

But he had an alibi and the ear of the judge. You'll never pin it on him, Violet reminded her.

Unless we can find the right evidence, Wynona responded. *Maybe being here isn't such a bad thing. If we can find something in the house that's suspicious, maybe we could convince Chief Ligurio to dig deeper.*

You want me to go exploring, don't you? Violet yawned. *I think it's my nap time.*

Please? I'll make cookies tonight.

Violet's nose twitched. *Snickerdoodles?*

Any kind you want.

Sold. Without another chitter, Violet slipped down Wynona's back to remain unseen from the other ladies in the room and

Wynona saw the mouse climb down the couch from her peripheral vision.

"Tell me, Mrs. Pearlily," Wynona said, trying to make sure no one noticed her familiar's escape. "How is Thallia feeling this morning?"

Mrs. Pearlily pursed her lips and shook her head. "She was so shaken up last night after being pulled in by the police." The fairy's manicured hand went to her chest. "And of course to lose Edana. That sweet little girl was just growing up. It's such a tragedy."

Wynona nodded her agreement. "It was tragic. Had she and Thallia been friends for very long?"

"Years," Mrs. Pearlily said in a serious tone. "Ever since they were little girls." She pinched her lips together and leaned forward ever so slightly. "Mr. Pearlily didn't love that Thallia was friends with a vampire, but when I told him that she came from such good stock, he allowed it."

"Good stock?" Wynona asked. "Who was Edana related to?"

"Well, you probably wouldn't know them, dear," Mrs. Pearlily replied. "Her family moved away several years ago, right after Edana graduated. But the Onyx family has been heavily involved in the stock trade. Those vampire senses have always been good at predicting the financial movements."

Wynona nodded, though she knew nothing of the sort. She'd have to do a little research when she got home. "And her relationship with Syn Ringer? Did your husband approve of that?" It occurred to Wynona that Prim hadn't asked any questions and she glanced over at her friend.

Prim's eyes were half closed and Wynona wasn't sure if the fairy was listening or not. This whole visit had been her idea. What in all of Hex Haven was she doing?

Carefully, Wynona reached over with her foot and bumped the side of Prim's.

Prim's eyes opened fully and she looked questioningly at Wynona.

"What was that, Mrs. Pearlily?" Wynona asked, pretending her attention had never been away. "I'm afraid I didn't quite catch what you said."

Mrs. Pearlily held up a finger and a moment later the door opened with their tea tray.

Wynona took note that Mrs. Pearlily obviously had better hearing than she did.

"Thank you, Dupe," Mrs. Pearlily said imperiously. She waited until the butler had left before pouring the drink. "Tea?" she asked Wynona, that light smile on her face again.

"Um...yes, thank you," Wynona said. There was something in Mrs. Pearlily's manner that was slightly off and she had to wonder if it was the question she had posed. Wynona had been after a reaction, of course. She needed to figure out who was lying between Syn and Thallia, but Mrs. Pearlily didn't seem eager to respond. "Thank you," Wynona murmured when she took the offered cup.

Prim took her cup and stood, wandering aimlessly around the room while she sipped the brew.

Wynona laughed a little uncomfortably. She had no idea what Prim was up to. "So...Syn Ringer? I spoke with him last night..."

Mrs. Pearlily stuck out her pinky finger while drinking her tea, then set down the cup on the saucer she held. "Syn Ringer never had a relationship with Thallia," she said with a shrill laugh. "I have no idea where you would have gotten that idea."

Wynona frowned. "Thallia said they were friends."

"Oh, I suppose they could be called acquaintances by some standards, but there was never anything more." Mrs. Pearlily took a leisurely sip. "Thallia has always had such a big heart. She can't turn away needy creatures, even if they're only looking to use her for her family name."

Wynona kept herself from pointing out that Mrs. Pearlily was the one who seemed fixated on using people for their name...but barely. "So he never dated her?"

"Goodness, no." Mrs. Pearlily laughed again. "Whatever gave you that idea?"

Wynona shrugged and drank her tea. It took effort not to make a face. Bagged tea never quite did it for her. The lemon balm was far from soothing, instead tasting stale and artificial. *Apparently, I've become a tea snob,* she thought to herself.

That was clear quite a long time ago, Violet huffed as she reentered the room.

Oh thank goodness, Wynona thought. *Did you find anything?*
Get me out of here and we'll talk.

"Ma'am?" The butler came back inside the parlor.

"Yes, Dupe?" Mrs. Pearlily asked.

"A Deputy Chief Strongclaw is here."

Mrs. Pearlily frowned. "Strongclaw? Is that a family I should know?"

"That's my boyfriend," Wynona said, setting down her cup and standing up. "Thank you so much for your time, Mrs. Pearlily, but I'm afraid I really must be going."

"Really? So quickly?"

Prim appeared at Wynona's side. "Yes. It's time."

Wynona's smile felt strained and she took Prim's arm. "We'll visit another time."

"Oh, please do," Mrs. Pearlily gushed. "Your family is such a wonderful...uh...family."

Wynona nodded, unable to verbally agree. "We're coming, Dupe," she told the butler.

The creature stepped back, allowing Wynona and Prim out into the hall. As they walked, Wynona felt Violet jump onto her leg and climb up onto her shoulder. *Steady?*

As I'll ever be.

"Wy!" Rascal called from the front door. He looked immensely relieved to see her.

"Hello, sweetheart," Wynona said loudly, giving Rascal a significant look. "Thank you for picking me up."

"Of course," Rascal said quickly, catching on without a word. "We wouldn't want you to be late for your next appointment, would we?"

"Nope." Wynona waved as she and Prim emerged into the sunshine. When the large front door finally slammed shut, she blew out a breath and her entire body slumped. "Oh my goodness, I was afraid we'd never get out of there. Violet said she found something."

"Oh, yeah?" Prim asked with a devilish grin. "I've got something better."

"Really?" Wynona asked, folding her arms over her chest. "It seemed to me that you spent the entire time walking around like a zombie rather than a detective."

Prim sniffed. "We all detect in different ways," she said, defending herself.

"And just how did you detect anything?"

Prim's grin was back and her pink eyes flashed. "You'd be amazed what plants will tell you if you use your manners."

CHAPTER 21

Wynona used her magic to set the last of the food on the table, then sat down herself. "Alright. Let's have it," she said to Prim.

Violet sniffed.

"Violet," Wynona warned. "I know you have news as well, but we'll get to everyone. Why don't you enjoy the cookie I promised you?"

Daemon, Rascal and Prim all sat around Wynona's dining room table. Celia hadn't been home when they'd arrived back at the cottage and Wynona had proceeded to fix everyone's lunch while they waited for the black hole to arrive. As far as Wynona knew, Prim and Daemon hadn't gone out on a date yet, but their chairs were noticeably closer together than normal.

Violet's nose twitched and she gave in, nibbling to her heart's content.

Wynona looked back at Prim.

The attention must have been exactly what the fairy wanted because she preened a little under all the gazes.

"Prim," Wynoan pressed.

"Alright, alright," Prim muttered. She fluffed her pink hair. "While dear old Mumsy was blabbering away about celebrities and such to you, I took a listen to the plants."

"You can actually *hear* plants?" Daemon asked, his awe evident in his tone. "I didn't realize they were sentient like that."

Prim nodded. "A common mistake. They're simple minded creatures, but they understand us, can follow commands and can usually communicate well enough to tell a creature what's been happening

179

around them." Prim's excitement became visible. "Especially conversations."

"And?" Rascal drawled.

Wynona knew he struggled with her best friend's dramatics. Getting straight to the point was more Rascal's style, especially when dealing with a case.

"And the begonia in the corner mentioned that Mr. Pearlily and Thallia fight...a lot."

Wynona frowned. "I think we could have guessed that, though having proof is helpful. He's a bully." She tapped her red fingernail on the table. "Though, I'm surprised they actually fight. It seems to me that Thallia is much more like her mother. I assumed he ran right over his daughter."

"In public maybe," Prim offered. "Thallia was always really big on public persona."

"That I can agree with," Wynona said with a sigh. "She's only working for me because she thinks it will get her in the public eye to be working for a member of the royal family."

Prim wrinkled her nose. "Are you kidding?"

Wynona shook her head. She opened her mouth to say more, then shut it. It probably wasn't fair to share everything that had happened in the interrogation room, though Wynona sort of wanted to vent a little.

"Huh." Prim pursed her lips. "I guess that explains why someone living on Daddy's dime would bother getting a job at all."

Rascal huffed a little, his brows furrowed in thought. "Did the plants say anything else? Fighting with her dad doesn't help us put her in jail."

Wynona gave him a look, but Rascal ignored her and Wynona forced her shoulders to relax. She had to admit that she had no idea how to prove Thalia's innocence. The deeper things got, the more it looked like the young fairy was guilty, and she'd already known that she wasn't exactly in touch with reality.

Still...the thought simply didn't sit well with Wynona. Thallia was naive and spoiled, but she wasn't a killer. *I think.*

Thinking isn't enough, Violet shot back.

I know, Wynona lamented. *But we're not making any headway toward an actual arrest either. The evidence seems to be a big moshpit of opinions rather than facts.*

Violet nodded, her mouth full of cookie.

"Fathers and daughters probably fight a lot," Daemon mused. "Did your...begonia...say what they would fight over?"

Prim nodded. "Apparently, he wasn't very fond of her friends."

Rascal snorted. "We knew that."

Prim's cheeks began to turn red. "Well, now you have proof."

Somehow I doubt the judge is going to take testimony from a plant, Rascal sent to Wynona.

She frowned at him and he shrugged. *Why are you so mad?*

Rascal looked at her cooly. *I thought we'd talked about this. You weren't going to put yourself at risk anymore.*

We did, Wynona said carefully. *In this case, I was trying to keep Prim from putting herself at risk.*

By endangering yourself and the chief's reputation.

Wynona leaned back. He was really upset about this. "I'm sorry," she said out loud, knowing the other two were probably wondering what was going on. "I was only trying to help."

A frustrated growl grew in Rascal's throat and he jumped to his feet, storming from the room.

Wynona's jaw dropped as she felt him shift into a wolf and leave the house. She ran after him, watching his dark body disappear down the drive.

At least he didn't go into the Grove of Secrets, Violet muttered.

"What's wrong with Wolfy?" Prim asked from Wynona's elbow.

"You going over to the Pearlilys made Wynona break a promise to keep herself safe," Daemon said from his place at the table.

Both women spun.

"Excuse me?" Prim asked tartly, putting her hands on her hips. "I didn't break any rules."

Daemon slowly stood up, his height suddenly feeling over-whelming in the small cottage. "The woman he loves made a promise not to put herself in danger, on purpose," Daemon said slowly, his black eyes boring into Prim's.

Wynona stepped back, feeling like an intruder in her own home. She was extremely glad Celia wasn't there. Things were a little over-crowded as it was.

"Your reckless behavior caused Wynona to run to keep you safe and put you in a house that our chief has already been warned to stay away from," Daemon continued.

Prim's cheeks were growing alarmingly bright. The red clashed terribly with her pink hair and eyes. "Well, how was I to know?" she demanded. "Nobody tells me anything."

"Did you bother to ask Wynona if it was okay?" Daemon pressed, now standing directly over Prim. "Did you ask *me* if you could be involved? Or did you just jump in without any idea what you were doing and risking any consequences because they more than likely wouldn't have affected you anyway?"

Prim's mouth opened and shut like a fish several times in a row before she clenched her jaw and fists. "Excuse me for trying to help," she ground out. "You can do the rest of this alone." Spinning on her toe, Prim marched for the door. "And you can forget dinner, buddy. I wouldn't eat dinner with you if you were the last paranormal on Earth."

A muscle in Daemon's jaw pulsed as Prim disappeared in her own vehicle. He looked to Wynona. "I'm sorry for the trouble. I'll be going as well." His words were soft, but the anger was evident.

"She doesn't mean it," Wynona said weakly. She knew better than most that Prim was often dramatic. It seemed to run in the whole species. When Prim calmed down, she'd definitely be willing to speak to the black hole again. But it might take some time.

"She can mean it," he said easily. "Because I meant what I said. She's reckless and doesn't think through her actions. I'm interested in what I've seen, but most of it was when she was under duress. She held to faith and showed a backbone most creatures couldn't dream of owning. She's started her own business and is fighting for a place in a world that mostly rejects her because of her physical deformity." He shook his head, sighing. "The flighty, naive Primrose Meadows I've watched lately isn't who I want to spend time with."

Wynona winced. "She means well."

"And when she decides to be who she's capable of being, I'll be here," Daemon said with a firm nod. "Until then, she needs to know that not all of us are going to put up with her nonsense." Without another word, he left.

The house was eerily quiet after the emotional turmoil of only moments ago. She opened her mind to see where Rascal was, but he was closed off to her. Her eyes stung for a moment and she slowly turned to walk back into the house.

"Do I get to make an entrance with the same dramatic flair that your friends left?" Celia asked wryly, coming from the back of the home.

Wynona paused. "What were you doing back there?"

Celia dusted off her skinny jeans. "Porting."

"You can port?"

If looks could kill, Wynona would have been burned to ash. "Of course I can port."

Wynona ignored the insult. It seemed that no matter how many bridges she built between her and her sister, Celia kept trying to burn them down again. Wynona folded her arms over her chest. "And just how long have you been listening to what was going on out here?"

Celia pursed her lips. "Long enough to know that your little fairy friend needs to suck it up. She's beyond annoying."

Some might say the same about you, Violet shouted from inside the house.

One side of Celia's mouth quirked up in a smirk. "I hear little mousy noises. Tell me, is your familiar making similar comments about myself?"

Wynona threw up her hands. "What is it today with everyone bickering? It's like being surrounded by toddlers."

Celia snickered and followed Wynona inside. "Guess you just bring out the best in all of us."

Wynona sent an equally scathing glare to her sister, but Celia was unmoved. Sitting down at the dining room table, Wynona put her face in her hands. "All I want is to get this stupid case over with, open the shop and let life go back to normal."

"Sorry, sissy," Celia drawled, sitting down and filling a plate with the uneaten food. "Your life is never going to be normal. Or hadn't you heard? You're the daughter of the resident king and you have more power than any one witch should." She paused before putting a cucumber in her mouth. "You'll always be in the center of attention."

Wynona huffed, but didn't argue. It wasn't worth it. She grabbed a strawberry and began to nibble on it. Her appetite was mostly gone, but there was nothing else to do at the moment. Prim's information had offered little in the way of new news and now everyone was gone. Who knew when they'd calm down enough to get back together...or when Rascal would speak to her again.

The thought of Rascal caused a sharp pain in Wynona's chest and she rubbed at her sternum. She hadn't meant to upset him. She understood that his wolf was protective and less logical than Rascal's human side was, but he was *so angry* lately and it worried Wynona.

She thought he had understood that she was protecting Prim, but he sure wasn't acting like it.

Had something gone wrong with the soulmate bond? Had Rascal changed his mind? Wynona had never been someone's soulmate before. They weren't an unheard of situation, but rare enough that despite all her reading growing up, Wynona wasn't sure what to expect.

I love you... she sent into the universe, hoping Rascal would eventually get the message.

I love you too, Violet sent back. She wiped her paws together, causing the last of the crumbs to fall on the table. *But I think you need to hear what I have to say now.*

Wynona nodded wearily. "Sorry. You never got to talk before everyone left."

Celia snorted.

Violet gave the witch the side eye, then turned back to Wynona. *I found an appointment book in Mr. Pearlily's office.*

Wynona's eyes widened and she leaned forward. "What?"

He had a late night meeting the night that Dralo was killed.

"What!"

Celia winced and covered her ears. "What in the world is that for?"

"His alibi is that he was home with his wife," Wynona murmured, ignoring Celia.

Exactly, Violet said triumphantly. She preened slightly. *And now we have proof he wasn't.*

"Except the judge won't take your word for it in court and somehow I doubt I can get a warrant issued on our little visit today." Wynona slumped in her seat.

Well, thanks a lot, Violet snapped.

Wynona shook her head. "You know I'm grateful. I'm just trying to think of how we can make this work. I believe you, Rascal and

Chief Ligurio will believe you, but a familar's accounting won't stand up in a trial and you know it."

Violet grumbled and began to smooth her fur.

"What exactly have you just figured out?" Celia pressed, her black eyes sparkling with interest.

Wynona hesitated. "I can't tell you the particulars," she hedged.

Celia nodded and waved with her hand. "That's okay. Vague is fine."

Wynona glanced at Violet, who shrugged. "The person I suspect of the murder has an iron clad alibi because someone else backs him up. Violet found his schedule and it shows he had a meeting the night of the murder."

Celia nodded, a slow grin building on her face. "In other words...he lied."

Wynona nodded in return. "Right. But I can't prove it."

Celia leaned back, tapping her nails against the top of a teacup. "Why not tail him?"

"What?"

"Tail him," Celia reiterated. "Follow him. See if he meets with anyone suspicious. Figure out what he's hiding. Even if he proves to not be the murderer, he's obviously hiding something." She leaned in close. "What is it?"

Wynona pressed her lips together. "I don't think I'd be very good at that. And Rascal wouldn't like it."

"Rascal ran off like a dog with his tail between his legs," Celia hissed.

Wynona stood up. "He was upset and had good reason to be. If you're going to insult him, I won't listen."

Celia put up her hands in surrender. "Fine. Dog boy is off limits. But following the guy is still a good idea. They won't know you're there, so there's no danger and you never know the...secrets...you might uncover."

Wynona let two breaths go by before she answered. "I'll think about it."

Celia's smirk was back. "You do that." She put her focus on the food and Wynona left the room.

What are you going to do? Violet asked, running after Wynona.

I'm going to look through Granny's grimoire and see if I can find a spell to help me be invisible.

Violet chuckled in delight. *Oooooh, this is going to be good.*

CHAPTER 22

Wynona grumbled and tossed the grimoire to the other side of her bed. "Nothing," she snapped, her patience at an end. "Absolutely nothing." Standing up, Wynona began to pace her room. "Granny could do almost anything! Why the heck doesn't she have an invisibility spell?"

Can't you just manifest it? The same way you do your other stuff? Violet asked, perched on the edge of the bed. Her nose was twitching as she watched Wynona go back and forth.

Wynona paused. "I could try, but it seems unlikely. Most of what I manifest has to do with manipulating objects around me. Like floating dishes or heating up water. How do I manifest invisibility?"

Violet shrugged. *Not a clue. I've never done this before.*

"Me either," Wynona grumbled, her shoulders stooping. She shook her head. "It's worth a try through, right?"

Violet watched.

Closing her eyes. Wynona took in a cleansing breath and let her magic race to her fingertips. The feeling was becoming more comfortable, though the first few seconds were still terrifying. One of these days, she was positive that she wouldn't be able to hold back the tsunami that came rushing down her arms every single time she brought it forth.

Visualizing herself in her mind's eye, Wynona systematically began to will her body to disappear. First her feet, then legs, torso, arms and finally her head. She could feel her magic swirling through her body, following the line she created in her mind. She was almost positive she was floating, her body felt nearly consumed with a euphoric sense of strength. Shifting her weight, she carefully opened her eyes and looked at Violet. "Did it work?"

Violet huffed. *No.*

Wynona threw down her hands, purple sparkles dancing on the floor. "Okay...so that's a loss. But what else can we do? I'm really not comfortable trying to follow Mr. Pearlily in daylight hours without some kind of protection."

Violet nodded and scratched behind her ears. *There's got to be something...*

Wynona walked over to the box of grimoires and casually glanced inside. An immediate sense of doom and intrigue hit her and she stumbled back.

You need to destroy that book, Violet said softly.

Wynona looked over her shoulder and nodded. "I think you're right. It calls and repels me at the same time and that terrifies me."

As it should. Violet scrambled down the bed. *Come on. Let's go to the shop.*

"Why?"

Because Lusgu should know how to destroy it.

Wynona frowned. "Can't we just burn it?"

I doubt it. Don't you think those witches put protection charms on those books? Some of them look to be hundreds of years old.

Warily, Wynona put her hand over the box and closed her eyes. Even when the black oiliness from the dark book hit her skin, she forced herself to stay in place. In another case, Wynona had managed to unlock a safe and sense the remnants of a magical locking spell. Now she was trying to do the same with the grimoires. "I don't feel anything unusual, other than the book itself," she whispered.

Violet scrambled down from the bed and climbed Wynona's leg. Once on her shoulder, she wrapped her tail around Wynona's neck. *Try again.*

More confident now that her familiar was helping, Wynona tried again.

Bring in a little magic. That's what you were doing before.

Wynona brought her powers up again, the electric sensation working its way down her arm. She tried to keep it slow this time, she didn't want to accidentally set anything off, but when the power got to her fingertips, her hand burst into flame. "Oh my gosh!" she cried.

Cut the magic! Violet screamed.

Wynona blinked, noting just enough to realize the fire wasn't burning her skin before the purple flames dissipated.

Violet was heaving with panting. *Don't ever do that again,* she said between breaths. *I don't think my heart can take it.*

"Yours and mine both," Wynona murmured. She studied her hand, but there was no sign of the flames or anything that would suggest she might be hurt. "That was really weird."

It had to have been some kind of reaction.

"Yeah. The flames were purple."

Exactly. Your magic reacted to something in those books. Could you tell what it was?

"No."

Me either. I still say we take it all to Lusgu.

Wynona frowned at her companion, then shrugged. "Fine. Let's go." She picked up the box, doing her best to ignore the push and pull of the dark books, and marched out the door.

The ride over felt wonderful with the breeze blowing against Wynona's hot cheeks and it helped calm her ire that she still couldn't get ahold of Rascal. She knew the Prim situation hadn't been ideal, but for him to just cold shoulder her like this was a bit extreme and hurt far worse than Wynona could have imagined.

He'll come around, Violet assured her as they walked inside the shop. *Give him time for his hissy fit and then he'll be back.*

Wynona huffed. "He's not having a hissy fit."

Tantrum? Man moment?

Wynona rolled her eyes and pressed through the dining room, into the kitchen. "Lusgu?" she called out, watching the corner. "Lusgu?"

The room was deadly silent and a shiver went down Wynona's spine. Three...three murders had happened in her shop now. It sort of made her want to pack up and move out, except that after her landlord had turned out to be the first murderer, she had managed a steal of a deal on her rent. Did she really want to turn that down?

A grunting noise caught her attention and Wynona saw the small figure she'd been looking for emerge from the corner wall.

She let out a breath she hadn't realized she was holding. "Hi... Are you doing okay?"

Lusgu glared at her from beneath his eyebrows. "What do you want?"

Wynona hesitated, but Violet smacked her tail against Wynona's neck to urge her on. "I'm looking for an invisibility spell, but couldn't find one in Granny's grimoire. Then we were trying to figure out—"

"You have Saffron's grimoire?" Lusgu's eyes opened wide and for the first time during the year he'd worked for Wynona, she could finally see what he looked like beneath the grim and stoic exterior.

"Y-yes?"

Lusgu shuffled over and grabbed the box from her, only to yelp and immediately drop it to the floor. He cursed. "What's in there?" he shouted.

Wynona was still staring in shock at Lusgu's change in behavior and barely registered that something magical had just happened. "I..."

"Wynona!" Lusgu snapped. "What's in the box?"

Wynona closed her eyes and shook her head to clear away her surprise. "Okay, hold on a minute." She pressed fingers into her forehead. "What just happened?"

"I want Saffron's grimoire," Lusgu said urgently.

"It's back at the house," Wynona responded.

"You said you had it!"

Wynona took a step back at his vehemence. "I do. But I didn't bring that one with me. It's the only grimoire I wanted and so I left it back at my place."

Lusgu walked around the box and stood toe to toe with Wynona. "Is it safe?" he demanded.

Wynona was still having a hard time following the conversation. This behavior was so out of character for her brownie. She was starting to get to know him, but now everything she thought she knew was flying out the window. "As far as I know."

"That's not good enough," he growled. Storming over to the backdoor of the kitchen, he grabbed his hat off the rack and slammed it on his head, causing his long ears to poke directly out to the sides of his head. "Take me."

Wynona put her hands up. "Hold on. We need to deal with this box first."

Lusgu cursed again and stared down into the cardboard. "What is it?"

"The other grimoires that Celia brought me."

Lusgu's head snapped her direction so fast it made Wynona jump. "Celia brought you these?"

Wynona nodded.

"And where did she get them?"

Wynona hesitated, but finally gave in. "I believe she took them from my mother's lab...uh...spell room."

He growled low, but there was almost an eerie chuckle among the dark tones. "Have you read them?"

Wynona shook her head. "No. I only wanted Granny's." Wynona wrinkled her nose. "Plus some of them contain...dark magic."

Lusgu nodded, his eyes still on the box. "It's to be expected."

"It is?" She shook her head. "Lusgu, what's going on? What are you not telling me?"

Instead of answering, Lusgu reached into the box and carefully picked up one of the grimoires. He studied the book hanging from his fingertips, turning it this way and that before tossing it over his shoulder.

"Hey!" Wynona cried, ducking out of the way. "What're you doing?"

He's plum loco, Violet said in awe.

It was your idea to come to him.

I had no idea he'd lose his marbles over a bunch of old spells.

Lusgu reached into the box and tried to pick up another one, but this time a burst of black sparks lit the kitchen and a boom louder than a cannon reverberated through the small space.

Wynona dropped to her knees, covering her ears. "What are you doing?" she screamed.

Lusgu didn't answer.

When Wynona finally managed to open her eyes, she gasped, rushing across the floor on her knees. "Lusgu!" She tentatively reached out to the body lying far too still on the hardwood floor. "Oh my goodness, please be okay."

Violet took a flying leap off Wynona's shoulder, landing on Lusgu's chest.

"Careful," Wynona warned.

Climbing up to his neck, the mouse nestled among the craggy folds. *He's got a heartbeat.*

Wynona blew out a breath. "What do we do?"

Can you try healing him?

"I don't know what's wrong," Wynona argued.

Violet came back out, resting on Lusgu's chest. *Well, figure it out quick because his heart is working, but his lungs aren't.*

Wynona's eyes were filling with tears so fast she could barely see at this point. "I...I don't know what to do."

Wynona.

Wynona took in a shuddering breath.

Pull yourself together, Violet said, though her tone was kind, considering the circumstances. *He needs your help. Your. Help. No one else can do this but you.*

Wynona nodded, wiping at her eyes. "You're right. You're absolutely right." She slowed her breathing this time, forcing her body to calm. "Okay." Putting a shaking hand on his chest, she squeezed her eyes closed and tried to concentrate.

The magic, usually so eager to move, didn't come the first time she called. Wynona shook out her hand and tried again.

Breathe, Violet demanded. *That's it. Just breathe.*

The usual electricity began to travel down Wynona's arm and the shaking in her hand increased. Wynona's entire body tightened as the magic hit her fingertips. Something about Lusgu was...different.

He pulled at her magic, sucking it right out of Wynona's hand.

What's going on? Violet asked, panic lacing her tone.

"I don't know," Wynona said through gritted teeth. "It's like he's siphoning from me."

Well, hold it back and get him healed. If he doesn't breathe soon, he's a goner.

"Working on it!" Wynona shouted back. The muscles in her face and neck began to ache with the effort and sweat trailed down her back. The magic pulse began to slow and Wynona regained control, though barely, of the powers.

Moving as fast as she dared, she began to send her magic through the tiny body, looking for any irregularity that the blast might have caused. When nothing abnormal caught her eye, she moved the magic back to the point of contact.

By this time, her entire body was shaking with the effort to keep the brownie from taking everything. Each time she had to pull back what was hers, she felt her strength drain a little more. "I won't be able to hold on much longer," she whispered in a breathless tone.

Come on, Lu, Violet whispered back. *Breathe, darn it!*

Not knowing what else to do at this point, Wynona sent a tiny shockwave of magic from her hand to the area of his lungs. Maybe he had simply been shocked out of his breath.

A loud, rasping gasp caught Wynona off guard and she was knocked onto her backside, her body collapsing against a cupboard and her magic snapping back like a tight rubber band. "Ow," she whimpered, rubbing her sternum.

"WY!" Rascal burst through the back door of the kitchen, his hair and eyes wild. "What happened?"

Wynona tried to climb to her feet, but her legs were shaking too hard and she collapsed back to the ground.

Rascal started her way, then stopped, his eyes caught on Lusgu, who was slowly climbing to his feet. "What did you do?" Rascal snarled.

Lusgu sneered. "Anything that's wrong with her has nothing to do with me," he shot back in a hoarse tone. Without another word, the brownie shuffled, a noticeable limp in his gait, back to his corner, disappearing into the portal.

Wynona was still breathing heavily and she looked to Rascal, ready for him to come wrap her in his arms. She loved his strength and needed it now more than ever. What had happened to Lusgu was a mystery and she wanted to talk it out and get another opinion. Rascal often had good logical insights and he simply made her feel heard and completed in a way she had never imagined.

"Are you hurt?" he ground out.

Wynona blinked. "What?"

"I asked...are you hurt?" Rascal's eyes were still glowing and there was hair on the back of his hands.

He's still angry.

Ya think? Violet grumbled. She wrapped her tail around Wynona's neck. *Dude needs a good kick in his—*

"No," Wynona said quickly, covering Violet's desire for violence. "I'm not hurt." *Not physically anyway.*

He nodded and backed toward the door.

"Where are you going?" Wynona cried, clambering to her feet. She held onto the counter top to steady herself since her legs were still struggling.

Rascal obviously noticed and took a step in her direction before stopping himself. His hands clenched and unclenched several times. "I...need some time," he said.

"Time?" she whispered, her knees growing even weaker as she realized he was leaving her.

Rascal nodded, then spun and took a leap out the door, turning into his wolf before he hit the ground.

Wynona didn't even feel the hardwood hit her tailbone when she landed back on the floor. "He left," she whispered incredulously. "He just...left."

Violet muttered and climbed down Wynona's shoulder. *This calls for chocolate.*

Wynona couldn't even answer. She pulled her knees up to her chest, wrapping her arms around them. After a moment, her head simply fell forward and a great wracking sob burst from her mouth. It was followed by another, and another, until one sob hadn't ended before the next began.

There was no way to tell how long Wynona sat on the floor, crying until she couldn't cry anymore, but when her tears were spent, she allowed herself to slide sideways, the floor cool beneath her cheek, and simply closed her eyes.

For the first time since escaping her family's castle, Wynona wasn't sure if she cared if she ever woke up again.

CHAPTER 23

Wynona knew that her eyes were red and puffy, but she had refused to heal them this morning. For some reason, the re-
minder felt necessary. Like a badge of honor over the fact that her
soulmate was in the process of rejecting her was something she needed to see when she looked in the mirror.

She pushed her dark glasses up her nose and squinted down the
street. Things had been such a mess yesterday that Wyonna hadn't
tried to find an invisibility spell again. In fact, she was terrified to
touch any of the grimoires at this point and had shoved the box in a
closet, covered them with more boxes and locked the door.

Granny's, however, was tucked under her mattress. Wynona
wasn't ready to touch it at the moment, but neither was she willing to
part with it. Besides...Lusgu had been interested in it and had sounded like there was something important in it. For now, or at least until
Lusgu was willing to speak to her again, Wynona would keep it semi-
close.

Good luck with that one, Violet muttered as she cleaned her
shoulder.

Maybe you could speak to him for me?

Fat chance. Violet rubbed her eyes. Apparently, she hadn't slept
well last night either. *He won't talk to me either.*

Wynona sighed and searched the street again. "I don't see him.
Do you?"

Violet shook her head. "Nope. He hasn't left the bank yet."

Wynona tried to take a calming breath, but her chest still felt
tight. She'd managed to follow Mr. Pearlily from his home to the
Shade Building and Loan, and was now waiting for him to emerge.

He must have had a decent amount of business, because Wynona had been standing at the corner for nearly an hour and her legs were beginning to ache.

She shifted her weight from one side to the other. "He can't stay in there forever. How long does it take to deposit a few checks?"

Violet twittered. *Do creatures even deposit checks anymore? Isn't it all done online?*

Wynona took off her glasses and rubbed between her eyebrows. "I suppose," she answered softly. "I'm just anxious, I guess."

Understandably, but you do know that your dark glasses and dark clothing make you far more conspicuous than if you'd just dressed normally?

Wynona looked down at her outfit. "I was hoping to blend into the shadows."

What shadows? It's the middle of the day.

Wynona's shoulders sagged and she shrugged. "I did the best I could with what brain cells were actually firing this morning, okay?"

Violet grumbled, but didn't speak anymore.

"Here he comes," Wynona hissed, putting her glasses back on. She leaned casually against the building where she was observing and stuffed her hands in her pockets, watching the tall man work his way through the crowd. When Mr. Pearlily came to the street, he hailed a cab and Wynona had a moment of panic.

As soon as he started getting inside, she rushed over and jumped on her Vespa. She nearly ran into a pedestrian as she tried to merge into traffic, but luckily, the creature simply cursed her out rather than making a bunch of noise, which would have attracted Mr. Pearlily's attention.

You're gonna get us killed, Violet shouted over the wind. She stood on her hind legs, arms holding onto the front of her basket and the wind blowing her fur away from her face.

I'm trying to keep up with our suspect, Wynona argued.

Same thing, I think.

Wynona ignored the sarcastic mouse and focused on the taxi making its way down the street. Luckily, Hex Haven wasn't such a major city that traffic was overly difficult to maneuver. The heart of their city held only four lanes, two in each direction, but the borders of Hex Haven spread wide, which was normal for paranormal cities. They often had to accommodate creatures who lived in forests and non-suburban areas, making cities wide, but not necessarily heavily populated in any one area.

"He's stopping," Wynona whispered, though she knew Violet couldn't hear. Pulling over, Wynona parked the Vespa and waited. She kept her helmet on, not wanting to risk showing her face until she knew where the fairy was headed.

Now in his smaller, fairy form, Mr. Pearlily floated just above the ground, his wings fluttering like mad, and marched up the steps of a grandiose building before pulling the glass doors open and disappearing inside.

Let's go, Wynona said, ripping off her helmet and grabbing Violet. "Do you know what this place is?" Wynona asked as she hurried over.

The library.

Wynona skidded to a halt. "Really?" She looked up at the opposing building and studied it. There in big, black letters was exactly what Violet had said.

Hex Haven Public Library

"How did I not know this was here?"

Probably because you've never actually just ventured around the city, Violet drawled. *You're always too busy creating teas and wreaking havoc.*

"I do not wreak havoc," Wynona argued.

I beg to differ.

"I'm trying to stop havoc," Wynona insisted as she carefully went up the steps. She had been in her family's library, but she had never been in a public one. She was curious as to what would be inside. Books, obviously, but would there be other things? Artifacts? Ancient pieces of magic?

Stop being dramatic, Violet scolded. *Get inside or you're gonna lose Mr. Pearlily.*

Wynona shook her head. She had nearly forgotten her reason for being there. Running up the steps, she took just a moment to make sure had caught her breath and then pulled open the door.

The smell of dust, paper and something much more ancient than the books hung in the air.

There he is, Violet whispered.

Wynona's eyes tried to search for Mr. Pearlily, but she couldn't seem to pull herself away from the books. Her family had hundreds of books, but this? This was amazing. Thousands upon thousands of volumes stood in stacks or bookcases, each and every one of them calling to Wynona, and she felt helpless to resist their pull.

WYNONA! Violet screeched.

Wynona jerked at the scream in her head. "What?" she asked, earning her a couple of odd looks from people wandering around the space.

Snap out of the gawking and get back to being a spy.

Wynona rubbed her forehead. *Sorry. I just...*

I get it. We'll come back. But we'll do it when our murder suspect isn't being suspicious.

Wynona nodded and finally looked around for her target. A flash of red hair rounded a corner and Wynona began to walk in that direction. She entered the stacks next to the one Mr. Pearlily had gone into. Walking carefully, Wynona tried peeking through the shelves, searching for him.

"I can't see him," Wynona whispered.

You might want to keep our conversations in your head at this point, Violet pointed out. She climbed down Wynona's torso and legs. *Hang on.* The purple body disappeared under the shelves in the direction that Mr. Pearlily should have been.

Wynona waited, her heart nearly jumping out of her chest every time a person walked by the front of her walkway. Currently, she was the only creature inside her row and she was sincerely hoping it would stay that way. She didn't want to have to explain her odd behavior to someone else, so being alone was definitely her preferred situation at the moment.

He's here, Violet said.

Where?

The next row over. Stay where you are. I'll keep an eye on him.

Wynona pinched her lips together. She had no idea what to do now. *What's he doing?* she asked.

Looking for a book.

Wynona rolled her eyes. *We're in a library. Of course that's what he's doing.*

Then why did you ask?

Putting her hands on her hips, Wynona let her head hang down. She was so bad at this spying thing. She wanted nothing more than to leave and pretend she had never been following the fairy.

But I can't, she reminded herself. *Thallia needs proof of her innocence.*

Or her guilt.

Wynona nodded reluctantly. *I still don't think she did it, but yes...either way. I'm hoping that being able to prove Thallia's innocence means we're proving someone else's guilt.*

Duck!

Wynona automatically ducked her head, then looked up. "What's going on?" she whispered.

He's at the top of the shelves, grabbing something. I was afraid he was going to fly over. Act natural.

Wynona grumbled under her breath, but straightened her shirt, then put her focus on the shelves. She began running her fingertips along the spines of the books in front of her, pretending interest. "What in the world is this?" she muttered, pulling a book off the shelf. "The Life and Times of Crones? Really?"

Focus, Wynona! What's wrong with you?

You asked me to look natural, Wynona argued back. *I'm acting natural.*

Violet sighed through their connection. *Your mind is somewhere else.*

Sorry. There was nothing else for Wynona to say. Violet was right. Wynona's heart and mind were anywhere but that library. She missed her friends. Prim had refused to answer any phone calls or texts since yesterday morning. Lusgu had stayed inside his portal. Daemon had given Wynona only short, curt answers that he was fine. And Rascal...well, Rascal was still missing in action.

She knew he had shown up at the tea shop yesterday because he had sensed her distress, but once knowing she was alright, he'd left again and no one, not even Daemon, had heard from him.

Wynona rubbed the back of her neck. Tension radiated through her shoulders and her head had been pounding since her crying session. How had it all fallen apart so quickly? All she had ever wanted was to run her tea shop, fly under the radar of her parents and maybe find some nice creatures to spend time with.

At first, Wynona had thought she'd accomplished just that. But the more time went on, the more life had gotten complicated. Her powers had emerged, Granny had died for the second time, Wynona's entire family history had been rewritten, she'd discovered a soulmate, her sister had left home and was living with her...and it all added up to Wynona being friendless and chasing possible murderers by herself as if she were some sort of secret spy, except she couldn't seem to blend in to save her life and she couldn't focus enough to see if anything was happening she should take note of.

Wynona's shoulders slumped. She knew what helplessness felt like...and this was it. Despair. Depression. It was all there and Wynona was tired of trying to push on. She wanted to curl up in bed, eat her weight in chocolate and let someone else save the world for once.

He's taking a book down.

Wynona grabbed the volume she had put back. *Which way?* She might want someone else to save the world, but right now...there was no one else.

Go back toward the entrance.

Wynona followed Violet's instructions until she reached an area with a dozen round tables and multiple chairs at each. Mr. Pearlily had taken a seat at the far table where no one would be able to disturb him. Wynona couldn't risk letting him see her, so she purposefully sat several tables away with her back in his direction. *Can you see what he's reading?* she asked Violet.

Working on it. It's big and heavy, whatever it is. Maybe he's looking up some ancient spell or something.

Remember, the murderer didn't actually use magic at the scene, Wynona said.

Violet grumbled, but acknowledged the point. *Almost there...*

Wynona opened her book on crones, but didn't read a word of it. She found herself holding her breath, waiting for Violet's answer. First the bank and now the library. There had to be some connection...but what? What would a businessman like Mr. Pearlily be doing at those two locations?

Shoot.

"What?" Wynona asked out loud before she could stop herself. She ducked her head into her book when the man across the way looked in her direction. *What did you find out?*

He's reading a book on eviction rules. The textbook is about the fine print of contracts. It must have to do with his real estate holdings.

Wynona bit back her groan, not wanting more attention. That more than likely explained the bank as well. What would a businessman like Mr. Pearlily be doing at the bank? Exactly what businessmen did at the bank. Business. He was probably looking into buying a new property or something.

Wynona snapped the book shut and marched it to the cart at the end of the shelves. *Come on, Violet. We're going home.*

The skittering of tiny feet came rushing across the tile and eventually climbed up Wynona's leg.

Wynona gave a wan smile to the front desk clerk and headed out into the sunshine. She pulled down her sunglasses from the top of her head, actually needing them in the brightness, and made her way to the Vespa.

Usually, riding her scooter was soothing, but Wynona found herself too wound up with emotions for herself to relax.

By the time they finally arrived back at the cottage, Wynona knew she needed to take a break from it all.

"I'm fixing a cuppa and taking a nap."

Violet didn't even bother with a returning quip, simply disappeared into her favorite hidey hole.

Using her magic, Wynona brewed herself some chamomile and rose, hoping the herbs would do their magic and help ease some of the anxiety coursing through her system.

Sipping the hot liquid, Wynona began walking toward her bedroom. A nap would hopefully ease the pain in her head the way the tea would ease her emotional pain. Maybe afterwards, things would look a little brighter and she could take charge of the case once more.

Just as she was walking into the hallway, the front door opened.

"Oh good, you're home," Celia called out.

"I'm taking a nap," Wynona answered, not bothering to turn around.

"Well, here. Take this first."

Wynona paused, closed her eyes for a moment to gather her patience and then turned. Celia was holding out a piece of paper.

"What is it?"

"A man called your cell phone while you were gone."

Wynona's eyes widened and she felt around in her pockets. Sure enough. Her phone hadn't been there. "Why didn't you let it go to voicemail?"

Celia rolled her eyes. "Because I'm nosy."

Clenching her jaw to keep from saying something petty, Wynona walked back and took the paper. "Thank you."

Celia smirked. "Of course." She winked. "Don't, uh...do anything I wouldn't do." With that, she headed to the kitchen.

Frowning, Wynona looked down at the paper.

Meet Mr. Pearlily at the shop tonight. Ten p.m.

Wynona turned the paper over, but there was nothing else written on it. "Celia?" There was no answer. Walking toward the kitchen, she peeked inside, but Celia was nowhere to be seen.

She ported somewhere.

Wynona sighed. "Of course she did."

What did she say?

Wynona squatted down and held out the paper for Violet to read.

Violet whistled. *You gonna go?*

"He probably saw me following him," Wynona muttered. Another sigh escaped. She was getting awfully good at those. "I suppose I'll have to."

You should tell Rascal.

Wynona hesitated. "I'll try, but he's been blocking me."

Violet just continued to look expectant.

Closing her eyes, Wynona tried to call her soulmate. *Rascal? Are you there?* Just as before, there was only a cavern of silence. She felt as if she were shouting into a vacuum of space.

Violet grumbled. *Fine. I'll go with you.*

"What if he's angry?" Wynona whispered.

Then I'll bite his wings off.

Wynona couldn't help but smile a little, despite her concern. She stood and took another drink of her tea. "I'm still taking that nap. I think I'm gonna need the strength in order to face the beast."

Oh, and bring your magic, Violet said as she skittered off. *I have a feeling we're going to need it.*

CHAPTER 24

*Y*ou're going with the black again? Violet scoffed.

Wynona closed her eyes. It seemed her patience was completely gone these days. "Violet," she said warningly. "If you don't like something, please just say so. My emotions right now are on the edge of exploding and I think we both know that that won't help me, or Hex Haven, if I truly have a breakdown. I'm still not sure how my magic didn't implode the kitchen last night, but I'd rather not test it out now."

For her part, Violet made a sheepish face. *Sorry. The snark just kind of...happens.*

"I know, and I love you for it, but right now I can't handle it. Please...for just a bit, take it easy on me."

Violet scrambled up Wynona's side and settled at her neck, draping her tail around for support. *We're in this together.*

Wynona's eyes pricked with tears, but she blinked them back. Everything was making her cry at the moment and Wynona didn't like it. She wanted to feel in control of herself and her surroundings, but nothing could be farther from the truth.

Giving her dark outfit one last look in the mirror, Wynona walked out of her bedroom. There was no point in hiding her activities tonight since Celia had been the one to give Wynona the message. Not to mention that Wynona hadn't heard Celia come home yet. She had no idea where her sister had ported off to, but apparently Celia had a life outside of their tiny cottage. One she didn't want to share with Wynona.

"Doesn't matter," Wynona muttered to herself. "Celia can do what she wants."

Let's hope.

Wynona did glance in the kitchen just to be sure Celia hadn't returned before going to the garage. She wasn't ready to port again yet. Wynona's emotions were too unbalanced at the moment for her to trust her ability to pull off such a difficult spell.

The night was cool and the ride helped Wynona feel ever so slightly better. She allowed the chilly air to enter and fill her lungs, helping Wynona to calm her nerves and prepare herself a little better for tonight. She had a feeling Mr. Pearlily simply wanted a chat in order to tell her to back off. He had more than likely seen her following him and wanted to let her know that she was crossing a line, which was true.

He'll probably threaten Chief Ligurio, Wynona thought as she pulled the Vespa into her usual spot at the back of the shop.

Probably, Violet agreed. *It's not going to be pretty, that's for sure. Are you ready for that?*

If you're asking if I'll cry, the answer is...probably. But I'll work through it. He has a right to be upset, but the fact that he's wanting to do it without an audience has me slightly worried.

Probably doesn't think he can threaten Ligurio's job if others are listening.

Fair enough. Wynona unlocked the kitchen door and slipped inside. Her eyes immediately went to the mess of pots and lids scattered all over the kitchen. Lusgu obviously hadn't been back to clean things up and until this moment, Wynona hadn't been brave enough to come back to the scene of his near death.

She felt responsible. If she hadn't brought those grimoires inside, he never would have been shocked. Wynona still had no idea what had caused the reaction, but whatever it was, she didn't want to experience it again.

She'd just killed her grandmother...for the second time...she didn't need to kill her janitor and friend as well.

Let it go, Violet ordered. *We can process everything later. Right now we have to let a fairy threaten and scold us.*

"Right," Wynona breathed. She glanced at her cell phone. She had ten minutes until Mr. Pearlily was supposed to be there. "Should I make some tea?"

Violet snorted. *Why? Do you really think he'd drink it?*

Wynona shrugged. "I don't know, but maybe it would help keep him from being too mean?" Deciding she wasn't ready to use her magic in the space, Wynona filled a pot and set it on the stove, creating a tray the old fashioned way.

Was it only a couple months ago that she had been so excited to finally be able to make tea using magic? It seemed like ages ago and the act of boiling water on the stove and putting it all on the tray by hand felt...awkward.

Just as the clock struck the hour, Wynona finished filling the tray. Taking a deep breath, she picked it up and walked toward the dining room. Turning, she used her back to press open the door and stepped backward. The room was dark, which explained why Wynona didn't see the large figure coming her way or the way the creature raised their hands up in the air in order to slam a hard object against her head.

With little more than the beginning of a scream, Wynona crumpled to the floor. The tray of tea landed underneath her chest and she had just enough consciousness to realize that the water was burning her skin before the thudding of feet caused her head to bounce a few times, pulling Wynona into a black place where her worries, fears and emotional pains, completely faded away.

What seemed like only moments later, Wynona felt herself being shifted and her head lolled to the side when she landed on her back.

"Careful!" someone growled.

Wynona knew she should recognize the voice, but it wasn't coming to her at the moment.

Well, if you'd been here, this wouldn't have happened, another voice snapped.

"Don't you think I already know that?" the deeper voice argued back. The tone was full of anguish and Wynona felt sympathy for the speaker. They obviously were in a great deal of pain.

The thought of pain brought to light the fact that her head felt as if someone was playing the drums in her brain...using garbage cans and baseball bats.

"How could this have happened?" a feminine voice whined.

Stupid girl. Can't she just shut up already?

"Step back," the deeper voice commanded. "I'll take it from here."

"What's going to happen?" the woman asked. "Should we call an ambulance?"

Wynona squeezed her eyes a little tighter. Their voices were really starting to cause her pain to worsen. But how did she ask them to all be quiet when she couldn't seem to move?

QUIET! the squeaky voice shouted. *We're hurting her!*

Wynona jumped at the command and her head knocked against the floor, drawing a groan out of her throat without her permission.

"Wy?" the deep voice asked softly. The pain was still evident, but now he sounded hopeful as well. "Can you hear me?"

"Yes," Wynona answered, though her voice came out breathless. It didn't sound like her at all and she tried to clear her throat, but it hurt so badly she cut it off. "Ow..."

Don't move, the squeaky voice said again. *You've been bashed like a rotten pumpkin. You need to heal yourself.*

"Well, that's a great way to get things started," the deep voice said sarcastically.

What do you want from me? the squeaker retorted. *This should never have happened!*

Whoever was arguing with Squeaker obviously had no come-back for the remark.

"I really think we need to call the ambulance," the feminine voice said.

"She can heal herself," the male said. "Waiting for an ambulance will take too long."

There was a shift in the air and Wynona felt the hair on the back of her neck raise up on end. The feeling was...pleasant and she decided she must be friends with whoever was talking.

"Wy," the man whispered against her ear, sending a shiver down her spine. "Please heal yourself. You've got a big cut on the side of your head and it's bleeding badly. Chief Ligurio is on his way with half the precinct and I want you alive and well when they get here."

If Vampy loses control, it's your job to hold him off.

"He's not a young vampire," the man growled.

Just sayin'.

The man grumbled some more, but Wynona couldn't understand the words. She was trying to open her eyes, but they were resisting and it was starting to make her panic. "I...can't..."

It's okay, Wy, Squeaky said in a softer tone. *Just relax.*

"I..." Wynona swallowed hard. She wanted to know what was happening. She needed to see who was speaking and why one was so angry and the other so sad. She wanted to comfort the angry one and tell him it was going to be okay even though Wynona didn't know why.

A warm palm landed against her cheek and the contact sent an even stronger pleasurable shock through her body. "I'm right here, Wy. It's going to be fine. Just relax and open your eyes."

He was comforting her? No, no, it should be the other way around. *Why can't I open my eyes?*

"Your head is badly wounded," the man said in that same soft tone. "You're struggling to think clearly." His voice broke at the end of his sentence and that same desire for compassion rolled through Wynona. His thumb caressed her cheek and Wynona leaned into the touch. "Can you feel the wound?"

No, Wynona thought.

"That's okay."

She stiffened. He could hear her?

"Yes...I can hear you," the man said slowly. There was a pause. "You don't remember." It wasn't a question, but an observation.

Remember what? Wynona asked. She knew her lips weren't moving and she still couldn't open her eyes to see who was talking. How could the man hear her inner thoughts?

"What's going on?" the woman cried. "How are you talking to her? She's lying so still!"

"Okay, okay," the man said. "Just take it easy. Don't get upset. You'll be able to remember soon, I'm sure. But you were hit on the head and it's muddling everything." That thumb went across Wynona's cheek again. "Instead of opening your eyes, I want you to use your magic. Send it to your head and heal the...spot that's been hit. Can you do that, sweetheart?"

Wynona didn't respond for a moment. He'd called her *sweetheart.* Her body responded to him. There had to be some kind of a connection, but why wouldn't she remember what it was?

I'm here too, Squeaky said. A small, warm presence climbed up Wynona's arm and across her chest, settling on her sternum. *I'll help you get started.*

A similar soothing sensation came from whatever was now sitting on top of her and Wynona relaxed a little, feeling like she was being cared for. Her fingers, which she hadn't been able to feel, were starting to tingle and the sensation slowly crept up her arms.

That's it, Squeaky insisted. *Feel the magic. Let it get stronger.*

Wynona wasn't sure what magic the creature was talking about, but she kind of enjoyed the tingling. It helped distract her from the pain in her head.

The creature moved, tucking up under Wynona's chin and resting directly on her skin, which felt slightly uncomfortable. The skin was tender and the weight, even of something so small, burned.

I know, Squeaky said. *Your skin was scalded, but touching you directly will help you heal. Bring the magic to this spot.*

Unsure what else to do but follow directions, Wynona imagined the tingling coming up until it settled just under her chin.

"That's it," the man said breathlessly. "That's it."

"How's she doing that?" the woman screamed.

"Strongclaw? What's going on?" another male demanded. His voice was also low, but very different from the one who was currently touching Wynona. The new voice was sharp and angry and didn't cause any type of pleasurable reaction at all.

"Stop!" the first man shouted. "You. Step back. Your crying isn't helping."

Wynona heard the shuffling of several footsteps mixed with whimpering.

"Chief. She's stuck right now and I'm trying to help her heal herself. Give me a minute."

You're helping her?

"Violet *and I*," the man growled in correction, "are working on it. But we need some time."

All the back and forth was making Wynona focus on her head again. The pounding was getting worse, though she noticed the burning on her skin had lessened.

No, no, no, Squeaky cried. *Don't let go just yet. We still need to do your head.*

A moan clawed its way up Wynona's throat and slipped out without permission. The pain in her head was becoming so sharp she was struggling to pay any attention to the voices at all.

Focus, Wynona, Squeaky demanded. *I know it hurts, but we're gonna make it better. Bring the magic back.*

There was a very tiny thumping against Wynona's skin and that same tingling started in her fingers again.

Don't lose it, Squeaky instructed. *Bring it up again, but this time, all the way to your head.*

Wynona could barely hear the voice at this point. All the sounds were muddling together, but she tried to focus as she was told. Multiple voices began to speak and she couldn't distinguish one from another, not even the deep one that pulled at her. He was just as lost as everything else.

The tingling wasn't as strong this time and moved much slower. Wynona tried to pull it upward, but the feeling was heavy...and her body was sinking into the floor...

"Don't you dare, Wynona!" the male shouted. "Don't you dare! Focus!" A slew of curse words flew through the air, but Wynona barely noticed.

The tingle began to slip back down her arm, but Squeaky thumped her chest again. *No! Pull, Wynona! Pull! Straight up to your head! Give it everything you've got! WOLF! Touch her skin again. Give her a point of contact!*

An anguished cry ripped through Wynona's consciousness just as that warm hand touched her cheek again. The shock of the touch went down her spine and caused a jump in the electricity in her arms.

That's it, Squeaky said. *Pull it up now. It's there. Pull it up.*

The voice was right. It was a little easier than it had been before and Wynona began to pull with a little more motivation. She really didn't like the sadness in the man's voice and if working on this would help him feel better, then she could stay awake long enough to do that.

"Come on, baby," the voice pleaded. "Come on. You can do it."

Wynona could feel herself growing faint again. The pull of sweet, peaceful sleep was so strong, but she resisted. She'd finish this first, then she would allow herself to sleep.

That's it. All the way up. Let it get stronger...

The tingle was back to where it had been, right at Wynona's neck, and this time Wynona gave it a little more of a push. It resisted again, but she needed to finish this. She didn't understand why, but for some reason it was important. Inch by tiny inch the feeling went into Wynona's jaw and then across her face.

The tiny creature climbed across Wynona's mouth and nose, stopping between her eyebrows. A light tapping occurred near Wynona's temple. *Right here. Direct it right here.*

The sensation was starting to dim, but Wynona held on as much as she could. The tiniest of tendrils squirmed past her eye and just touched the edge of the spot Squeaky had indicated.

The pounding in Wynona's head eased the slightest amount.

"That's it!" the man shouted, then dropped his voice. "Again, Wy. Do it again."

Mustering what little strength she still had, Wynona broadened the tendril just a little more. With each push, the pain in her head slowly began to retreat and Wynona found her energy restoring at the same pace. The process was grueling and intriguing at the same time and by the time it had finished, Wynona was as exhausted as she was exhilarated.

Her eyes finally fluttered and she managed to open them to Rascal's brightly glowing golden ones. The despair on his face made her want to weep, but she wasn't sure she had the energy for it. Her mind was back, but it had taken everything out of her to heal it. Her hand shook violently as she brought it up to touch his stubbly cheek. "You came..." she rasped.

A heavy sob broke free from Rascal and tears poured down his face. Without a word, he wrapped his strong arms around her and pulled Wynona into his chest. She knew they had a lot to talk about, but right now wasn't a moment for words.

Closing her eyes, Wynona gave herself to the weariness and simply let him hold her. She knew there was a room full of people looking for answers, and she would provide them...but not right this second. They could wait.

CHAPTER 25

Wynona leaned her head against the headrest, her eyes half closed as Rascal drove her home. His hand tightened on her thigh.

"You doing okay?"

Wynona nodded. "Fine."

He grunted and his thumb twitched back and forth against her pants. "Wy...we...need to talk."

"I know." She closed her eyes. "But I have a feeling tonight isn't going to be the best time."

Rascal sighed. "I know. I just wanted you to know that I'm ready when the time's right."

"Okay." She rocked back and forth as the truck moved. She could tell when they'd reached the dirt road before her house as the rocking grew more intense. She felt the truck slow down as Rascal tried to take care with her being under the weather, until they finally came to a halt.

Her eyelids were heavy and she'd barely managed to open them by the time Rascal was around to her side of the truck, opening her door.

"I got ya," he said in a low tone. Reaching across her, he unbuckled the belt and then put an arm under her legs and around her back, lifting Wynona out with ease.

"I can walk," she protested weakly. The truth was, it felt amazing to be in his arms and she absolutely did not want to leave.

Let him carry you. Violet huffed, settling farther into Wynona's neck. *He earned it.*

Rascal gave Wynona a smile which was only a hint of his usual self. "Listen to the lady," he teased.

Wynona studied the dark rings under his eyes and the bloodshot colors. She had thought her life had been rough, but Rascal had obviously had it difficult as well. She reached up, running her finger tips along his facial hair growth. "You haven't been sleeping. I wish I could heal that."

Rascal grunted and banged on the front door with his foot. "Sleep'll come...eventually."

The door cracked open, then slammed against the wall. "What in the world?"

Rascal walked inside, pushing Celia to the side just a little. "She needs to lay down and I'm being followed by a crowd."

"What?" Celia screeched.

Wynona winced. Her head was definitely better, but she was still a little sensitive to noises. She'd been hit hard. Ultimately, Wynona felt that it was a miracle she was still alive. The cuts and burns on her chest had healed first when Violet had managed to get Wynona to use her magic. But it was the hole in her skull that had caused the most trouble.

Wynona hadn't been able to move or recognize anyone during that time and without Violet and Rascal's mental connections, she would surely have died.

"Your sister nearly lost her life only a few minutes ago," Rascal said in a low tone, still holding Wynona tightly to his chest. "Perhaps you could bring down the screaming and prepare for a room full of guests? I don't think Wy's up to it."

Celia's jaw dropped and she looked at Wynona. "What's going on? Is he serious? Did Mr. Pearlily try to kill you?"

"Mr. Pearlily?" Rascal growled.

Wynona patted his chest in a calming manner. "We can talk about it when Chief Ligurio gets here."

"Deverell is coming?" Celia asked weakly, her face suddenly more pale than normal.

Wynona frowned. "Yes. Is that a problem? They're all coming."

Celia's lips thinned and she shook her head. "No big deal." She came toward them. "Put her on the couch... What's your name again?"

Wynona wanted to roll her eyes, but she didn't want the headache that would come with it. "Rascal."

"Right. Rascal." Celia pointed to the seat. "Set her down and I'll get some tea and a blanket."

"I've got the blanket," Rascal said tightly. "You take care of the tea."

"Anything in particular?" Celia asked, pausing before she left the room.

Wynona hesitated. Who was this? It couldn't be her sister. Celia's sarcastic personality would never worry about getting Wynona tea, even if she had nearly just died. "Um..."

Celia rolled her eyes. "It's not like I'm going to poison it, sis. What do you want?"

Aaaand, she's back. You need to almost die more often. We got a split second of 'Nice Celia' and it almost gave me hope.

Rascal growled.

Celia shook her head and started walking. "Guess you get what you get."

Gingerly, Rascal set Wynona on the couch, then lunged across the room for an afghan laying in a heap on the floor. "Here." He arranged it on her lap. "What else do you need?"

What she really wanted was for him to sit down and continue holding her, but Wynona was afraid of pushing her luck. She still had no idea what Rascal had decided during his short break from her and though he had taken care of her in the last few minutes, she wasn't sure if he was planning to stick around.

He huffed and sat down, pulling her into his chest. "Like I said, we'll talk about it, but for now...just know that yes, I'm an idiot, my wolf is mostly to blame and no, I'm not going anywhere."

Wynona burst into tears and buried her head against his shoulder.

"Shhh..." he whispered in her ear, rubbing her back. "It's gonna be okay."

Wynona shook her head. The tears were wreaking havoc in her skull, but she couldn't seem to stop. All the emotions and pain had come to a head and the timing couldn't have been worse.

"Alright, Ms. Le Doux," Chief Ligurio said sharply as if to prove her point. "I know it's been hard, but we need to know what happened."

Celia came back, glaring at the officers streaming into the house. "She nearly died, Deverell. I think you could be a little more compassionate."

"Thank you," Wynona murmured when Celia handed her a teacup and saucer.

"Oh, because that's your specialty?" the vampire growled.

Celia turned to the chief and put her hands on her hips. "At least she isn't risking her life around me. Can the same be said for *you*, Chief?"

"Please stop," Wynona said softly. All heads snapped in her direction and Wynona closed her tired eyes. "Celia, we need to talk about the case. You're welcome to stay here or go shut yourself in your room, but no more fighting. They're doing their job and Chief Ligurio is a friend of mine."

The room grew quiet and Wynona cracked her eyes open to see Celia and Chief Ligurio still glaring.

"She's not out to hurt me, Chief Ligurio," Wynona added. "Please respect that." She watched his jaw clench, but ultimately the vampire nodded and walked stiffly to a chair before sitting down.

"What happened tonight?" he asked, his tone completely changed from a moment before.

Wynona took a deep breath and straightened herself. She needed to do this without Rascal's help. She'd made another choice, and this one had almost had deadly consequences. Apparently, whatever inner sense had helped Wynona solve those previous murders had completely left her. The harder she tried to help, the more she messed things up.

"I received a note earlier from Mr. Pearlily, saying to meet him at the shop tonight."

Those red eyes narrowed. "I thought we discussed meeting people by yourself. Have you learned nothing?"

Wynona held up a shaky hand. "I know. But this wasn't a stranger and I had assumed Mr. Pearlily had simply caught me following him earlier in the day and wanted to threaten your job about it."

Chief Ligurio's eyes flamed. "Tell me this is a joke," he said in a deadly tone.

"Pretty sure she's got the concussion to prove it's not," Celia said breezily from the corner she'd chosen to sit in. One long leg lay over the other and she bounced her foot with a smirk on her face. "I took the message myself. Mr. Pearlily called her phone and gave me the orders." She opened her eyes dramatically wide. "He didn't sound like much of a threat."

Chief Ligurio and Rascal were both growling so loudly that no one could speak over the noise.

"Chief!" Wynona shouted, then rubbed her forehead. "Chief. Violet discovered something in Mr. Pearlily's appointment book two days ago when Prim wanted to visit Mrs. Pearlily."

Chief Ligurio closed his eyes and hung his head. "Okay..." he said in a defeated tone. "I think maybe we need to start earlier than tonight. Go back to this meeting with Prim." Chief Ligurio's dark head came up and he pinned Rascal with a glare. "Why didn't I know about this?"

Rascal raised an eyebrow. "I believe we've talked about this."

Wynona frowned and looked between the two men. She was obviously missing something.

Later, Rascal said. *It'll all be clear when we talk...alone.*

Wynona nodded. She turned back to the chief. "I'm sorry I didn't keep you informed. The last couple of days have been rough and I should have checked in, you're right."

Celia snorted, then studied her nails as if she hadn't made a noise at all.

Wynona sighed and proceeded to share the whole story with the room full of officers. There was a lot of grunting, huffing and general murmuring while she spoke, but Wynona pressed on. Just like she had been prepared earlier to take on Mr. Pearlily's wrath, she knew she needed to be willing to deal with the police's...and especially Rascal's.

This isn't your fault, he sent her way. He'd been listening in on her thoughts all evening and Wynona was too tired to put up her wall, so she chose not to scold him about it. That part of her brain had felt empty for the last twenty four hours, so she was almost grateful at this point to have the comforting presence back.

It is, she admitted. *But I was doing the best I could.*

He tightened his arm around her, tucking her just a little deeper into his shoulder. "So now what?"

Chief Ligurio tapped his foot on the floor. "I'm not sure. Where does this leave us? I'm assuming you didn't actually get a look at the person who hit you?"

Wynona shook her head. "No. I had no idea I wasn't alone in the shop."

Hey!

Wynona looked at Violet apologetically. "Sorry. I meant I didn't realize my guest was there."

Violet sniffed and began cleaning her ears.

"No idea at all," Rascal pressed. "You're not usually caught so unawares."

Wynona nodded. "I know. I came in early for the meeting through the back. There were no cars out front and I put together a tea tray, hoping it would help keep Mr. Pearlily from being so mad about my following him." She shrugged. "I was completely expecting one thing and so wasn't looking for another."

Chief Ligurio rubbed his forehead. "What were you hit with? Did you see how big the creature was? Anything at all?"

Wynona rubbed the side of her head. "I'm not sure. I would guess a large piece of wood. It could have been a bat or just something similar. The blow seemed to come from above me, so it very well could have been a man or a large woman." She blew out a breath. "I was walking backward into the dining room and didn't even fully turn around before I was hit. I'm pretty sure I landed on the tea tray, which is why I was burnt and cut as well."

Chief Ligurio turned to Celia. "And your story? You said you took the message?"

Celia raised an eyebrow. "I did. But that's all there was. The phone rang. I took a message."

"And the voice? Are you sure it was Mr. Pearlily's? Have you ever met him before?"

Celia huffed and gave Chief Ligurio a cool look. "Are you questioning my intelligence?"

"I'm questioning the whole situation," he barked back. "They're not difficult questions, Ms. Le Doux."

Celia's eyes narrowed. "And I answered them."

"Not fully."

One side of Celia's lip curled. "As much as I think is necessary."

Wynona jumped when a blur passed in front of her and Chief Ligurio stopped, looming over Celia. "Are you willing to play with your sister's life, Celia?" he asked in a low tone. "Does the one creature who was willing to take you in not deserve more than your sarcastic answers?"

Celia's cheeks were nearly as red as Chief Ligurio's eyes as she glared back at him, her nostrils flaring. "The creature who called," she said tightly, enunciating each word carefully, "had a deep, husky tone. I've only seen Mr. Pearlily from a distance, so I have no idea if that's his natural voice or not."

Wynona studied the pair. There was something happening beneath the surface there, but that wasn't what had her attention. Slowly, she straightened. "Chief Ligurio?"

"Yes?"

"Could you move across the room again?"

Celia and Chief Ligurio both looked over at Wynona. "What?"

Rascal. Would you stand by the couch and try to hit him as he runs past? Wynona's mind was churning. She had an idea and needed to think it through.

Rascal gave her a questioning look.

"Please?"

Making a face, the shifter stood and walked to the edge of the couch.

"Chief, would you please use your vampire speed to run past Rascal?"

One black eyebrow went up, but Wynona pleaded silently. Looking as excited as Rascal, the vampire took off.

Rascal swung wildly as the vampire flew past him, but he wasn't even close to hitting his boss.

"Did you just take a swing at me?" Chief Ligurio demanded.

Rascal turned to Wynona. "Is that what you wanted?"

She nodded. "I know who the murderer is."

All eyebrows went up.

"I think."

"How definite is this?" Chief Ligurio asked.

Wynona pinched her lips in thought. "We...I need to talk to Thallia. After that, I'll know if I'm right."

Chief Ligurio looked at his watch. "Looks like Thallia shouldn't have been sent home from the shop. The Pearlily family is going to have to pull another all-nighter."

Violet grumbled. *Unfortunately, they're not the only ones.*

CHAPTER 26

Wynona yawned and tried to hide it behind her hand, but she knew every person in the room caught the movement. They were in the interrogation room waiting for Thallia and her family to show up. Chief Ligurio had asked for Mr. Pearlily to be brought in as well in order to ask him about the phone call situation, though the entire team felt sure he wasn't the one on the other end of the line.

It was evident that Wynona had been set up, but by whom? She had a pretty clear idea, but accusing someone of two murders and an attempted murder wasn't something you did unless you were absolutely certain.

"Need something, Ms. Le Doux?" Chief Ligurio said in amusement.

Wynona gave him a sheepish smile. "Sorry. It's been a long day."

"And there's no tea for that?"

Rascal gave a warning growl and Wynona patted his knee. "It's okay, he's just teasing."

Rascal huffed.

"The problem, Chief, is that if I drink matcha now, I'll probably stay awake for much longer than I need to. Plus, I'm pretty sure most of my exhaustion is from healing myself and there's no tea to cure that."

He chuckled and crossed one leg over the other. "So how is it...living with Celia?"

Wynona's eyes bugged out. "Excuse me?"

The vampire quickly shook his head. "Nevermind."

Before Wynona could try again, the door opened. "Chief? She's here."

"Bring them in."

Thallia walked in, her head hanging down and her feet shuffling on the floor.

Wynona stirred. She hated to see someone so down and it tugged at her heartstrings.

"Ms. Pearlily," Chief Ligurio said firmly. "Will your lawyer be joining us?"

Thallia looked up from under her eyelashes. "No. My father said I'm on my own."

Chief Ligurio huffed. "Have a seat, miss."

Thallia's bottom lip was hanging out so far it barely looked attached and Wynona was reminded of a young child being caught with their hand in the cookie jar. Except, Thallia wasn't a young child and she wasn't the murderer.

"Thallia," Wynona said softly. "Would you please tell me why you were at the shop earlier this evening?"

Thallia looked to the side. "I...I was out for a late night walk," she whispered. "I've been having trouble sleeping and didn't want to listen to my parents fighting, so I decided to walk around downtown."

"And?"

The fairy's wings slumped even farther. "And I heard a scream coming from inside the shop." Her misty eyes came up to meet Wynona's. "Two murders had already happened and I was afraid it was another one, so I ran inside."

"How did you get in?" Wynona interrupted.

"The front door was wide open," Thallia said with a shrug.

Wynona frowned. "It was wide open?"

Thallia nodded. "I didn't notice until I looked over because of the scream, but yeah."

It was closed when I drove around back, Wynona sent to Rascal.

He nodded, keeping his eyes on Thallia.

"And what did you find inside, Ms. Pearlily?" Chief Ligurio asked.

Thallia's eyes filled with tears again. "I couldn't see anything, so I flipped on the light and...you were on the ground, Ms. Le Doux. Your head was bleeding and your purple mouse was running in circles, squeaking so loud I could barely think."

"You didn't see who hurt her?" the chief pressed.

Thallia shook her head. "No. The kitchen door was closing and I heard footsteps, but I didn't chase them." She pressed back into her seat. "I...was scared they'd hit me too."

"It's okay," Wynona encouraged. "But what did you do next?"

"Your mouse was still screaming, but I didn't understand it, so I sort of just stood there. I wasn't sure if you were alive or dead and I didn't have my phone on me." She wiped at her eyes. "I couldn't get pictures or anything and then suddenly your mouse ran out of the shop and disappeared."

Don't, Wynona sent to Rascal. She could see his eyes beginning to glow at Thallia's lack of concern over Wynona's well being. Her inability to get pictures shouldn't have trumped taking care of an injured woman and Wynona was grateful the young lady had forgotten her device at home.

He growled slightly, but didn't move.

"Five minutes later, the mouse came back with a wolf." Thallia's eyes went up to Rascal. "It was you."

He nodded. "She was the only one there when I arrived. I could smell there had been another creature, but by the time I got there, I couldn't tell what kind or how long they'd been gone."

Chief Ligurio tapped his fingers on the desk. "Do you have any other witnesses, Ms. Pearlily?"

She shook her head miserably. "No."

"Thallia, I have a question," Wynona said, leaning back casually. "Your friend, Edana." She tilted her head. "Did your father like her?"

Thallia scoffed. "Edana hardly went near my father. She was ter-rified of him."

"Really? What did he do that scared her?"

Thallia shrugged. "Nothing, other than being himself. Dad isn't the easiest man to get along with and anyone who's been to my house more than once has heard him yell at people. Edana hated conflict and avoided Dad at all costs."

"We talked to Syn," Wynona hedged.

Thallia's demeanor was coming back to normal as she sneered. "Oh? Then you saw what a skunk he is."

"Actually, he says you were using him as a way to escape Dralo's abusive control," Rascal threw out.

Wynona shot him a look when Thallia went crazy. *Thanks a lot. She had it coming.*

Wynona mentally rolled her eyes. "Thallia, I think it's time for us to stop lying to each other."

Thallia snapped her mouth shut. "What do you mean?"

"You were dating Syn, weren't you?"

The young fairy just stared.

"You did it, not because you liked him, but because your father hated him."

The staring continued.

"In fact, the reason you got a job at the shop was because you knew it would upset your father...right?"

A muscle in Thallia's wing twitched, but otherwise she didn't speak.

"I believe you were with Edana the night she died," Wynona con-tinued, her words slow and deliberate. "But you weren't hiding from Syn and you weren't brainstorming about Dralo. Dralo was com-pletely innocent in all this. He had no idea you were cheating behind his back and Syn had no idea you didn't truly love him."

Thallia's face stayed stoic, but she leaned back slightly. "Where are you going with this, Ms. Le Doux?"

Wynona leaned forward a little. "I believe you were working on creating some drama. The very drama you claimed you wanted to sell about me, to the tabloids."

Those teal eyes hardened and Thallia folded her arms over her chest.

"You needed something to help you break free of your family. Something that would give you a spotlight and a way to leave your family in a dramatic way. You have no marketable skills, and your father was starting to notice that you were spending much more money than you should have been. Money which was going to Dralo's luxurious lifestyle."

Thallia chuckled darkly, all pretense of her crying gone. "It was happening right under his nose and he never knew."

Wynona nodded. "Right. And you needed a way to leave that would protect you. So you began dating Syn, knowing your father would eventually find out. His famous temper would give you fodder for the gossips and when the story went viral, you could use the fame to get out of the house without getting in trouble." Wynona leaned back again. "Your father would be too busy fighting to fix his public reputation to cut off the money the way he was bound to if he discovered your fraud too soon."

The fairy shrugged. "So? It's not illegal."

"No. It's just self serving."

"Every creature for themselves," Thallia said easily. "If I don't look out for me, no one else will."

"And were you looking out for Edana when you shared your news with her?"

Thallia stilled.

"Because Edana, like Dralo, ended up being a victim for another reason...didn't she?"

Chief Ligurio's head was snapping back and forth between the two women. "Wrap it up, Ms. Le Doux," he snapped.

"Thallia's flaky public persona has made her a media darling, or at least someone no one would suspect of such a devious plan, which is why it was so brilliant." Wynona hated what she was about to say next. "But counting on her dad's temper didn't work, because what Thallia didn't count on was her mother's love."

"I'm so lost," Rascal muttered.

Thallia's breathing began to speed up and her face flushed, letting Wynona know she was on the right track. She hated it.

"Her father would have eventually caught on," Wynona continued. "And Thallia's plan probably would have worked. But Mrs. Pearlily caught on much faster than her husband and had no idea it was all a fraud."

"Mrs. Pearlily killed Dralo?" Chief Ligurio snapped. "How do you know?"

"The papers," Wynona said, her eyes still on the angry young fairy. *Where's Daemon?*

Rascal pulled out his phone and punched in a few things before tucking it back in his pocket. *On his way, but it'll be a few. Be careful.*

Wynona nodded her understanding. "The flutter of papers on my desk. Have you ever noticed that Mrs. Pearlily constantly flutters her wings?" She waited while the chief nodded. "Her husband doesn't. When he's emotional, his wings stiffen just like his muscles. Mrs. Pearlily was talking with Dralo in my office and the fluttering scattered the papers. It wasn't a stealing situation. She had lured Dralo there under the pretense of a secret meeting with Thallia. I had just interrupted his chance to see her earlier, so this meeting was a way to...stick it to the man, so to speak. Dralo's dark sense of justice was caught by getting that meeting with his girlfriend in the very place he'd been kicked out of."

Thallia's wings began to twitch heavily.

He needs to hurry! Wynona said frantically to Rascal.

I have my stun gun. It's okay.

"So your mother killed Dralo..." Chief Ligurio started.

"Because she thought getting rid of the boyfriend would put Thallia back on the straight and narrow." Wynona stuck her chin in the air, trying to show a confidence she wasn't feeling at the moment. "Syn ended up being safe because Thallia broke up with him, and he'll probably never quite understand how that saved his life."

"She thought Dralo was beneath me," Thalli said with a dark smile. "And she was right. He was." She shrugged. "But he served his purpose. I just caught the attention of the wrong parent."

"And Edana?" Chief Ligurio asked.

Wynona sighed and rubbed her forehead. "Edana was Thallia's confidant. Mrs. Pearlily probably suspected that Thallia was on to her and when Thallia spent the night, Mrs. Pearlily took care of Dralo, then went after Edana."

"And you know this one how?" Chief Ligurio asked in exasperation.

Wynona turned to look at him. "Remember how I had you race across my room tonight?"

He nodded.

"You were too fast, even for shifter reflexes."

He nodded again.

"Mrs. Pearlily was wrong, wasn't she, Thallia? You hadn't told Edana anything. You weren't quite sure yourself about what was going on, just that your mother was acting odd and your dad was being too slow. So you didn't warn Edana and when your mother brought her to my shop, Edana went willingly."

The tears in Thallia's eyes were much more genuine this time.

"If she was scared of Mr. Pearlily, the vampire wouldn't have stuck around and her speed would have ensured her escape. No...the person she met was someone Edana thought she could trust. The one adult in the Pearlily household who seemed nice."

"What about her size? Dralo was hit from above. As were you. Mrs. Pearlily is half your size," Chief Ligurio pressed.

Wynona nodded. "Curious, isn't it? That we've never seen her human form?" Wynona's black eyes turned to Thallia, whose cheeks were growing flushed. "Is there something...different about your mother's human form, Thallia? Something that might make her capable of killing someone twice her height?"

Chief Ligurio cursed under his breath and grabbed his phone. "Is Mrs. Pearlily here with her husband?" he shouted into the speaker. His jaw clenched at the answer. "Well, get her in here now. Take several officers. Consider her armed and dangerous."

Thallia slowly stood. "You can't bring her in," she said in a low tone. "She was protecting me. Her only child!"

"Your mother is a murderer," Wynona stated clearly. "She killed your boyfriend, your best friend and she tried to kill me."

"How do you know it was her?" Thallia challenged, her wings spread tightly behind her. Fire was licking the tips of her fingers and Wynona wished Daemon would hurry again.

"Stand down," Rascal said, holding his stun gun up. "Put your powers away, Thallia. Now."

"She's the only person who's ever believed in me!" Thallia shouted. "You can't have her!" Without warning, Thallia burst into flame and Wynona squealed.

"Where's Skymaw!" Chief Ligurio bellowed.

"On his way!" Rascal called back. He released the taser, but the heat from Thallia's flames were too much.

Wynona stumbled back, protecting her face. There had to be something she could do. She had no idea that fairies could be consumed in flame the same way a demon could. She really needed to get back to that library and have some quality research time.

If we live through this, Violet cried. *My fur is being singed.*

Wynona put her hands up. There had to be a spell or something she could do. She tried imagining water, but nothing happened. Meanwhile, Thallia was starting to walk in their direction and fire was spreading across the floor.

"Get behind me," Rascal shouted, shoving Wynona between him and the wall.

"Let me try to contain her," Wynona shouted back.

"It's too dangerous," Rascal answered.

"Then watch my back." Wynona stepped to the side and brought her hands out again. The only thing she could think to do was create another protective barrier, but instead of covering her and the men, she created a dome around Thallia.

The heat from the flame stopped immediately, though Wynona's body broke out in a sweat anyway as she held the magic in place.

Thallia screamed and pounded her flaming hands against the barrier.

"Can you pull out the oxygen?" Chief Ligurio panted. He wiped at his own sweaty forehead.

"I'm not sure how, but I can try," Wynona said through gritted teeth.

"No need!"

Without warning, the purple bubble and flaming fairy were gone. Thallia collapsed to the ground, unconscious, and Wynona felt as if someone had sucker punched her when Daemon stole the magic from the room.

She began to go down, but Rascal caught her around the waist, pulling her upright. "Thanks." She gasped.

Rascal just held her tighter. "Get some cuffs on her," he shouted to the officers pouring into the room.

A hex's thread was wound around Thallia's wrists and Wynona breathed a little easier when Daemon released his hold on the room.

"What's the news on the mother?" Chief Ligurio asked.

Daemon shook his head. "Haskill was just arriving when I did. She wasn't home."

Wynona's heart fell. "She knew. She knew we'd figured it out and she's running."

Chief Ligurio growled. "Not on my watch," he said tightly, marching toward the door. "Pull out the matcha, Ms. Le Doux. We've got a long night ahead."

CHAPTER 27

"Thank you," Wynona said to whatever officer was handing her a glass of water. She drank it far more quickly than was polite, but her body still felt excessively dehydrated after the encounter with Thallia.

"I had no idea fairies could burn like that," Rascal grumbled, slumping into the seat next to her.

Wynona shook her head slowly. "They can't...I don't think. At least, I've never heard or read about it." She stared at the paper cup in her hands, her mind churning as she went over the situation again...for what seemed the hundredth time. "I think I need a better education on creatures than the one I have."

Rascal rubbed her back. "That makes two of us. I've learned more since you joined our force than in the ten years prior." He gave her a half hearted smirk. "What is it about you that brings out all the crazies?"

Wynona glared. "Ha. Ha."

His smile grew and he almost looked like himself again, which gave her hope that they would come back from...whatever it was that had pulled them apart.

Okay... Violet said, coming back from the bathroom. *I think I got most of the soot out of my fur. But let me tell you, the two don't mix well, so don't expect me to be around the next time you want to play with pyrotechnics.*

"I'm not eager to repeat it myself," Wynona assured her familiar. She bent over and put a hand on the floor, allowing Violet to climb on.

Rascal reached over, but hesitated, then dropped his hand before taking the creature. His relationship with Violet had been just as hurt as his bond with Wynona. They were seriously going to have to figure this thing out if life was ever going to get back to normal.

Chief Ligurio came back into the room.

But not until this is over, Wynona lamented to herself.

"Okay. Dad and daughter are both in custody. Their lawyer is here, screaming about the injustice of it all..." Chief Ligurio sighed. "In other words, I think we're on the right track."

"And they don't have any idea where Mrs. Pearlily might have run off to?" Wynona asked.

The vampire shook his head and brushed a hand over his dark, now unruly hair. "She's not one to go on trips by herself, apparently. She's always been dedicated to her family, so they don't have any ideas as to where she might go to hide."

"Isn't there anything we can do?"

"The highways are blocked," Rascal assured her. "There's an APB out, and we're watching the airport over in Cauldron Cove. There's not much else we can do."

Wynona pursed her lips in thought. "She could have gone to the Grove of Secrets..."

Rascal's head jerked her way. "No one ever comes out of there."

"I know, but...if someone was desperate enough, they might give it a try."

Chief Ligurio scoffed. "I don't think she would simply commit suicide this quickly. My guess is she's close to home. She put too much work into saving her daughter to simply disappear for good. She's probably waiting and watching, hoping we'll calm down so she can get back to work."

Doing what? Violet asked sarcastically. *Killing the rest of the population so Thallia can be queen?*

Hush, Wynona said, though there was little reprimand in her tone. She had never personally experienced the love of a mother, but at the moment, Wynona was wondering if her own mother's apathy wasn't preferable to a parent who was willing to kill innocents in order to force their child into compliance. A sudden thought popped into Wynona's head. "We need to talk to Mr. Pearlily about where he really was the night of Dralo's murder," Wynona said softly. She was so tired at this point, she was surprised she could keep her eyes open at all...or that her brain was still running. "Was he covering for his wife? Or himself?"

Chief Ligurio nodded. "Right. I'd forgotten that one." He waved them toward the door. "He's in interrogation room number four."

Wynona stumbled slightly when she got to her feet and Rascal wrapped his arm around her waist.

"You need to go home," he growled.

"We need to finish this," Wynona answered back. "I'm tired of this case taking over. I want my business and my life back."

He grunted in approval and together they walked out of the office and down the hallway.

Daemon came toward them with long strides. "Wynona," he said by way of greeting. "I brought you something." He held out a box with familiar gold writing on the top.

Wynona smiled. She took the offering and breathed deeply. "How did you know the raspberry croissants were my favorite breakfast food?"

He grinned. "When I sent another officer to the imp's, I made sure he got the answers he needed. I'm sorry I don't have any tea for you, but..." He shrugged. "The person who makes the tea is busy."

Wynona waved him off. "That's alright. These will certainly help bring my blood sugar back up and I can find tea in Amaris's desk when she gets in this morning."

"Well done, Skymaw," Rascal said in a low tone.

"Boss," Daemon responded with a nod. He reached his long arm over and opened the room door. "Shall we?"

Wynona straightened her shoulders, refusing to go in leaning so heavily on Rascal, and walked inside. She wanted to devour the fresh pastries in her hands, but she would refrain...mostly. If Mr. Pearlily and his lawyer thought Wynona wouldn't eat at all during their little chat, they were dead wrong. She needed something and Daemon's sweet gesture was just the ticket.

As usual, Wynona sat in a chair by Chief Ligurio and Rascal stood just behind her shoulder. *Want one?* she asked him.

Rascal subtly shook his head. *Later.*

She nodded and took one out, then froze, realizing the weight that was usually sitting on her shoulder was gone. *Violet?*

My pocket, Rascal offered, still keeping his head toward Mr. Pearlily and Mr. Muskgaver. *She fell asleep.*

Wynona let out a small sigh of relief, then delicately bit into her food. It was a credit to Chief Ligurio that he didn't even flinch at the fact that she was eating during an interview, obviously recognizing how much Wynona needed some sustenance.

He did, however, give her a sideways look and raise his eyebrows as if to ask if she were ready.

Wynona nodded, her mouth too full to answer.

Clearing his throat, Chief Ligurio began speaking in the official tone he used in public. "Mr. Pearlily," the vampire began. "You understand that we're searching for your wife in connection with the murders..."

Mr. Pearlily scoffed and folded his large arms over his chest. "I don't know how anyone could think my wife would have anything to do with this mess. You're barking up the wrong tree, Ligurio." The fairy's eyes drifted to Rascal. "Sorry, guess that applies more to you, huh?"

Wynona sent calming vibes immediately when she heard Rascal growl. Really, the dog jokes from other people were getting tiresome. Could no one think of anything new? Poor Rascal always seemed to be the one picked on when it came to low blow insults.

Good thing I can handle it, he replied to her thoughts.

Good thing you didn't growl in response.

He has to learn that I'm the predator...not him.

Wynona mentally shook her head. *Wolves...*

"Are you aware that your daughter has confirmed our suspicions?" Chief Ligurio asked casually.

Mr. Pearlily stilled and his lawyer jumped into action.

"Chief Ligurio, unless you have solid proof, I suggest you be careful with your accusations," the small creature said hesitantly.

"We have the evidence we need for the courtroom," Chief Ligurio said, moving on as if the information wasn't important, though the way Mr. Pearlily blanched, said remark had completed its goal. "But what I want to talk about is *you*, Mr. Pearlily. The night of Dralo's murder, you told us that you were home with your wife." Chief Ligurio typed on his computer, not really going anywhere, but appearing to be pulling up information. "We have information that says otherwise and wanted to allow you the opportunity to amend your statement."

The Pearlily family lawyer stammered. "We...uh..."

Mr. Pearlily's pale face darkened and he snapped his fingers at the small man, who instantly shut up.

Wynona's eyebrows went up. Apparently, Mr. Pearlily had more power than she thought.

Leaning forward onto the desk, Mr. Pearlily narrowed his eyes at Chief Ligurio. "Why don't you tell me what you know and we'll see what we can work out, hm?"

Chief Ligurio scoffed. "See what we can work out? You think your activities are going to find a way past my desk?"

What's he talking about? Wynona asked Rascal.

He's posturing. Hang tight.

Wynona leaned back, hoping she looked confident, even though she was in the middle of eating a croissant and had no idea what was being argued over. What activities? Mr. Pearlily hadn't told them what he'd been doing.

Mr. Pearlily tapped the desk with his knuckles, looking as if he were weighing his options. Finally, he leaned back. "I don't think I should say anything else. My...associates...wouldn't like it."

"Then we'll plan on seeing your wife *and* you in the courtroom," Chief Ligurio said easily. He closed his laptop and began to stand.

Wynona quickly scrambled to follow, but Mr. Pearlily stopped them.

"I can't tell you what you want to know."

Chief Ligurio paused. "But?"

Mr. Pearlily's eyes darted to Wynona and then back to the chief. A sinking feeling started in her gut. "But there's someone who will vouch for me."

No one had missed the look and Chief Ligurio's jaw clenched in anger. "Then you had better send him my way." With renewed energy, he stormed out of the room with Wynona and Rascal hot on his heels.

"Your father is into something," Chief Ligurio said in a tone so low Wynona could barely understand. "His fingers have been in the last two cases and I don't like it." They walked into his office. "Shut the door."

Daemon immediately complied.

"Don't you have something to do, Skymaw?" Chief Ligurio snapped.

"Ms. Le Doux is my first priority," Daemon said bravely. "If you recall my promotion and my promise."

Chief Ligurio huffed but said nothing more.

Wynona was glad for the company. "You're right, Chief," she said, sitting down and settling the box of pastries on the desk. "Though, I can't imagine what it is. Celia mentioned as much when we talked about her leaving the family. He sent her on several odd errands. She delivered envelopes, and later some of the families had noticeable problems."

Chief Ligurio rubbed his forehead and pushed his hair out of his face. His usual pristine appearance had disappeared several hours ago. "We'll come back to that later. I don't have enough information to pursue anything and right now there's a murderer on the loose who needs to be brought in." He sighed. "However, what that conversation does tell me is that Mr. Pearlily was covering for himself that night. I don't think he had any idea his wife didn't stay at home like a good little prisoner."

"Agreed," Rascal added. "His attention has been on his business. It was probably why he was so slow in discovering all the problems with his daughter."

Wynona nodded. "Mrs. Pearlily, who was always around and had nothing else to draw her attention, is the one who noticed and took action." Wynona made a face. "Unethical action, but action nonetheless. She might have even figured that her husband wouldn't notice any of her activities because he was so focused on whatever this thing is with my dad."

"If Pearlily and President Le Doux are getting together, I think it's safe to say other big figures in the community are involved as well," Rascal said softly, his eyes on Wynona.

She nodded. Sometimes she really resented being part of that family. "I think you're right."

He gave her a little wink. "Of course."

Wynona smiled back. She had missed his winking.

Chief Ligurio tapped a pencil against his desk. "I think we've re-hashed things enough tonight. We've got watches all over the city and beyond. There's no one else to talk to and we've pounded all our evidence until I don't want to hear it anymore." He stood. "I'm going home to sleep. I suggest you do the same."

Wynona was slower to climb to her feet. The short sugar burst from the croissant was already fading. "I think I could use some rest myself."

"Prepare yourself, Ms. Le Doux," Chief Ligurio said as he held open the door. "This case might almost be over, but I have a feeling something else is just beginning."

Hating the fact that he was right, Wynona only nodded as she walked out the door.

"And it probably wouldn't hurt to tell your sister as well."

The words were so soft that Wynona stumbled slightly, trying to stop and listen, but instinct told her not to acknowledge the comment. Chief Ligurio and Celia had been a thing at one point in time, but family politics had put a wedge wider than Spell Summit between them. Now they butted heads like two centaurs in a fight ring.

Chief Ligurio's comment, however, told Wynona what she had suspected for a while. Those feelings were far from dead, though neither of the people involved would admit it any time soon.

"I'm driving you home," Rascal warned her. "And sleeping on your couch."

Wynona started to protest, but he put up his hand.

"Until Mrs. Pearlily is behind bars, I'm not leaving you unprotected." He shrugged. "Or at least until your magic is more reliable."

Wynona nodded. "Thank you," she said softly. Leaning around him, she smiled at Daemon. "And thank you. I'll see you soon."

Daemon gave her a mock salute as Rascal took her hand. Wynona let herself be led safe and protected in Rascal's company. She didn't want to think anymore, didn't want to feel. She simply wanted to give into the exhaustion calling her name. She'd deal with the full fallout later today, after a much needed date with her bed.

CHAPTER 28

Wynona slowly forced her heavy eyelids open. She had slept like the dead and the sun was just coming up outside her window. *Ugh.* Pushing up onto her elbows, she let herself adjust to the dimness of the room. Glancing at the wall clock, she realized the sun was setting, not rising. She'd literally slept all day.

Lazy lugabed, Violet teased.

"Aren't you the one always saying you need your beauty sleep?" Wynona asked just before yawning.

Yeah, well...you're not done quite yet.

Wynona scowled and sat upright. Her head spun and she had to wait a moment before dropping her legs over the side. Pressing a hand to the side of her head, Wynona moaned a little.

"Wy?" Rascal called from outside. He knocked. "Are you decent?"

"Come in," she croaked.

Rascal was at her side in an instant. "What do you need? I can tell your head's hurting."

She nodded. "Yeah. Hang on. I'm gonna try and heal it." She held still and called her magic up. When Violet climbed up her back and nestled against her neck, Wynona's shaky control settled. She was obviously still weak from the injury yesterday. Magic apparently healed the wound, but couldn't seem to speed the recovery. Wynona sighed as she felt the headache subside.

Rascal relaxed as well. "Good evening, sleepyhead," he said with a tired smile.

Wynona knew her smile couldn't have been much better. "Did you sleep at all?"

He shrugged. "A bit."

The rings under his eyes were darker than before, so Wynona knew he was fudging the truth. "You need rest," she insisted.

"After we catch a killer."

"You can't protect me from everything," Wynona insisted.

"No, you're right." Rascal put his hands on his hips. "But I'll protect you from what I can and right now, this is something I can do."

"Rascal..."

He raised his eyebrows.

"Are we...are we okay? Are you regretting...us?"

His shoulders sank. "No," he said hoarsely. "I would never regret that. But there's a...thing with my wolf... We're..." He pushed out a harsh breath and shoved his hands in his wild hair. "The moon...it's..."

"Wynona? Are you awake?" Celia poked her head in the door, only giving Rascal a cursory glance. Once she saw her sister was up, Celia came in fully and leaned against the doorjamb. "How are you feeling?"

"Better," Wynona said. She stood and paused, waiting to see if her vision would spin again, but her healing had helped tremendously. Slowly, she walked across the room. "But I think I need to eat."

Violet scampered around Wynona's feet and hurried down the hall. *You snooze, you lose!*

Wynona grinned as her familiar disappeared from view.

"Actually..." Celia drawled.

Wynona paused and turned around.

Celia made a face and wiggled her fingers around her head. "You might want a mirror first."

Wynona's hand came up to her head and she realized her hair was wilder than Rascal's. She winced, not even wanting to think about what Rascal was seeing.

Nothing but a beautiful woman.

She gave him a grateful look. "I'll be right back."

Prideful, Violet sent her way. *Absolutely shameful, Wynona. You've seen me with messy fur.*

Not the same thing! Wynona argued.

Violet snickered.

Making it into the bathroom, Wynona quietly groaned when she saw what she looked like. Medusa could have been her twin. *Think magic can fix this?* she asked her familiar.

Doesn't hurt to try. You're getting better.

As of yet, Wynona hadn't tried to use her magic for her personal looks, but today might just be the day to start. Channeling the electricity, she used one finger to focus a very small stream and pointed over and around her head, taming her hair into submission, fixing her mascara and glossing her lips. "Much better," Wynona said, smiling at her reflection. "But I'll need to change the clothes the old fashioned way." Shifting materials was definitely going to take more practice than simply straightening a headful of knots.

"There she is," Rascal said when she opened the bathroom door. His smile was still tight, but at least she was seeing it more often.

Wynona ran her finger under his eye. "Want me to see if I can fix this?"

He shook his head. "Good old fashioned sleep will take care of it...eventually." He took her hand. "Come on. Let's feed you and make plans."

"What are we planning?" Wynona asked as they walked into the kitchen.

"How to catch Mrs. Pearlily," Celia answered.

Wynona stopped. "We're going to set a trap?"

Rascal made a face. "I don't like it."

"Of course not," Celia argued. "It'll probably mean having Wynona be bait."

Wynona nearly fell into a chair at the table. "Bait? Really? What makes you think she'd risk coming after me?"

Celia brought a plate of pancakes to the table. "Because you're the one who figured it all out."

"But Mrs. Pearlily doesn't know that."

Celia shook her head and went back to the kitchen. "She knows."

"Prim was with me that day."

"She knows!" Celia insisted.

Wynona put her face in her hands. "This is crazy. After this case, I'm officially quitting."

Good. The pay stinks, Violet added.

"Wait...you're getting paid?" Rascal asked in fake surprise.

Wynona smiled, but it was more because it was the first joke she'd heard from him that sounded like his old self. "Yeah...I get five bucks for every killer I bring in."

"So you're like a bounty hunter," Rascal finished. "Niiiice."

"You need better weapons," Celia said wryly. "A purple mouse isn't exactly fearsome."

I'll show her fearsome...

Wynona cleared her throat. "Did you cook this, Celia?"

Celia dropped off the syrup and a plate of bacon before sitting herself. "Yeah. It's no big deal."

"I didn't know you could cook."

Celia kept her stoic look, but her pink cheeks showed her feelings. "I...spent some time with the cook when Mom and Dad weren't looking."

Wynona gave a commiserating smile. "Which was often."

Celia nodded. "Which was often." She grabbed a stack of flap-jacks and piled them on her plate.

Wynona had to admire her sister's appetite. It was twice as much as Wynona ate. The meal was done in relative silence and Rascal made sure there was no bacon left by the end. The sustenance went a long way in helping Wynona feel stronger, though she still thought she could sleep for the next week and not be bothered by it.

"Okay..." Celia rubbed her hands together and pushed her plate to the side. "On to more exciting things."

"Yeah...murder is very exciting," Wynona drawled.

Celia's sharp grin was more than simply devious. It was downright dangerous. "So she's a fairy."

Wynona nodded.

"And she's already killed two people."

Wynona nodded again while Rascal huffed.

"She beat you over the head with a baseball bat."

Rascal's growl echoed through the room.

"Easy, Wolfy," Celia said. "I'm simply laying out the facts."

Wynona put her hand on his leg. "Yes. She must have been hovering over the ground, though I couldn't feel the air from her wings. Otherwise she's too small to hit me at the angle she did."

Celia nodded. "Have you noticed the pattern here?"

Wynona raised her eyebrows and looked at Rascal before going back to Celia. "Uh..."

"The shop," Celia insisted. "*All* the attacks happened at the shop."

Wynona paused. "She has a way inside," she breathed. "How did I not see that?"

Celia shrugged. "Probably the blow to the head. I've heard they hurt."

Wynona rubbed her forehead. "Each and every attack. I mean, I knew they'd all happened there, but I hadn't put together that it meant she had a way inside. Thallia even said the door was wide open. There was no forced entry, which is part of why Dralo's burglary idea didn't make sense. And Edana met her there as well, meaning she knew that Mrs. Pearlily had access." Wynona turned wide eyes to Rascal. "But how? How did she get a key?"

Celia practically cackled. "I know this one."

Wynona's head snapped in her sister's direction. "What?"

Celia stuck her nose in the air in triumph. "Did you really think I'd sit around doing nothing while you went to the station? Just because Mr. Sourpuss didn't want me to come along didn't mean I wasn't going to try and solve the case."

"Why didn't you say something before?"

Celia gave her a look. "You were half dead and slept all day. When did you want me to tell you?"

"Fine, fine." Wynona waved her hands in the air. "Tell us now."

Celia leaned in, her eyes glowing with excitement. "Sequoia Pearlily is the majority shareholder in the corporation that bought your building when what's-his-name went to jail."

Wynona's jaw dropped. "What?"

Celia nodded. "And the best part is...her husband has no idea. He's got this massive real estate company and his wife uses it to get herself all the inside deals, since he can't keep his mouth shut. And he has no idea she's the one buying all the properties."

Wynona slowly shook her head while Rascal whistled low.

"How in the paranormal world did you figure that out?" he asked, his eyes narrowing.

Celia smirked. "I'm guessing you don't really want to know." She studied her nails. "A girl has to have some secrets, you know. And when you've grown up doing the dirty work for a dark wizard...you pick up a few things."

Wynona reached across the table to rest her hand on her sister's. "One of these days we need to address what Dad's up to."

Celia jerked away. "Good luck with that. I want nothing to do with him." She stood. "Now. Let's go to the shop and see if we can set something up."

"Now?" Wynona asked, jumping to her feet.

No time like the present, Violet said, scrambling down from the table. *She's devious. I like it.*

Rascal stood as well. "I need to get the chief in on this."

"Then call him," Celia called over her shoulder. "But I'm not waiting."

"If you think you're doing this without me, you're crazy or stupid," Prim said from the doorway. "I don't know which." She was in her human form and stood with her legs spread and arms folded.

"When did you get here?" Wynona asked.

"I came to check on how you were healing and your tulips outside said Sissy was forming a plan." Prim shrugged. "So I sat and let them share everything they heard." She grinned. "Tulips never could keep a secret."

"I don't like this," Rascal warned.

"Don't be such a fuddy-duddy," Celia shouted from the garage. "Call the big bad vamp and he can meet us there. But let's get this show on the road so that Wynona doesn't have to look over her shoulder for the rest of her life." Celia's dark head came back inside. "I'd deny it in court, but I'm growing just a little fond of her." In the blink of an eye, she was gone again and Wynona heard an engine start up.

"She has a car?" Prim asked.

Wynona shrugged. "I don't know. There isn't room for one in the garage. My Vespa's in there."

The roar of a motorcycle burst through the room and Celia sped down the driveway in a cloud of dust. The silence that followed was deafening.

"No wonder she and Chief were an item," Rascal grumbled. "He's always had a thing for the edgy girls." He took Wynona's hand, who was too shocked to move on her own. "Come on. Let's get over there before she does something we'll all regret."

"I'll meet you there!" Prim called, rushing back to her own vehicle.

"I think I awoke in an alternate universe," Wynona said dazedly as Rascal guided her into his truck.

"As long as we're still together, I'm just fine with that," Rascal said. He kissed her nose and stepped back. "Buckle up, beautiful. We're after a killer."

CHAPTER 29

The shop was dark and slightly ominous as Wynona and Rascal pulled up. "Pull around back," she said softly.

Rascal followed orders. His large truck took up nearly the entire alley. There was barely enough room to open their doors and climb out. Celia's motorcycle was right next to the kitchen door and she was waiting, leaning casually against the building.

As Wynona and Rascal approached, an unsettled feeling came into Wynona's stomach. It was strong enough that she paused and put a hand on her belly.

"What is it?" Rascal asked, stopping with her.

"I don't know," Wynona responded honestly. "I just...I have kind of a bad feeling about all this."

Rascal's eyes began to glow and he took a hard look around the alley, sniffing the air as he went.

Celia's footsteps joined them. "What's the hold up?"

"Wynona has a feeling," Rascal said, still searching the area. "I don't see or smell anything."

"There's no one here," Celia scoffed. "Nothing has moved since I got here. Now unlock the door and let's see if we can set up something."

"You're right," Wynona said, rubbing her forehead. "I just... Sorry...I guess I'm still overly tired."

"Which is completely understandable, but you'll sleep much better if we get this finished once and for all," Celia pressed. "Come on."

Wynona followed her sister back to the building, then unlocked the door and let everyone inside. "Should we get Lusgu?" Wynona asked Violet. She hadn't managed to see the brownie since he'd been knocked unconscious from the grimoires. Wynona was worried about him, but she also couldn't force him to answer when she called. His portal seemed to be safe enough from what happened inside the shop, but she didn't want to risk him getting hurt if she didn't have to.

Violet poked her nose up from Rascal's pocket. *I'll go talk to him.*

Rascal took her out of his pocket and carefully set the mouse on the ground, where Violet promptly raced across the floor and disappeared into the corner.

Wynona took a deep breath, then turned to walk toward the dining room, but nearly ran into Celia, who was standing watching the corner with a shocked look on her face.

Celia pointed to the spot. "What in all of purgatory just happened?"

"Lusgu, my janitor lives there."

"He has a permanent portal?"

Wynona nodded.

"Can you go in?"

Wynona shook her head. "No. I've tried knocking and entering a couple times, but only Violet seems immune to whatever wards he has up."

Celia's eyes narrowed and she was silent for a moment before shaking her head. "You're surrounded by some of the oddest things and you don't even know it."

"You have no idea," Wynona murmured. She pushed open the door to the dining room and flipped on the light. "So now what?" she asked as she walked to the center. When no one answered, Wynona spun around, but she was alone. "Rascal? Celia?"

"I'm afraid they aren't coming, dear."

That sinking feeling was back and Wynona felt as if she might be sick. They had come to set a trap, but it appeared they had walked into one instead. Slowly, Wynona spun. "Hello, Mrs. Pearlily."

The fairy's usual ingratiating smile was gone and now it was as sharp and calculated as any villain Wynona had ever run into. *Rascal? Can you hear me?*

That sinister smile grew. "I'm afraid he can't."

Wynona's eyes bugged out of her head. "How can you hear me?"

Mrs. Pearlily tapped her temple. "I'm not quite an ordinary fairy," she said simply, then clasped her hands in front of her. "Though, no one but my daughter knows. She...inherited...a few of my family gifts that tend to run through the female line, so there was no way to hide it."

"Mr. Pearlily has no idea, does he?" Wynona asked. She needed to keep the fairy talking. Wynona wasn't the least bit prepared for this and had no idea how to handle it. What extra powers did Mrs. Pearlily have? And how could Wynona protect herself against them?

Apparently, she could read thoughts and she had also kept Celia and Rascal from following Wynona into the dining room. *Maybe I just need to address her as another witch until I know more.*

"I had plans for you and I, you know," Mrs. Pearlily said as she slowly began to walk across the room.

Wynona immediately brought her magic to her fingers, purple sparks falling to the carpet as she moved to counter the woman's movements. "I'm sure you did. They went awry, didn't they?"

Mrs. Pearlily rolled her eyes. "I wasn't actually trying to kill you last night," she argued. "Sometimes my...powers...get a little out of control." She smirked. "I'm sure you know all about that, don't you?"

Wynona tilted her head. "I'm far more in control than I used to be," she defended. Maybe if she could intimidate Mrs. Pearlily, it would hold her off long enough for Chief Ligurio and the rest of the precinct to arrive. She brought her hands up and rested them on a chair, showing off the dancing current. "Are you sure you want to do this? It doesn't have to be a fight, Sequoia. Someone's bound to get hurt." Wynona hoped that using Mrs. Pearlily's first name would help put them on more even ground. Obviously, the fairy had a false sense of connection and Wynona was absolutely going to exploit that.

Sequoia's smile was confident and not the least bit intimidated. "I'm afraid that someone is going to be you and your friends, but I wanted to speak to you by yourself before I had to take care of you."

Wynona spread the purple up her arms. "Why? We hardly know each other."

"But we could have," Sequoia insisted. She sidestepped again. "Between our powers and our connections to the right people, you and I could have ruled beyond the borders of Hex Haven."

"You really think you're a match for my father?"

Sequoia scoffed. "Your father. He has no idea what's going on right under his nose." Sequoia began to walk away from Wynona, waving a careless hand in the air. "He thinks we don't know about his secret meetings or his plans, but anyone with any sense and an ear in the underworld knows exactly what's happening." She spun. "And he won't succeed."

Wynona folded her arms over her chest. "You're so sure? How do you plan to stop him?" Wynona had no idea what Mrs. Pearlily was referring to, but it gave them a direction in the conversation and if Wynona managed to survive this ambush, it might help them figure out what to do about President Le Doux.

Mrs. Pearlily opened her mouth, then stopped and her face lit up. "You have no idea, do you?" Her laugh was shrill and painful, like claws on a chalkboard. "You don't know what your father is doing!" Sequoia leaned forward in her amusement and Wynona took the opportunity to put more distance between them. "STOP!" Mrs. Pearlily shouted and Wynona obeyed. She didn't want to anger the insane woman...yet.

"Alright," Wynona admitted carefully. "I don't know what he's planning. Would you care to enlighten me?"

Mrs. Pearlily shook her head, her smile back. "No. I don't think I will." She shrugged. "After all, what would be the point? You won't survive our little meeting here, so I'm not going to waste my time explaining it all." She made a face. "It's very tedious, after all."

"But you also have plans," Wynona urged. "Tell me, why did you want me to be a part of them? Was Thallia also part of them? You worked so hard to keep her from making a stupid mistake with her life when it came to Dralo. What part is she supposed to play?"

"Like I said," Mrs. Pearlily responded, "she inherited some family powers. They would have been useful." Her face darkened. "But her shallow stupidity is making it difficult to keep her useful. She'll ruin herself in the media before I can make my move and while my reputation is spotless, hers will be too tarnished to have her at my side." Mrs. Pearlily gave a beleaguered sigh. "I suppose with you and her out of the picture, I'll simply have to find other help. It's so difficult these days."

"Your reputation won't stay untarnished if you kill me," Wynona added. "The police know it was you. They know you killed Dralo because your husband hadn't caught on to Thallia's antics. They know you killed Edana because you thought she knew too much."

"Yes..." Mrs. Pearlily pursed her lips. "That one was unfortunate. Her family could have been useful, but only if they all believed my public persona. I was sure Thallia had shared her suspicions, but apparently, I acted in haste." Mrs. Pearlily tilted her head in a careless gesture. "I'll take better care next time."

"How will you manage to do anything after this spectacle?" Wynona pressed. "The whole paranormal world will know your involvement. Killing me won't stop the rest of the police station from taking you in or declaring your activities to the public."

"I won't be able to stay in Hex Haven, that's for sure," Mrs. Pearlily said with a shake of her head. "But that doesn't mean I can't start over somewhere else. A new name, a new hairdo." She grinned. "And maybe even a new husband. This one has gotten difficult."

"And what about Thallia?" Wynona asked softly. "She's your daughter."

Mrs. Pearlily dropped her gaze and shrugged. It was clear she was trying to pretend she didn't care, but even an evil mother apparently loved her child. "She made her choices," Mrs. Pearlily defended. "I tried to help, but she's continued to push me away." Her eyes came up and hardened in a way that let Wynona know their time of chatting was coming to an end. "Besides, the police have her. I can't save her and myself, so..."

The implication was clear. Mrs. Pearlily was going to do what she needed to do in order to keep herself free and above the nasty fallout of the killing spree.

The fairy put one hand in the air and snapped her fingers. "Now...I think we've chatted enough, dear. I'm terribly sorry that you felt so compelled to search for answers, but at least now you have them."

Wynona's eyes kept darting around, her senses on high alert. What had happened when Mrs. Pearlily snapped? It had to mean something, but she couldn't figure it out.

Mrs. Pearlily simply stayed still, smiling as if this had all been a lark.

Wynona's nose twitched. She could smell...something. She took in a deep sniff, frantically racking her brain for recognition. The smell grew stronger and her head snapped toward the kitchen. "No..." she breathed.

Mrs. Pearlily laughed again, sounding like fingernails on a chalkboard.

"What did you do?" Wynona demanded, her body surging with emotional magic.

"What do you think I did?" Mrs. Pearlily taunted.

Wynona fought the desire to scream. "Fire..." she whimpered. "You started a fire."

CHAPTER 30

Wynona's first thought was to run to the kitchen and make sure her loved ones got out, but she knew better. Just as Rascal and Celia had been kept from coming in, Wynona was positive she wouldn't be able to get out. She'd have to trust their ability to survive long enough for her to take care of Mrs. Pearlily. And she would take care of the fairy. Wynona was done with being a pawn. She was tired of creatures who thought they could simply walk over those around them, willy nilly.

Her father being the main one and now Mrs. Pearlily. Both of them had the same aspirations and Wynona knew she was one of the few who had the power to put a stop to it.

This one first.

Wynona still had very little training in offensive magic, but she decided now was the perfect time to start training. Wiggling her fingers, she built a large purple ball in her hand and threw it at her unprepared companion.

"Oof!" Mrs. Pearlily was thrown backward, the spell sizzling against her dress and burning a few holes when Mrs. Pearlily slammed into the antique teacups cupboard, shattering dozens of cups.

Wynona winced at the loss. *They're just things,* she reminded herself. *They can be replaced.* With Mrs. Pearlily indisposed, Wynona reached toward the kitchen door and began to use her magic to pull it open.

It resisted, still stuck in whatever magic Mrs. Pearlily had used. "Come on," Wynona ground out. She tightened her grip, every muscle in her body tensed until she felt ready to snap, and pulled.

The door shook, but didn't move.

Sweat began to pour down Wynona's neck when she saw the smoke coming out from under the door. The entire kitchen must be engulfed in flames at this point. "Please have made it out the back," Wynona whispered, still tugging on the door.

A low, gravelling laugh caught her attention and Wynona's efforts waned slightly. The sound grew harsher and louder and movement forced Wynona to stop yanking on the door and turn.

Her eyes widened and Wynona had to swallow a scream when the creature rising from the floor unfolded itself. "You're a demon," Wynona managed to utter, though she was scared into near paralysis.

Mrs. Pearlily, nearly unrecognizable at this point, laughed. The chalkboard sound had turned to gravel and shook the walls. Just like her daughter, the fairy was engulfed in flames, but instead of simply being a burning fairy, Mrs. Pearlily was something...more. She was nearly seven feet tall with muscles usually associated with a centaur. Her dress was torn to accommodate her new shape and her wings hung clear to the ground. Each twitch of the appendages sent a skittering of fire in a new direction and the back wall of Wynona's dining room began to go up in flames, starting with the curtains, which took little encouragement to become ash.

"Want to reconsider your desire to take me in?" Mrs. Pearlily asked in a low tone.

Wynona realized she was speaking to the voice who had tricked Celia into thinking they were Mr. Pearlily. There was nothing feminine about the creature in front of her. "Never."

The creature shrugged. "Demons don't have a conscience," she explained. "That was the best gift my father could have given me. Too bad for you that your grandmother ruined yours."

"Caring for others has made me stronger," Wynona argued back. She began trying to figure out how to fight the creature. Fire wasn't going to work. Water? "I pity you."

Mrs. Pearlily didn't like that response and her roar brought down any remaining dishes that were still hanging onto the shelves.

Wynona screamed and covered her head, her protective bubble coming up just in time to stop a fireball aimed directly at her chest. Wynona's breathing was coming so quickly now that she was seeing black spots in the side of her vision. *Get yourself together!* she screamed internally.

With the forcefield holding for the moment, Wynona put her focus back on the door. She could hold off Mrs. Pearlily for a moment, but her family might be out of time. That door needed to open now.

Closing her eyes and ignoring the fire banging against her bubble, she put her focus back on the door. She allowed her senses to roam over the magic stopping the door from opening. Just as before, when she'd tried to open a safe, Wynona could see tiny flashes and realized Mrs. Pearlily had essentially cast a net over the door. It was built with some kind of black magic that felt a little like metal. Definitely something from her underworld repertoire.

But how to open it?

Wynona's bubble shook and she opened her eyes, jerking when she realized the entire shop was now in flames. The wooden tables and benches, the couches and afghans, the decorative pillows were long gone and the throw rug was disappearing.

"WYNONA!" came a bellow from the kitchen area, followed by a loud round of hacking and coughing.

"Rascal." Wynona nearly collapsed. They were still alive. She checked the net again. Why could she hear them?

Another roar shook the building and Wynona turned to see Mrs. Pearlily throwing and slamming furniture around the room. The demon was completely out of control at this point. She wasn't flinging fireballs, and she wasn't trying to kill Wynona. She was simply destroying, which was the very thing demons did best.

Rascal, can you hear me? Wynona shouted into the space in her mind. She knew there was a possibility that Mrs. Pearlily could still hear her, but if she'd lost herself to the needs of her demon side, maybe it didn't matter.

WY! You're alive!

I'm here, Wynona said as calmly as she could. *I'm trying to get the door to open. Stand back as much as you can. Her spell is weakening because she's lost herself to her demon.*

DEMON? He raged.

Wynona shut down the communication. She needed to concentrate. Weakened or not, it was still going to be hard to handle. She closed her eyes again, adding more strength to her bubble to keep the fire and debris from hitting her, and went back to the magical net.

She searched, one chain at a time, starting at the bottom, to find a point she could break. There had to be something...there!

Wynona barked out a laugh, then immediately forced herself to focus again. Even with her bubble, the room was getting too hot. She was going to pass out from the heat if she didn't get out of there...now.

Wynona knew her next step was rudimentary at best, but she didn't have any other ideas. Imagining her magic as a set of wire cutters, she began to work on the weakest link. It took a few tries, but she managed to get it cut.

A yelp let her know that Mrs. Pearlily had felt the cut. Opening her eyes, Wynona's heart sank when the demon was looking directly at her. Her time to work had officially ended. Crouching down to avoid the couch being hurled her direction, Wynona sent hundreds of wire cutters toward the door. *Snap! Snap!* They began working their way through the metal threads and with each one, Mrs. Pearlily screamed.

"WY!" Rascal's voice was louder. The spell was growing thin.

"Take cover!" Wynona screamed.

Mrs. Pearlily picked up the china cabinet and instead of throwing it at Wynona, aimed at the door. Wood splintering on wood made Wynona's eardrums hurt and her gut clench.

Heat burst through the room as the kitchen fire was released, only to be met with another fire.

Rascal? Where are you? Wynona could barely breathe. Even her bubble wasn't enough at this point. The shop was a total loss. There wouldn't be anything that could be salvaged at this point. The only reason she was still alive was because of her magic, but with each moment, Wynona could feel herself growing weaker. It was becoming too much, holding off the fire and keeping oxygen in her space.

On the floor, Rascal finally answered.

Wynona blew out a breath and got down on all fours. She peered into the flames and saw a black mass headed her way. The blanket was sizzling and Wynona knew the wet fabric was the only reason Celia and Rascal were still alive.

Throwing out her hand, she put a bubble over them and began to pull. Rascal was cursing in her mind, but she couldn't answer him and drag them in at the same time. With a final *pop,* she pulled them into her space and tore off the blanket.

Celia collapsed, coughing and heaving against the floorboards.

Rascal gulped in air, his face bright red and his clothes nearly burned off his back. His skin was cracked and bleeding and Wynona immediately burst into tears.

"Not yet." He gasped. "Not yet. We have to get out first."

Biting her cheek so hard she tasted blood, Wynona nodded. She would get them out, then heal him. "Come on," she whispered. "Stay close."

Staying on the floor, Wynona picked their way through the stubble, avoiding the worst of the fire, and made their way to the front door. She could hear Mrs. Pearlily shouting and screaming and now working her way through the kitchen with all the pots and dishes.

The sounds of the destruction were as terrifying as they were re-lieving. As long as the demon was in the kitchen, she wasn't near Wynona.

"Wait!" Rascal shouted when Wynona reached up to open the front door. He grabbed the last of the blanket they had used to survive. "It's hot." Using the fabric, he gritted his teeth and jerked the door open.

Wynona threw herself over Rascal and Celia when the air hit their spot and they were thrown out the door in the explosion. Her shield burst when they landed on the sidewalk, each rolling in a slightly different direction.

The heat coming from the shop was so intense that the sky looked wavy, but Wynona couldn't bring herself to move.

"Wy," Rascal whispered. He crawled over to her. "Wy, are you al-right?"

She didn't speak right away, just taking his hand and squeezing it. It was one of the few parts of his body that didn't have terrible burns. "Hold on," she finally whispered. Her throat felt raw and her lungs didn't want to work, but Wynona knew she wouldn't be able to concentrate unless Rascal was well.

"You don't have to—" Rascal stopped his protest and groaned as his skin healed and knit itself back together. He was still covered in soot and flushed with heat, but the fresh pink of his back was a welcome sight. "Thank you," he said, his voice much more normal now.

Wynona coughed and nodded. "Celia?"

"Yourself first," he insisted.

Wynona shook her head and rolled to her side. Celia was laying just a few feet away, not moving except for her chest, which rose and fell in short, erratic bursts. Wynona grabbed at the grass, trying to crawl over.

"I've got you," Rascal said, trying to pick her up. His strength, however, was still weak and he stumbled.

"Let me."

Wynona looked up to see Daemon standing above them.

Prim stood at his side, tears streaming down her cheeks as she looked down, then up, then down again. "Oh, Nona..."

Rascal tried to pick Wynona up again, but collapsed again to his knees.

"I've got her," Daemon said softly. He knelt and carefully gathered Wynona in his arms before standing back up. "To Celia?"

Wynona nodded, not trusting herself to speak without coughing.

Daemon walked over and knelt down and laid Wynona by her sister. Chief Ligurio's red eyes came up from his place on Celia's other side, his face tight with tension. "Anything you can do, Ms. Le Doux?" he asked, his voice low and shaking slightly with anxiety.

Wynona took her sister's hand. Celia didn't have the same burns that Rascal did, but her lungs hadn't held up to the smoke very well. The healing was quick, but Wynona knew that Celia would feel weak for quite some time.

Celia blinked and made to sit up, but her arms shook.

"Easy," Chief Liguirio scolded. He made to reach out, but stopped himself.

"Not until that demon is sent back to where it belongs," Celia said through gritted teeth. She got herself sitting upright and looked at the building. The fire lit her face before she turned to Wynona. "Heal yourself," she snapped. "We have work to do."

"What do you think you're doing?" Chief Ligurio shouted as Celia began to climb to her feet.

"Wynona," Celia demanded. "Come on."

Hating it, but knowing her sister was right, Wynona closed her eyes and focused on the cuts, bruises and burns she had sustained. More than anything, it was her energy that needed to be replenished, but magic couldn't help that. Reaching for Daemon, Wynona climbed to her feet, leaning against her friend. "What now?"

"You need to use your purple shield thing to contain the fire," Celia said quickly. "Otherwise we're going to lose the whole neighborhood."

Wynona glanced at the other buildings and realized her sister was right. Already her neighbors' paint jobs were looking scorched. It wouldn't be long now before the fire spread. She reached out, but her magic sputtered. "I...don't know if I can."

Celia scoffed. "You're supposed to be the greatest witch we've ever had."

"Lay off," Rascal said as he limped their way. "She just finished saving your life."

"And she needs to save a few others," Celia argued back. She swayed and Chief Ligurio put an arm around her waist. Celia flinched, but didn't argue. "My magic isn't enough and I can't create a shield." Her black eyes slammed into Wynona's. "This is all on you. If you think Mom and Dad won't use this as an excuse to take us back, you're an idiot. Do it now, or you're going to lose everything you've worked so hard for."

Wynona clenched her jaw and closed her eyes. Her magic had responded to Celia's harsh, but truthful speech. Reaching out, she took Rascal's hand and squeezed it tightly. She needed something to ground her since Violet..."VIOLET!" Wynona screamed, realizing Lusgu and her familiar were still inside.

Rascal tightened their connection and pulled Wynona back into his chest. "She was still in the portal. We have to assume they're safe. But they can't come out until you've put out the fire."

Wynona nodded, her tears coming in a torrent. She forced her eyes closed again and let herself lean into Rascal. She didn't know how he had the strength to hold her up, but she wouldn't worry about it for now.

Normally Wynona did everything she could to contain her magic, but this time, she knew she wouldn't be strong enough. It was time to open the floodgates. She welcomed the tsunami and felt her body jolt when the magic slammed into her with the weight of a sledgehammer.

"You've got this," Rascal whispered in her ear.

Her best magical performances had all happened when she had imagined the scene in her mind, and Wynona did just that. She built a mass of purple above the shop and slowly, carefully, began to let it drip like paint, until it surrounded the building on all sides. Her whole body was shaking as the strength of the fire tried to escape the confines of the shield, but Wynona held tight. Lusgu, Violet and all the shops on her street depended on it. She *refused* to fail them.

A collective sigh let her know her plan had worked, but it still wasn't over. "How do I put it out?" she asked.

"It needs oxygen to survive," Daemon announced. "Won't it simply starve inside the bubble?"

"Not fast enough," Chief Ligurio growled.

He must have seen what was coming because just as Wynona moved to open her eyes, she felt something slam into the shield.

"What is that?" Prim screeched.

"I believe it's Mrs. Pearlily," Rascal answered.

"Hang on," Celia said. She grabbed Wynona's other hand and another burst of power went through Wynona's failing body.

"What are you doing?" Rascal demanded. "She can't take any more."

Celia didn't answer. Instead, she closed her eyes the same way Wynona had and her body tensed. "Air. Is. My. Specialty," she ground out.

Wynona felt something foreign work its way through her system and then leave in a rush of wind. The air swirled up next to the shield and through the combined magic, passed straight through.

She watched in awe as a funnel began to build at the top of the bubble, causing the fire to swirl into a tornado. Wynona tightened her knees, the power of the storm pushing against her wall.

"Just a little more," Celia said through her clenched jaw.

Wynona's fingers felt broken as Celia squeezed her so hard, but finally, *finally,* the air funnel headed straight up, moving through the shield for several long seconds with a fierce hissing noise.

Everyone waited anxiously for several seconds before the fire left in the space sputtered and died out. Leaving a burnt shell and an unconscious demon in the rubble.

Celia was panting and fell into Chief Ligurio, who was still waiting by her side. "There," she said breathlessly. "It's done." Black eyes rolled into Celia's head and she promptly passed out.

Chief Ligurio's vampire reflexes kicked in and he swept the witch's feet up, holding her gently against his chest. "Call the clean up crew," he ground out as he walked past Daemon. "Strongclaw, you and Ms. Le Doux get back to the house. Now."

"Not until I know they're alright," Wynona said weakly.

I'm fine, Violet responded. *We can't come out yet. But go home. I'll see you soon.*

With the last of her fears assuaged, Wynona's knees buckled. Strong arms she recognized, but that weren't the ones she wanted, picked her up and headed toward Rascal's truck.

"I'll be by as soon as I can," Daemon assured her as he buckled her in. "Until then, you'll be in good hands." Daemon nodded across the seat as Rascal climbed wearily into his spot.

"Thanks," Rascal muttered.

"Anytime, boss," Daemon replied. He winked at Wynona. "Always enjoy holding a beautiful woman in my arms."

Wynona almost smiled when Rascal sighed. "I don't even have the energy to growl," he told his officer. "Get out of here."

Daemon gave Wynona another grin before closing her door.

"Let's go home," he told her.

Wynona leaned her head back. "I don't think I'm going to leave for at least a month."

Rascal chuckled in an exhausted tone. "That's the best thing you've said in a long time."

CHAPTER 31

H er tiny cottage had never been such a welcome sight when Rascal parked his truck in the driveway. "Celia's motorcycle is still at the building," Wynona said. "She'll be so upset. What if it got burned?"

"We'll figure all that out," Rascal assured her. "Right now, we have other things to focus on."

Wynona nodded and climbed down from her seat. Her legs barely held her, but Rascal wasn't in much better shape. They held hands while they went inside where Chief Ligurio was helping Celia onto the couch. She must have woken up during their drive over.

"Do you need another healing?" Wynona asked her sister.

Celia shook her head. "No. I need sleep."

"And tea," Wynona insisted.

"Not happening," Rascal said firmly.

Wynona smiled and squeezed his hand. "This one won't take much energy." Wiggling her fingers, she had the tea prepare itself and only waited a few minutes before the tray had landed on the coffee table with four steaming cups before she sat down herself. "We'll all feel better after this," Wynona assured them.

Rascal sighed. "You shouldn't have wasted your strength."

Wynona leaned her head against his shoulder. "It's never a waste to help people," she said right before breaking into a large yawn. "Plus, the tea will give us energy to finish what we need to." Wynona looked at Chief Ligurio. "Sorry I don't have a drink you'd prefer."

He grunted. "It's fine."

Wynona sipped her brew and closed her eyes. It seemed like it had been too long since she'd simply sat and had a hot cup of tea.

"What's in this?" Celia asked, glaring at her cup.

"Blackberry and ginger," Wynona informed her. "It'll help your body heal."

Celia made a noncommittal noise, but picked up the cup and sniffed at it.

"She's not going to poison you," Rascal said tightly.

"Granny had a tendency to add...*extras*...to her tea," Celia mused. "And since she was your teacher, I had no way of knowing if you would be the same."

Wynona frowned. "What?"

"Later, ladies," Chief Ligurio said in his official police voice. He set his own cup down and leaned his elbows onto his knees. "Right now I want answers."

Wynona glanced at Rascal, who shrugged. "You want to tell it, or me?"

Wynona sighed. "I suppose it should be me, since I'm the one who was in the room with Sequoia."

Chief Ligurio gave her his full attention and Wynona braced herself. There were going to be a lot of questions.

Forty five minutes later, they managed to reach the point where Wynona, Rascal and Celia had been thrown out of the shop by the air hitting the fire.

"You were lucky the whole thing didn't come down on your head," Chief Ligurio muttered.

Wynona nodded. "I agree. But I think Mrs. Pearlily was doing something to keep it up. There was too much fire too fast for it to have not collapsed."

"Speaking of..." Rascal cleared his throat. "Where was the fire department? Didn't someone call them?"

Chief Ligurio snorted. "Tending to a false alarm on the other side of the city."

"Seriously?" Wynona asked. "Don't we have more than one engine?"

The chief shook his head. "We're paranormals, Ms. Le Doux. Ninety-nine percent of fires don't even respond to water, and I have a feeling Mrs. Pearlily's would have been the same."

"Underworld fire doesn't respond to water," Celia added. Her head was leaning back against the couch and her eyes were closed. "It has to be oxygen starved or spelled out."

Wynona fought the slither of jealousy in her gut. There were proving to be large gaps in Wynona's education, even with all the reading she'd done growing up. Celia, however, had obviously been given access to a lot more useful information.

"So we have a confession?" Chief Ligurio clarified.

Wynona nodded. "Yes. We pretty much had it right, except Mrs. Pearlily was up to much more than simply trying to save her daughter some future heartache. She had full plans to take over the paranormal world."

Celia huffed. "Idiot."

Wynona laughed lightly. "It seems that those who want the power are the ones who would be the worst to have in power."

Rascal tucked her a little deeper into his side. "I hate how true that is."

"But she did admit to killing Dralo, because her husband wasn't paying attention to the problem. And she said killing Edana was a hasty mistake since the vampire didn't know anything, but what was done was done." Wynona sighed at the useless loss of life. How creatures could simply view others as expendable was lost on her. "And I wasn't supposed to be killed, the hit was a warning. She mentioned that her powers sometimes got out of control." Wynona shrugged. "We all saw that at the end."

"So let me get this straight...she was half demon?" Chief Ligurio clarified.

Wynona nodded. "Yes. She couldn't hide her affinity for fire, so she told people that was her power, which gave her the powers she needed to be useful to Mr. Pearlily, who had wealth and connections she wanted to use." She shrugged again. "Anyway, Thallia gave us a glimpse when she burst into flames. She doesn't shift into a full demon like her mother, but she inherited enough of the powers that Sequoia wanted to use her in her power play, but Thallia was behaving too much like a spoiled child."

"And her husband?" Rascal asked.

"He's in cahoots with my dad, but oblivious to everything else." Wynona yawned again. "Sorry."

"And you figured all this out by realizing her wings had scattered the papers in your office?" Chief Ligurio said with a frown. "It seems like a stretch."

"It was that and your vampire speed," Wynona clarified. "Edana would have been much faster than Mr. Pearlily. Not to mention, she wouldn't have met with him in the first place. All Edana knew was that Thallia was following some ridiculous plan to get her dad's attention and so when Mrs. Pearlily called and wanted to chat, I have no doubt that Edana jumped at the chance to help. She had no idea that Mrs. Pearlily had other powers that would destroy her."

"There were no signs of fire at any of the scenes," Chief Ligurio argued.

"She couldn't risk that," Wynona responded. "Both Mrs. Pearlily and Thallia had fire powers. It would have been too easy of a clue. It all had to be done without fire of any kind. Which is probably why she just nixed the use of magic at all."

Chief Ligurio nodded slowly. "I can see that." He blew out a harsh breath and leaned back against the couch. "I feel like we caught one criminal, but all it did was unearth something deeper."

"Agreed," Rascal stated. "The president is up to something and others are looking to beat him to it." He turned to Wynona. "But what?"

Wynona looked to Celia.

Celia never even opened her eyes. "I have no idea," she murmured. "Don't look at me."

Wynona squished her lips to the side. "Mrs. Pearlily knows, but she told me it would be a waste to share because I was going to be dead." She shivered slightly and Rascal kissed her temple. "That woman was officially insane."

"Most underworld creatures are," Chief Ligurio grunted. He stood. "Strongclaw. After tonight, sleep. Then come in and get those reports done."

Rascal nodded.

"Why after tonight?" Wynona asked.

Celia chuckled and cracked an eye. "You're so naive."

Wynona frowned. "What am I missing?"

"There's an eclipse tonight," Rascal whispered, his eyes full of worry.

Wynona jerked upright. "It's the spring solstice."

"Happy birthday," Celia said sarcastically. She stood up and began to saunter toward the hallway. "You're blessed to get to live another year."

Wynona shook her head. "I totally forgot."

"Oh, and I have a present for you," Celia said before disappearing. "But I think it can wait until tomorrow." With her signature mischievous grin, she was gone.

"I hate to say it, but I need to go as well." Rascal gave her a quick peck and stood up.

Wynona watched him, her worry starting to build. "Does the moon affect your wolf?" she asked softly. The front door closed, letting her know Chief LIgurio had seen himself out, though it probably didn't matter since the vampire knew more of what was going on than Wynona did anyway.

Rascal nodded. "I...I'll explain it all tomorrow, okay?"

Wynona studied him...his tired countenance from not sleeping lately and the weariness from their ordeal just a few minutes ago. He needed sleep. For about a week. "Okay." What else could she say? He was a grown man and was asking for her trust. She had trusted him implicitly before their breakdown, and she wanted to feel so now, but her bruised heart was having trouble.

It'll all be okay, he assured her. *One more day. Just give me one more day.*

Wynona nodded. She didn't trust her voice to speak any more. She did squeak when Rascal surprised her by grabbing the back of her neck and stealing a fierce kiss, worthy of the predator he housed inside himself.

"I love you," he growled. Then turning, he ran for the door.

Tears pricked the back of her eyes, but Wynona refused to let them fall. *He'll be back,* she assured herself. *He'll be back.*

Too worried and too tired to do her regular bedtime routine, Wynona turned, grabbed a throw pillow and curled up on her side on the couch. She pulled an afghan from the back of the couch and tucked it up to her chin. For the first several minutes, her concern was stronger than her exhaustion and she struggled to get her mind to calm. It jumped back and forth between Rascal, her ruined shop and Violet. How she was going to come back from this, Wynona had no idea, but she also knew she'd be able to think better if she could simply sleep.

Sleep, Violet cooed. *We'll work it out. Rascal's safe. I'm safe. Lusgu's safe. You're safe. Sleep. I'll see you tomorrow.*

With one last breath and a flash of purple fur in her mind's eye, Wynona finally drifted off into nothingness.

CHAPTER 32

Wynona woke up with a crick in her neck, but the rest of her body was doing much better than it had been the day before. Her stomach growled and she smiled, then winced as she stretched her neck.

Use your magic.

Wynona's head jerked, tugging on the knot. "Ow," she whimpered.

Violet snickered. *Use. Your. Magic.*

Looking up from under her eyelashes, Wynona gave a self deprecating grin. "Good morning."

Violet preened from her place on the coffee table. *Morning. Now fix your neck so we can have a proper conversation.*

Wynona brought a trickle of her magic to her fingers and the kink disappeared. She sighed in relief, then reached over to let Violet climb onto her hand. "I was worried for you."

I know, but Lusgu and I stayed at his house. It was fine.

Wynona cuddled her friend. "How did you get here?" Violet stood on her hind legs and turned her twitching nose to the kitchen.

Only then did Wynona notice all the sounds coming from her home. "Lusgu?"

"Don't you ever cook a proper meal here?" he grumbled. "Or clean?"

Wynona smiled, then stood up and walked over. Bending over, she wrapped her arms around the brownie. He only reached her waist, so the bend was pretty deep, but Wynona didn't care. She was too happy to see her grumpy employee. "Thank you for keeping her and yourself safe," Wynona whispered thickly.

Lusgu never reached around to hug her back and his huff at her words said he was annoyed...as usual...but neither did he pull away, and Wynona decided she would count that as a win.

She finally stood and wiped at her eyes. "Did your home suffer any damage?"

He shrugged. "Only the door."

"How did you get here?"

He glared. "I had to move it somewhere."

Wynona's eyebrows shot up. "You...you moved your house here?"

Violet chittered. *Next to the broom closet.*

This house is getting awfully crowded, Wynona lamented.

Tell me about it.

Wynona slumped. *Sorry. I didn't mean to broadcast that. It'll be fine. I'm sure.*

Violet scoffed. *If you say so.*

"Can I help with breakfast?" Wynona asked, trying to change the subject.

Lusgu's beady eyes rolled as well as any teenager creature and he shuffled off, Wynona's broom following behind him.

"Guess we're getting served this morning," Celia said in a chipper tone as she flounced to the table.

"I don't like feeling like I'm not helping," Wynona murmured.

"Enjoy it," Celia ordered. "For once in your life, just sit back and let someone else handle it."

Wynona twiddled her thumbs, trying to do just that, but it felt wrong. She didn't like being waited on, but she also was still recovering, so she tried to simply be grateful.

Later, with her stomach full and happy, Wynona allowed herself to take an extra long shower, essentially washing the events of the last week off her shoulders. She practically felt like a new woman once done.

Not knowing the plan for the day, she wore jeans and a T-shirt, deciding she would simply relax until she knew otherwise. It was her birthday, after all...though Wynona wasn't going to remind anyone of that.

Can you meet me at the shop?

Wynona blinked. "Rascal?"

His deep chuckle echoed in her mind. *Yes. Can you come to the shop?*

Okay, she sent back, finally remembering to not speak out loud. "Looks like we're headed to the shop," Wynona told Violet. She paused. "I guess that's technically not correct anymore." Her good mood wavered, though she gave Violet a tremulous smile. "I don't think anything is salvageable."

Let's go see. On the bright side, I guess this means we get to do a makeover?

Wynona nodded, though the thought didn't cheer her up. She had loved her shop. The old wood, the uneven floors, the old and cozy feeling of all the furniture she had picked...it was like her home. When Celia had tried to redo it, it had felt like a personal part of Wynona had been washed away, which was why she'd been so adamant Celia change it back.

The shop was the same. Wynona's heart and soul had gone into creating her business. She'd been looking forward to going back to work once this case was over and now she would have to wait...again.

"Maybe it won't be so bad," she told Violet as they walked down the hall. "I suppose all the killing at the shop had kind of put a damper on the place anyway. This means we can start anew."

That's the spirit. Violet curled her tail around Wynona's neck. *Grab your keys and let's go.*

Wynona picked up her keys. "Lusgu, I'm going to the shop. Is there anything there you want me to check for?"

The brownie scoffed. "Not likely."

Wynona nodded, totally understanding how he felt. "I'll be back in a while."

"Wait!" Celia called, running in their direction. "I'm coming too. I need to get my motorcycle."

"Speaking of which," Wynona began. She put her hands on her hips. "Where in the world did you get a motorcycle?"

"I've always wanted one," Celia said with a smile. "Now come on. The day's wasting."

Wynona sighed. "There isn't room for the two of us on the Vespa. Can't you just port there?"

Celia shook her head. "Nope. Not this morning." She wiggled her fingers, her silver magic dancing between her nails. "I'm saving it for something else."

Wynona frowned, but Celia didn't give her time for questions. "Come on!"

Sighing, Wynona rubbed her forehead. "Maybe we should let her drive and we'll port."

Not a chance. Just suck in, I guess.

Wynona shook her head. "Whatever." She walked out to the garage and the two women squeezed onto the small seat. "You sure you want to ride like this all the way to the tea house?"

"Just go already," Celia grumbled, repositioning herself.

"Alrighty." Wynona turned the key, revved the engine and pulled out into the driveway. The twenty minute drive was uncomfortable to say the least and they garnered more than a few odd looks, but no one fell off and Celia's cursing was kept to a couple of choice moments, so Wynona decided the experience wasn't a complete disaster.

Rascal's massive truck was already parked in front, so Wynona pulled in front of him and put the scooter into park. She and Celia untangled themselves and climbed off.

"Morning," Rascal said, his signature wide, care-free grin back in place. He sauntered over and bent to give her a kiss on the cheek.

Wynona was momentarily stunned into silence. He looked...completely normal. His hair was slightly messy, the dark rings gone, his golden eyes glowed with humor and the tension that had been lining face had melted away. "What... How?" she stuttered, not quite sure how to phrase what was trying to form in her head.

"Yeah..." Rascal rubbed the back of his neck and gave her a sheepish smile. He looked around and it was the first time Wynona noticed just how many people were milling around. Half the police department must be there, sorting through the rubble, and members of the media were milling about, taking pictures and asking questions. Several of them eyed Wynona, but none ventured her way.

"Don't worry," Rascal assured her. "Chief made enough threats that no one should bother you for an interview...for at least a week anyway." He made a face. "We're pretty sure that's all the time he could buy you."

"Thank you," Wynona said softly. She leaned into Rascal's side, his arm around her waist. "I'm not ready to talk to anyone yet."

"We figured." He kissed the side of her head.

They stood for a quiet moment and Wynona recognized several faces in the working crowd. Chief Ligurio was just inside the burnt out door of the shop, shouting orders. Daemon was in the dining room, visible through the missing front window. He also seemed to be ordering people about and Wynona relaxed, knowing that her friends were taking care of things. She just didn't have it in her to deal with it today.

"You're going to have to start from the ground up," Rascal said in a low tone. He shifted Wynona in front of him, pulling her back against his chest. His mouth rested right next to her ear. "That can either be very exciting or very scary."

She laughed, wiping a stray tear. "Or a little of both." She felt his grin against her hair.

"I'd like to think it will be exciting...because I'm hoping you can make a new start in all aspects of your life."

Wynona paused. "I don't understand." She spun to look at Rascal for an explanation.

He left his hands at her waist and smiled down at her. "The last few days have been...difficult," he said with a dark chuckle.

Wynona raised her eyebrows.

"I don't know how much you know about shifters, but as a wolf, the full moon always affects me a little, but an eclipse over a full moon is...something else." He cleared his throat and shifted his weight, obviously uncomfortable with the topic. "The wolf becomes stronger than the man and..." He cleared his throat again.

"It's okay," Wynona encouraged softly. "You can tell me."

Rascal chuckled. "Well, I kind of have to tell you, because our relationship is what made things so difficult."

Wynona frowned, slightly hurt at his words. "What did I do? Was it because I was in danger those couple of times?"

Rascal shook his head. "I'm sorry how I reacted to those. My wolf is overprotective and because we were getting close to the eclipse, I was having trouble controlling him. It's why I finally left. He was so upset at you getting hurt I could barely hold him back. And..." Rascal scrunched his nose and dropped his voice. "And his desire to claim his soulmate was overwhelming."

Wynona felt heat climb her neck and into her cheeks. "Claim his soulmate?"

Rascal nodded. "Yeah...I know it sounds archaic, but..." He shrugged. "I'm an animal. Nothing's archaic to them."

Wynona let her forehead fall to his chest. "I'm so sorry. I had no idea."

"And I didn't want you to," Rascal assured her. He pressed his lips into her hair. "I didn't ever want you to feel pressured or rushed. Our timeline is just that...ours. My wolf is part of me and he will always be willing to claim you, but I absolutely didn't want one random night in our lives to dictate the rest of them."

"Thank you," Wynona whispered. She leaned back. "I thought—"

"I know," Rascal finished for her. "And I hate that I left you like that, but I wasn't sleeping and was barely in control. Being around you was too much."

"You couldn't sleep at all?" she said, aghast.

He shook his head. "No. The wolf would have taken over."

"Oh my goodness, Rascal. How did you manage it?"

He grinned. "By planning this very next moment."

Wynona's eyebrows went up.

"That new start?"

She nodded.

"Now that I'm not under the influence of anything except how I feel about you," his eyes began to glow, "I was hoping we could start a new journey for your business..." He brought their foreheads together. "And start a new journey for us."

"Rascal..." She breathed.

"Wynona Odessa Le Doux...I love you. I love you so much I can barely breathe. I love how determined you are to help the underdog. I love how you gather friends that everyone else is afraid to be friends with. I love watching you grow with your powers. I love seeing you overcome every obstacle that lands in your way and come out stronger for it." He leaned back just enough for them to look into each other's eyes. "I want to be part of that. I want to be by your side as you do all those things, but I *don't* want to have to keep saying goodbye at night. Will you make me the happiest shifter in the paranormal world by marrying me?"

Wynona could barely breathe and her eyes were filling so quickly with tears that she could barely see as well, but she didn't care. "Yes," she whispered. "Yes!" Leaping up, she wrapped her arms around Rascal's neck and planted her mouth on his.

True to form, Rascal easily caught her and time stood still while he returned her kiss, celebrating the very best birthday present she had ever received...other than her freedom the year before.

Never in her wildest dreams would she have dreamed this would be her life. It wasn't perfect. It was messy and difficult and Wynona knew more than most that there were still tough times ahead, but *this* moment was perfect. Perfect and amazing, and it gave her hope for all that she would have yet to face with her father and rebuilding her business. She could do this. *They* could do this. It was going to be so good.

When they finally came up for air, Wynona's eyes widened and she looked around in awe at the purple sparkles floating in the air around them. "Oops," she said in a small laugh.

Rascal just shook his head and smiled.

Clapping caught their attention and Wynona jerked her head toward the crowd, who had obviously stopped to watch the spectacle she and Rascal were making. Her cheeks were flaming as cameras went off and the entire police force stood smiling and clapping for the newly engaged couple.

"Strongclaw!" Chief Ligurio shouted.

"Yes, sir?"

"Aren't you forgetting something?" the vampire asked, one black eyebrow perfectly arched.

Rascal cursed under his breath and reached into his pocket, pulling out a ring box. "I think I got a little too excited about your answer," he said by way of apology.

Wynona wiped her tears and held out her shaking hand. "I don't even care," she said. "The ring isn't..." Her words trailed off when he fitted a large, stunning white diamond solitaire onto her finger. "Ooohhh," she breathed. "Oh my goodness."

He laughed. "What was it you were saying?"

Wynona whacked his arm with her other hand. "It's...so much more than I imagined."

Rascal took the hand she was staring at and kissed her palm. "You deserve it."

She reached up on tiptoe for another sweet kiss. "Thank you."

If you two are done smooching, perhaps you could come get me out of the basket now?

Wynona closed her eyes and hung her head. "I'm so sorry," she told Violet, hurrying over to grab her familiar out of the front basket on the scooter. "I didn't mean to leave you. I got distracted."

"It was my fault," Rascal interrupted. He held out his hand and Violet climbed on, joyfully allowing herself to be tucked into his front pocket.

I'll forgive you. Violet sniffed. *But just this once.*

"Thank you," Rascal said with a wink at Wynona. "I appreciate it."

"Are you two going to set a date?" Chief Ligurio asked, crossing the last few feet of grass to stop beside them. Daemon stood at the chief's side, grinning widely.

Seeing the black hole reminded Wynona of her best friend. "Prim's going to kill me," she murmured, grabbing her phone out of her pocket. She heard Rascal answering the chief while she texted Prim the news. But before Prim could answer back, a loud roaring brought their chatting to a screeching halt.

Celia, riding her motorcycle, came bursting out of the alleyway too fast and skidding to a stop right in front of Wynona's scooter. Pulling off her helmet, Celia shook out her hair, looking a little too pleased with herself. "Congrats, sis."

"Thank you," Wynona said sincerely.

"I guess this makes my birthday present even better."

Wynona looked at Rascal, but he shrugged. "What's that?"

Celia's mischievous grin grew. "I'm moving out."

"What? Where are you going? How can you afford to move?" Wynona blurted out.

"I've got a job," Celia said, her chin rising in the air. "Where do you think I've been porting to every day?"

"Wow..." Wynona nodded slowly. "Good for you. What are you doing?"

Celia pulled a card out of her back pocket and held it out to Wynona.

Celia Le Doux

Interior Decorator

"Interior decorating?" Rascal asked.

"No wonder you were rearranging my house," Wynona said with a laugh.

Celia shrugged. "I was trying to give you a free makeover, but...perhaps it was too soon." She glanced at the building. "When you're ready for my services, let me know."

"I will," Wynona assured her.

"Well...I guess I'll see you around then." Celia glanced slyly over Wynona's shoulder, where a certain vampire still stood. Throwing a wink his way, she put on her helmet, revved her engine, and took off down the street.

"Hey, boss?" Daemon asked. His hands were in his pockets and he was rocking back and forth on his heels.

"Yeah?" Chief Ligurio asked, his eyes on the retreating motorcycle.

"I think maybe someone should pull her over for speeding..." Daemon said carefully.

Wynona bit her lip to keep from laughing and Rascal coughed to hide his, but it still took Chief Ligurio a moment to recover.

When he finally came back to himself, he growled...loudly...glared at Daemon and marched back to the house.

Daemon shrugged. "I tried." With another smile, he turned and walked away too.

With everyone else gone, Rascal wrapped his arms around Wynona's waist again. "How would you like to go back to the cottage and rest and cuddle the rest of the day, Ms. Le Doux?"

"Hmmm..." Wynona made a considering face. "Would you be there?"

Rascal nuzzled her neck. "That was kind of the whole point."

"Then I think it sounds wonderful."

"Great." He began leading her to the truck. "We'll have Skymaw get your scooter later."

"I need to tell you something, though," Wynona hedged as she climbed into the passenger seat.

"What's that?" Rascal waited at the open passenger door.

"Um...Celia might be moving out, but I, uh, have a new roommate."

He scowled. "What?"

"Lusgu moved in."

Rascal's jaw dropped. "You're kidding."

Wynona shook her head. "No. He moved his door from the shop to my kitchen."

Rascal blinked several times. "Unbelievable." Muttering the word over and over again, he closed the door and began to walk to his seat.

Wynona laughed to herself. Yep. Life was messy, difficult and never quite turned out how she hoped, but they could handle this. They could handle anything...as long as they were together.

Don't Miss Wynona's Next Adventure!
"Stir in a Murder"

Just when she's ready for a new start,
a murder turns life on its head...

New beginnings abound in Wynona's life as she plans her future
with Rascal and rebuilds her shop from the ground up, all while her
relationships continue to evolve with those closest to her.

With Celia out of the house, but a new roommate taking her place,
Wynona feels as if she's often walking on egg shells in her own
home. Lusgu is a mystery that Wynona can't quite unravel, though
his proximity makes her more curious than ever.

When a dragon shifter, who happens to be an old friend of Lusgu's,
is accused of murder, Wynona realizes this might be her chance to
peel back a few more layers of the brownie's history.

With Violet and Rascal at her side, Wynona dives into a world of
science and magic as she tries to clear the dragon's name, and keep
herself alive for her future wedding at the same time.

Grab Your Copy Of
"Stir in a Murder"

CPSIA information can be obtained
at www.ICGtesting.com
Printed in the USA
LVHW080746191122
733589LV00031B/1477